More praise for *Schmidt Delivered*

"[An] adroitly conceived variation on the novel of manners . . . The book's singular achievement [is] to quietly nudge the novel of manners in a more provocative direction. He does this in part [by] rendering a superficially unlikeable protagonist with the same humanizing fullness other authors save for likable ones. . . . [*Schmidt Delivered* is] about the way we live now as reflected in the distorting funhouse mirror of the way we lived when everyone stayed on his side of the class divide."

—*The New York Times Book Review*

"[Begley's] textured portrait of bewildered Schmidt is a triumph of empathy and compassion. . . . He describes the ultra-rich, ultra-sybaritic Hamptons scene with dry relish."

—*Publishers Weekly* (starred review)

And acclaim for *About Schmidt*

"Begley again demonstrates that he can reveal the complexities of society and personality with a clear eye and graceful style. . . . More than meets the requirements of graceful fiction."

—*Time*

"Comical, tough, unsparing; it is as if Louis Auchincloss had exchanged the kid gloves for brass knuckles. . . . Interesting and nervy."

—*The Washington Post Book World*

"Mesmerizing . . . Evocative . . . Begley has created a terribly funny, touching, infuriating, complex character. . . . [He] uses his intimate attunement to the language, habits, and assumptions of the upper class to reveal the tiny cracks in the system and to excavate the subtle cruelties and disarray that lie beneath the surface."

—*Los An[illegible]mes*

"Witty . . . Begley has a flair for lies [illegible]d, assured tone makes its flashes [illegible] striking."

Also by Louis Begley

MISTLER'S EXIT

ABOUT SCHMIDT

AS MAX SAW IT

THE MAN WHO WAS LATE

WARTIME LIES

SCHMIDT DELIVERED

Schmidt Delivered

LOUIS BEGLEY

BALLANTINE BOOKS • NEW YORK

A Ballantine Book
Published by The Ballantine Publishing Group

www.ballantinebooks.com

Library of Congress Catalog Card Number: 2001118324

ISBN 0-345-44083-8

This edition published by arrangement with Alfred A. Knopf, a division of Random House, Inc.

Manufactured in the United States of America

Cover design by Min Choi
Cover photograph by Maura McEvoy

First Ballantine Books Edition: November 2001

10 9 8 7 6 5 4 3 2 1

for N. *and* J., *later*

Vedrò mentr'io sospiro
Felice il servo mio?

—LE NOZZE DI FIGARO

SCHMIDT DELIVERED

I

YES, it's Schmidtie here. Hello hello. Yes, this is Schmidtie speaking.

He had knocked the telephone off his night table and was groping under the bed for the receiver. People shouldn't be calling a retired gent before nine. Or was this some sort of bad news? Charlotte!

I hope this is not an inconvenient time.

The speaker's voice was agreeably deep, with a mystifying rough intonation at the edge.

You don't remember me.

Terribly sorry, I'm not good at recognizing voices.

Look, there's no reason you should remember me, though people usually do remember my voice. I'm Michael Mansour. That's right, in this country I pronounce "Man-sower," not "Man-soor." Anything to make it easy for the natives. We met yesterday, at the Blackmans' party. You know who I am?

Now Schmidt had his bearings. Of course, the billionaire investor who backs Gil's films. Egyptian, or something, but lodged firmly toward the top of *Forbes* magazine's list of the richest tycoons in America.

Of course. I've read about you, more than once. The king of bottom fishers.

Ha! Ha! I like that—you made a pun, right? But that's just how I make money. I'm a friend of Gil's, he gave me your telephone number. I'd like you and your wife to come over for lunch on Saturday. My house, at one-thirty, unless you want to take a dip in the ocean before we start drinking. Gil says you're his best friend. He's told me what kind of lawyer you were. I'm sorry we never got to work together. Anyway, Gil's friends are my friends. So you'll come? Excuse me, you're sure you remember meeting me? By the way, I've got a pool, too, if you don't like the ocean.

Considering Mr. Mansour's grandeur, this diffidence was touching.

Of course I remember, replied Schmidt, reaching for a high level of amiability. Elaine introduced us. Actually, the young woman I was with is my friend, not my wife. She's not here just now. Could I call you after I've checked with her?

He was telling a white lie. Carrie was right there, resolutely asleep, her head buried under the pillow. It would take more than the three rings of the telephone and Schmidt's talking sotto voce to Mr. Mansour to wake her when she was like that.

Your friend is gorgeous. Charming too. I figured she was your wife, and not your daughter, because she doesn't look like you. Anyway, congratulations! I want you to bring her, but come alone if she's busy. I can always have you over together another time.

I'll be in touch.

Having taken in the further news that Mr. Mansour was no longer to be found at his East Hampton residence, which he had abandoned to the more recent of his two wives, Schmidt wrote down the unlisted number. Not to worry, he would keep it to himself. Ah, the Crussel house on Flying Point Road in Water Mill? Yes, he knew how to find it all right. Yes, and find memories in that house as well, that the visit might endow with a new meaning not untinged with new bitterness, but he saw no point in mentioning that to Mr. Mansour so early in the morning.

The original owners of the house in question, Mr. and Mrs. Crussel, had been important clients of Wood & King, the firm where Schmidt had been a partner until he retired. A trusts and estates colleague, Murphy, took care of them, just as he watched over the modest affairs of Schmidt and his late wife, Mary, but Schmidt, who specialized in representing insurance companies in the loans they made, was usefully situated, in a manner of speaking, as the Crussels' neighbor who knew them socially. It fell upon him, therefore, to be the firm's unofficial emissary charged with maintaining and developing them as clients, through more frequent and more assiduous attendance at their lunches and dinners than would have otherwise been his style. Occasionally, as though leading a Great War charge *à outrance*, he had gone so far in his devotion to professional duty as to propel a giggling and squealing

Olga Crussel into the surf and hold her up, with both hands, while she bobbed in the unthreatening breakers. These exploits established in the Crussel household his reputation for gallantry and limitless strength as a swimmer; they also gave the authority of revealed truth to his occasional, offhand assurances that his partner, Murphy, knew what he was doing and could be relied upon.

Schmidt was pleased to recall that the house, of which Mr. Mansour was now the owner, was one of the few subjects about which the Crussels had not asked his opinion. A prizewinning Brazilian architect, a friend of a niece of the Crussels, had designed it. He had come out with her for a Fourth of July weekend and stayed in the large clapboard cottage that then stood on the site and that had been the Crussels' beach house ever since they came to the Hamptons. Sizing up the opportunity for new business—the large fortune, although discreet, was hardly unknown to connoisseurs of such matters—he made a rapid drawing of what he would, if the property were his, put in the place of their current dowdy home: a large, loosely flowing aquatic structure corresponding to Olga Crussel's inner self, with reception rooms and decks for entertaining in full view of the ocean and Mecox Bay, between which this astonishing acreage was located. Olga took the bait. For a Swiss banker, whose family had been, since the days of Calvin, a pillar of Geneva's patriciate, Jean Crussel was a prodigy of speed when he really wanted to make up his mind. Besides, he doted on his wife. The decision to go ahead was made on the spot, without so much as a call to Murphy or Schmidt or Olga's pet decorator.

The cottage was torn down during one terrifying week, but construction of the new house dragged on. Getting it finished and moving in turned into the Crussels' race against senility and death. The old couple won the first leg: before the platoon of round-the-clock keepers and nurses had to be brought in, they did have two years' worth of showing off, at party after party, the Brazilian's construction, which in Schmidt's opinion—but perhaps he was unfair, having grown to like a good deal the unmourned old cottage—resembled nothing more than a motel crossed with an ocean liner a drunken skipper had carelessly run aground on the beach.

Jean and Olga were childless; the collateral heirs owned perfectly adequate summerhouses nearby and elsewhere. They put the property on the market and waited for years, unwilling, in the way of the very rich, to lower the asking price. That an even wealthier new man had at last put cash into the heirs' pockets and, presumably, stood ready to pour more millions into this raped dune was bound to be a very good thing for the local contractors, and for tradesmen in New York, London, and Paris. Perhaps for the economy, worldwide. Schmidt imagined that Mr. Mansour had already excised various sly improvements Jean Crussel made as soon as the Brazilian, busy with commissions for other masterpieces, had turned his back: remote-control switches that made the venetian blinds in the bedrooms go up and down and devices that adjusted slats without human intervention in relation to the angle of the sun, aluminum ramps and no-slip surfaces positioned strategically inside the house and on the decks to prevent a fall that might shatter decalcified bones, and the cabaret room with its circular dance floor on which Jean and Olga had daily practiced the tango and the paso doble under the surveillance of a teenage Arthur Murray instructress. He might have even put down a new deck at the shallow end of the pool to conceal the twin pink Jacuzzi tubs. That's where the spider-thin husband and wife, sometimes in the company of other octogenarians, soaked naked, lifting their candid and blissful faces to the forenoon sun. The revolution in all of this, thought Schmidt, remained to be seen and admired.

Should he nudge Carrie and awaken her? He decided against it. Instead, he advanced his hand cautiously under the covers, ran it over her breast, felt for her armpit, which was moist from sleep, let it linger there while with his nose he ruffled the rush of her black curls on the pillow, and quietly got out of bed. It was a pity. Right now he could do it, without the help Carrie was willing to give him even while she groaned with impatience. Failure going to bed, a makeup session in the morning: both the symmetry and the thought that, if he did wake her, she might attribute the satisfactory situation to his bladder rather than to his libido, were discouraging. He put on his pants and shirt, waited to put on his shoes until he was on the stairs, squeezed four oranges so that Carrie could have her glass of juice right away if she came down before he returned, did not drink any himself because he preferred to have it with her at breakfast, and drove to the post office and then to the candy store, where, each morning when he was in Bridgehampton, ever since poor Mary and he had first started coming there, he picked up the *New York Times.* The remaining errand was to get croissants, an important change in Schmidt's routine. Until Carrie decided, at the beginning of his long convalescence, that freshly baked croissants from Sesame, where her friend, formerly a fellow waitress at O'Henry's, had begun to work, would boost his morale, despite their outrageous price, he had invariably eaten for breakfast one-half of a toasted English muffin spread thinly with bitter orange marmalade. The other half he saved for the next day. Without question, the new regime was a huge, habit-forming gastronomic improvement. It had also brought about frequent chance encounters with Gil Blackman, whose own morning addiction was to scones, and introduced Schmidt to a daily spectacle he thought was perfect material for one of those hard-edged or, as some would say, downright nasty movies Gil had been making.

Had Schmidt dared, he would have presented a treatment to him in writing: It's a few minutes short of nine o'clock. The Mercedes station wagons, Range Rovers, BMWs, and Jaguars have assembled on the gravel in front of Sesame's locked front door. Men with two days' growth of beard are kissing women wearing what would seem to be cotton nightshirts and flip-flops. These women have rushed here straight from bed, you can still smell it on them, before they brushed their teeth. Also a Toyota, which looks out of place. The fellow in it might as well be invisible. He doesn't kiss anybody and nobody greets him. In fact, he has parked off to the side, but he's in the way so he gets dirty looks. Imperceptibly, a line forms. At nine sharp the door opens. Easy does it. God help you if it looks as though you might want to cut in. This crowd would tear you limb from limb. They're into serious fun. Now not all the women are in nightgowns: they've been joined by others in riding clothes with no breasts and hair that looks as if it's been soaked in chlorine, women in sweat clothes so wet you think they've actually been running, and fat guys with tits and horn-rimmed bifocals in tennis whites who may or may not make it to the tennis court. Little girls got up like scaled-down sluts, with chipped lacquer on fingernails and toenails, whine about bagels. Tomatoes, two of which go at what the fruit stand one hundred yards down the road would charge for eight of the same size; little plastic containers, five dollars a pop, of oil and vinegar with salt and pepper settled at the bottom, just stir and pour this dressing over the tomatoes or the lettuce and arugula that are also available in little Baggies at one dollar per leaf; prebrowned sausages ready to eat as soon as they're warm (assuming a pair of hands can be found to put them into a frying pan and on the stove, otherwise don't bother, just serve them "at room temperature"); mineral water and fruit juice in bottles like champagne splits for consumption on the premises or in the waiting Range Rover. Wads of hundred-dollar bills. Give me three pounds of this, give me a quart of that. These commands are barked at the imperturbably polite boys and girls behind the counter, as though no mode of address other than the imperative exists. The boys and girls write it all down very neatly. A lanky old codger with blue eyes that have seen better days and a thin mouth diffidently picks two croissants from the basket. He hesitates. The purchase is too paltry.

Should he just stuff them in the pocket of his cotton jacket and walk out, instead of bothering the help about a four-dollar transaction? Nuts, he won't shoplift, but he'll show respect. One of the bony women lets him back into the line. He lays the croissants on the counter, asks for fresh goat cheese from Vermont and, because he likes it and it's suitably expensive, a wedge of English blue.

But Schmidt doesn't write his version of Ali Baba's cave or tell his friend Gil about it. For all his bluff manner, Mr. Blackman is very sensitive. Schmidt fears that he might be offended by Schmidt's point of view on these morning proceedings in which they are both such regular participants.

Back in his own kitchen, at breakfast with Carrie. Her presence is a miracle. Worshipful Schmidt knows that she is naked under the gorgeous ruby-red silk man's bathrobe made up for her by a shirtmaker in the place Vendôme whom Schmidt's father favored. Schmidt had her measured for it in Paris, during the spring vacation. There is no resource of her sallow and triumphant body yet unexplored by his eyes, lips, and hands. Her voice, hoarse and weary but tender as a mother's when she nurses and coos at a child, fills his memory. When the jazz station he listens to on his car radio plays a Billie Holiday song, Carrie becomes so absolutely present that he blushes. Prudence, above all, prudence. But after he has kissed her on both cheeks, his hand somehow finds its way under the silk, touching the undersides of her breasts, and then the nipples, which harden immediately. The hand wishes to descend, toward Carrie's flat stomach. He restrains it, already reassured. If she remembers how it went in bed last night, she has forgiven him. Or she has forgotten—she fell asleep long before he did.

Hey Schmidtie, a woman called. She said she is Mr. Mansour's secretary and asked if we have a fax machine. She wants to fax directions to his house. I said you'd call her back. Who's Mr. Mansour?

A very rich man, friend of Gil's. You saw him at their house. Bald, on the small side, and tanned. Some sort of Egyptian Jew, I think. Or maybe he's Moroccan.

Yeah, I saw him. Was he standing next to Gil most of the time? That guy undressing all the girls with his eyes?

No doubt, especially you. He telephoned first thing this morning and invited us to lunch on Saturday. I said I'd ask if you want to go. He's divorced recently. This may be part of filling out his new social life with a few new faces. Or maybe it isn't. He's got so much money he can order guests from a caterer.

He thinks we're married?

He did. I explained that we aren't.

And he still wants us both? Mr. Schmidt and his Puerto Rican girlfriend?

Of course, he does. He wants dreary Mr. Schmidt only because he'll bring his delicious friend. He thinks you're beautiful. He told me. Everybody does. Beautiful and insanely adorable.

Don't shit me, Schmidtie. He asked for me because he thinks I'm your wife. Hey, no that's not it. He wants me there to wait on tables!

How many variations of this exchange have they gone through? Like "Greensleeves" played into your ear over and over when the dentist's receptionist puts you on hold.

Carrie, he said, you shouldn't think like that. You are a gorgeous, young American citizen. If you really have the silly idea that people look down on you because you're living with an old guy who isn't your husband, let's fix it. Please consent to become the beautiful, adorable, and proper Mrs. Schmidtie Schmidt! All you need to do is say yes. My people and I will take care of everything else.

She looked away. One afternoon, almost two years back, soon after he had recovered from the accident, while they were out on the back porch, he had taken her hand and whispered, Please be my wife. Everything seemed right for it. Bryan, her part-time boyfriend, was out of the way, cleverly dispatched to work on the house Schmidt had inherited in Palm Beach, to restore it to its pristine condition. He had as good as put that repulsive fellow into long-term storage! Neither he, nor Bryan's predecessor, Mr. Wilson, would handle Carrie's body again. In the case of Mr. Wilson, who had bounced off the windshield of Schmidt's totaled car, Schmidt liked to think that was a dead certainty.

She had stared blankly at him, then as now, but even so he had gone on to argue his case.

Look, it's all come together. Charlotte has her Jon Riker. They're married. He's made an honest woman of her. He says that, not I! I've given her money and furniture and silver out of this house. Everything she wants—for the time being anyway! They'll drift away from me, farther and farther. Why shouldn't you and I be married? Come on, sometimes I even think you love me. Maybe almost as much as you loved Mr. Wilson!

As always, when he showed the poor judgment or bad taste to mention Mr. Wilson, or she brought him up herself, big tears appeared in the corners of her eyes and ran down the sides of her nose. He kissed it dry.

Man, she said, what's with you? You know I love you. I've loved you since the first time. Hey, I practically had to rape you! I want to live with you. But I can't marry you. Jesus, you're more than forty years older! Even your daughter's older than me. What happens when we can't do it anymore? I'm supposed to lie in bed at night and play with myself while you read?

I hope that won't be for quite a while, he answered. Remember how you asked me whether people could love each other and not do it all the time? I told you they could. They get used to showing their love in different ways, they give each other pleasure.

Like how? Fingerfucking me? Thanks a lot, I had that with Mr. Wilson when he couldn't get it up no matter what I tried. Hey Schmidtie, we're doing fine. Just leave it alone.

Sure, he'd resolve to leave it alone, if only to avoid being reminded how completely right she was and what desolation awaited him down the road if he wasn't lucky enough to die soon. But the subject had a queer way of forcing its way in, for instance when anything concerning money came up. Soon after she moved in, and time and again afterward, he told her that she didn't need to be a waitress; it would take forever to save enough to put herself through college. Of course, he knew he was exaggerating. More was at stake for him than the date on which she would receive her diploma. Why not quit, he pleaded, and let me pay for your education? What's the point of refusing my help? Her invariable reply: You want to turn me into a gold digger. Thereupon, just as monotonously, he'd tell her that was nonsense; they were living in the same house and eating the same food anyway, just like a husband and wife. The least he could do was to make it possible for her to enjoy those privileges that his wife would be entitled to as a matter of course. She would shake her head and say, I'm not your wife. Charlotte and Jon will say they had me figured out all along. I'm after your money!

Inspiration came to him at the end of one of those dreary exchanges. He would hook her by the gift of a tiny BMW convertible, the car she thought was the coolest in the world. The sales manager delivered it in person to the house during lunch and, as arranged, left the keys on the seat. As soon as they had finished eating, Schmidt said, Look, there is something in the driveway I want to show you.

At first she just stood there, staring very seriously at the little car. Only after he repeated twice, Go on, it's yours, did she look to him for permission, open the door on the driver's side, ease her body in delicately, as though the chassis were going to break at the least false move, and run her hands over the steering wheel, the glistening dashboard, the black leather.

Why don't you take it out for a spin, he asked. We'll have coffee when you come back.

Instead, she got out. When she had finished kissing him, standing on tiptoe, her arms around his neck, she whispered, Oh, Schmidtie, this is so bad, I just can't say no to this car. You come too. Let's take this baby for a ride.

She put the top down. Somewhere on an empty stretch of Route 114, heading from Sag Harbor to East Hampton, past the road that leads to Cedar Point, looking for all the world like a child before the Christmas tree at Rockefeller Center, she floored the gas pedal. The car shot forward. Schmidt waited until the needle was back at sixty and put forward his proposition: Wouldn't it be nice to drive this car to Southampton College and back? You'd make me very happy, I want a college girl in the house. That way we would go on living here. I hear the courses in psychology are pretty good. You could major in that and get the diploma you need to be a social worker. If that still interests you. They have courses in acting and creative writing too. How about it?

He held his breath while she made a face. The grimace changed slowly into a smile, and she spoke.

Hey, you'll have a live-in college girl! I guess it beats fucking a waitress. Shit Schmidtie. You would ask me now. How can I say no to you?

A great idea, because it had worked. She liked the college, even let him help with her papers. An invitation from Mr. Mansour was hardly the most romantic of contexts in which to press his suit. Nevertheless, there he was, trying once more.

Carrie, my love, he said, swallowing the last piece of his croissant. I've just asked you again to marry me. Aren't you going to say something?

Yeah, I am. Thanks a lot, Schmidtie, but please drop it. We're OK the way we are. Nothing's changed. You're too old. I'm too young. We'd give Charlotte a heart attack. Your friends would flip out.

The Blackmans adore you, ventured Schmidtie. And they're practically my only friends.

That was true. Everybody had dropped him when Mary died, or he had stopped seeing them.

No reply.

But what about the estimable Mr. Mansour? Shall I say yes?

It was a mistake to have told Carrie that Mansour was very rich. That had only made her shy, not curious. Perhaps it would be less frightening to meet this fellow on her home ground. Therefore, he added, Would you rather invite him to dinner here? Or to lunch, on a day when you don't have classes?

Schmidtie, what's the matter with you? You've got rocks in your head? I don't know how to entertain. What's this guy's house like?

It's in Water Mill. Right on the beach, very modern and, in my opinion, too big and rather silly. I knew the old couple who built it. Before they became senile, I used to go over there quite often. Now they're dead.

OK. We'll go. But you'll tell me how to dress.

Schmidt dialed the number. A male voice with an identifiable Mediterranean accent informed him that he had reached Michael Mansour's residence.

Will you please tell Mr. Mansour that Mr. Schmidt and Miss Gorchuck—he still found it difficult to repress a giggle when, as was usually necessary, he spelled her name—will be glad to come to lunch on Saturday?

Somebody, perhaps Mr. Mansour's punctilious secretary, had been at work. Instead of giggling back or showing surprise, the voice replied, I will tell Mr. Mansour, and went off the line.

Carrie was hanging up on him too. It had taken her no time to dress, as she wore nothing under her blue jeans and shirt and combed her hair with her fingers. Ah, "That brave vibration each way free"! She ran down the stairs two steps at a time, blew a noisy kiss in Schmidt's direction, and was out the door. Film studies. She had enrolled in a special summer program. The class she was going to was a workshop. She wouldn't be back until midafternoon.

Each change in Schmidt's routine was like a mountain he was at first unwilling to climb, even if the result might be an improvement, such as greater comfort and efficiency or better value for his money. This was especially true of separating himself from an employee or disappointing a tradesman. Thus, he had not let go the Polish brigade of garrulous, familiar, and obese cleaning ladies, whose arrival on Wednesday mornings, in leisure clothes of bizarre colors surely chosen to match the paint of their gas-guzzling cars, heralded the two-hour passage through the house of a benevolent tornado that blew away dust but otherwise had little to do with cleaning and had constituted, in the period between Mary's death and the advent of Carrie, his principal contact with the world.

Likewise, Schmidt continued to buy his fruit and vegetables from the merchant who had "always" sold them to him; his flashlight batteries, nails, screws, and small household appliances at the hardware store on Main Street; and his liquor and wine from the store owned by a young man whose parents, before they retired to Florida, had supplied the best groceries and meat in town. It was of no interest to Schmidt that most longtime residents preferred the slightly fresher produce at the roadside stand where a Fra Angelico Virgin come alive, in a T-shirt with HI! stenciled on it, denim skirt, and dirty sneakers, weighed the tomatoes and new potatoes, smiling at you over neat arrangements of melons and suchlike grown in the adjoining field by her boyfriend, a fitness freak with sunken eyes and cheeks. Indeed, Schmidt would sooner attend Saturday morning services in the Sag Harbor synagogue than buy a vacuum cleaner or a bottle of bourbon at the mall outside Bridgehampton. Examples of his mulishness in small matters multiplied. As he set to washing the breakfast dishes, a task he did not in the least dislike but one that took up time, he reflected on the advantages of hiring a housekeeper or some other sort of domestic employee—the word "servant" having become proscribed with such force that even Schmidt bowed to it—who would relieve him of that and other chores, even making the bed and picking up in the bathroom, when, as this morning, Carrie bolted out of the house, as well as shopping, setting the table for meals, and, perhaps, even cooking. Or he could engage a couple. The man would get the newspaper and the mail, do yard work, polish every piece of brass and wax every unpainted wood surface in the house, and strive in general for that impression of perfect stasis Schmidt had not yet achieved in his house and surrounding property, a condition that would compel the sharpest and most discerning eye to concede that not a pebble in the driveway or a single piece of garden furniture had ever been disturbed. The space over the garage could be fitted out for just such a couple.

He put the last plate in the dishwasher and went out to check on the garden and the pool. Something was probably wrong with the water filter. Schmidt didn't like the fan of tiny bubbles issuing from the return lines. It would be best to have the pool-maintenance service make sure air wasn't getting into the system. Another annoying and time-consuming phone call that someone other than he could be making, possibly the combination houseman-and-yardman husband. The difficulty, if indeed there be one, wasn't that a full-time housekeeper would look down her nose on the Polish brigade and ask to get those ladies fired, a disloyal act Schmidt had no intention of performing. He knew he could be stern enough to impose Mrs. Nowak and her colleagues on whomever else he engaged. They would be like a covenant that runs with the land, a part of the social contract. Only Carrie's feelings stood in the way. Class consciousness of Colony Club ladies? Schmidt thought it was rudimentary in comparison with Carrie's. He read as a clear signal, for instance, her refusal to set foot in O'Henry's or to shop in Bridgehampton: the poor child didn't think that she was any kind of success in the eyes of her former coworkers and the army of locals who filled the tanks of her and Schmidt's cars, mowed the lawn, vacuumed the pool, fixed the plumbing, painted the shutters, or did any of the other vastly overpriced chores required for Schmidt's general enjoyment of life. Far from it, she thought, not inaccurately, that she was considered by them a traitor to her class. The expression was his and not one, Schmidt realized, that either she or they would use, having recourse instead to some up-to-date synonym for "floozy." Naturally: a Puerto Rican waitress from Brooklyn comes out to the Hamptons to pocket big tips and after a year gets tired of plates covered with scraps of red meat and uneaten fries and even of shacking up with Bryan or some other local stud. So she gets herself a better job—laying a rich old guy, someone it's all right for the locals and the migrant lumpen proletariat to rob blind but not to fraternize with. That had surely been the initial analysis made by the Polish brigade. But the ladies got used to Carrie during Schmidt's convalescence, and she got used to them. Whatever might be their a priori moral or social judgment of Carrie, he felt certain they couldn't help seeing that she was a good egg and was treating him right. But so long as they lived in this place, with the folk memory of their history so fresh, how was he to get her to think of herself as the lady of the house and make her comfortable with any other staff he might hire?

As soon as he had recovered from his accident, he had a five-foot wall of delicately colored weathered old bricks built to surround the pool. The flagstone deck was replaced by more old bricks, and red and pink climbing roses and rosebushes were planted inside the wall. A get-well present to himself. The roses prospered and were in full bloom. Bogard, the gardener, kept an eye out for hornet nests. So far they had been lucky: neither hornets nor bees had come to visit. Schmidt tested the temperature of the water with his hand. Perfect for him but on the cold side for Carrie. It was a beautiful but cool July. Reluctantly—in part because he had never been able to get out of his head the remark of a publisher friend of Mary's that a morning of heating the pool costs as much as the best seat at the opera, in part because he liked the cold for himself and wouldn't have cared if others, Carrie alone excepted, stayed out of the water, and also because he disliked the noise—Schmidt turned on the heater, took off his clothes in the changing cabin at the side of the pool house, dove in, and began doing laps. He had given up counting long ago. The effort to keep track distracted him from thoughts about anything else. Instead, he regulated himself according to the clock suspended on the brick wall. His intention was to swim fast every day for thirty minutes, unless it rained so hard that getting into the water seemed too absurd or he heard thunder nearby.

It really was too bad he had only Gil and Elaine Blackman to turn to for company, and Gil sometimes seemed too chummy with Carrie for his comfort. In the old days, he had liked, had in fact been proud of, Mary's milieu of publishers and writers. He certainly preferred it to the equally closed world of Wall Street lawyers, and he hardly knew anyone else in or near Bridgehampton other than the eternal Blackmans. Well before Carrie, Mary's friends made him feel that, deprived of her prestige, on which account he was forgiven his mostly silent presence at their lunches and dinners, he was of no use to them. Most of the lawyers among his acquaintance were practicing partners in first-class New York law firms just like his old firm, a handful taught at Columbia or New York University, and an even smaller number, a couple of classmates and one former partner, had become federal judges. He hadn't kept up with them. And their wives, their dreary wives! If you put aside the few aging beauties among them, who had kept the self-assurance and good humor that having first-rate looks when you are young can give you for life, about the only good thing you could say for them was that they were women. Schmidt resolutely preferred women to men.

Were there former colleagues, active and retired partners of Wood & King, who liked him, with whom he could reestablish some sort of ties? He thought that, on the whole, their feelings toward him were pleasantly benevolent. The exception, of course, would be Charlotte's husband, Jon Riker. If by some miracle that fellow could push a button and electrocute his father-in-law in his own swimming pool, there wasn't a force great enough, Schmidt thought, not even Wood & King's presiding partner, that could keep his big fat finger off the button. As a practical matter, none of this mattered. His old legal pals didn't happen to pass their summers or weekends anywhere nearby, and, to Schmidt's surprise, until he divined that she didn't especially care to live nearer to Brooklyn and her parents, Carrie showed no interest in the suggestion he had floated that they get an apartment in New York. And suppose they did, how would he go about launching them as a couple? Would he arrange a round of cocktails, little dinners, and theater outings? He had been used to seeing his partners mostly over lunch. The wives he saw twice a year, at firm dinners for partners and their spouses—since they had begun to take women into the partnership, spouses were no longer necessarily wives—and the firm outings for all lawyers and concubines of any sexual orientation designed to promote good fellowship through a day of tennis, golf, and drinking. It had suited Mary to keep her distance from his firm, and Schmidt wasn't sure that left to himself he would have preferred to be more gregarious. Even if Carrie were not in the picture, it would have been awkward, and perhaps not possible, to live down his past aloofness, to become one of the boys. But imagine Jack and Dorothy DeForrest—or even the W & K man-of-the-world Lew Brenner and his wife, Tina—invited to a small dinner at Schmidtie's brand-new penthouse to meet Miss Carrie Gorchuck. They would get through the meal and the coffee and brandy all right, though the men might be too unsettled to cluster as usual in the corner of the living room to talk about the firm's finances, but afterward, what a fuss! Schmidt with a girl younger than his own daughter, yes, younger than Jon Riker's wife! No, she's not a lawyer. I asked what she did and she came right out with it; she was a waitress until that old goat came along and made it worth her while to give up working. Beautiful as the day is long, absolutely—and then, depending on the speaker, a further graphic detail might follow—but, you know, with just a touch of the tarbrush. Some sort of Hispanic. Yes, Puerto Rican. It was just as well that the issue didn't need to be faced. The very young partners—

and certainly the associates—would think the new Mrs. Schmidt was a ten. But what was Schmidt to them or they to him?

He executed a very correct turn and looked up at the clock. Twenty-five minutes. To keep going for another five was intolerable, not because it was hard but because it was too boring. Another daily defeat. Cut short the swim, skip the exercises intended to tighten the stomach, fall asleep over *The Decline and Fall of the Roman Empire.* He climbed out, dried himself, and, with the towel wrapped around his midriff, out of habit, although there was no risk of an unannounced visitor who might surprise him in his nakedness, lay down in the sun. Really, it couldn't be simpler: just like Carrie, he was déclassé. Since deep down the last thing he wanted was to rejoin his class—even if giving up Carrie weren't the price—he must look for a social life elsewhere. Alas, not among the waitresses and busboys at O'Henry's or the chattering Ecuadoreans and Dominicans who trimmed his hedges and picked up broken tree branches. He was too old for the former; the latter didn't speak English. Not among the funny men and women with oversize smiles who sold local real estate, placed insurance, or fixed your teeth in an emergency, if you couldn't go into town. They were too unattractive. He needed to find people who belonged to no class and, indifferent to his loss of status or simply too ignorant to understand, might be drawn in by his availability and style. That was supposed to be the one advantage of a comfortable retirement. You want Schmidt at lunch? You've got him. Someone's asked you to fill a table at the gala benefit for the opera at fifteen hundred dollars a seat? Schmidtie's check is in the mail. Couldn't Carrie's looks do it for them? In his youth, they might have been adopted by members of café society, like the Greek shipowners who had been his father's clients. Was there still a café society, even though El Morocco and the Copacabana had vanished, and the "21" Club kept changing hands like a used car? Exposure to articles on "lifestyles," which had spread inside the *New York Times* like a malignant growth, and the occasional furtive dips into a weekly New York publication that had made a specialty of studying the vulgar rich, with reporting by young persons some of whose parents he had known, led Schmidt to believe that there did exist a similar subclass, completely outside society as he had once understood it, composed of parvenus—not especially beautiful or idle—sitting on mountains of vastly appreciated shares in companies they had started or bought on the cheap. With his billions and Levantine aroma, Michael Mansour was surely in it. Perhaps other friends of the Blackmans qualified. One would have to see.

The telephone rang in the house. Let it go. Until recently, when Carrie's mercilessly teasing compelled the acquisition, Schmidt had had no answering machine, on the theory that if anyone really needed to reach him it was easy enough to call again. Now that he was the owner of such a contraption, he compensated by listening to messages only rarely—when he thought Carrie might have left one. The ringing continued. It was someone persistent, who took into account the possibility that he was in the garden. He might answer in time if he ran, and then he might not. He remained on his deck chair. Carrie wouldn't be calling; she was in class and, anyway, didn't have the telephone habit. What if it was Charlotte? He had planned to call her himself, a little later. Nobody else mattered; it wasn't as if there were still the chance of his getting a new assignment or, that miracle of miracles, a brand-new client. He would have liked to wipe the slate clean of the last years of his practice, before Mary's illness brought him to retire early: a shrinking workload, feelings of helplessness (although he had not done anything to lose clients; how could he have prevented the consequences of his specialty's having gone the way of the telex machine?), guilt, and shame about not having enough brains or energy or force of personality to drum up business of some other sort. A number of fellow financing lawyers he knew and respected had done just that. In the jargon of the profession, they "retooled." Loneliness and not knowing what to do with his time were a cheap price to pay for early retirement, for having been set free. Besides, a couple more years, and he would have had to leave the firm anyway. Without the miracle of Carrie to console him. It wasn't as though anyone at Wood & King might have suggested that he stay on past the mandatory retirement age. Had anyone thought of calling it the Drop Dead date? In fact, it was likely that the younger partners might have agitated to have him pushed out if he hadn't made everybody's life easy and negotiated his own departure. People's lack of imagination was wonderfully surprising: these partners in their forties or early fifties, didn't they foresee that what they did to their elders would be done to them in not so many years? More brutally, in all likelihood. Schmidt and his contemporaries had been brought up in a tradition of almost filial respect for their elders. If they had neglected to transmit a halfway effective simulacrum of those feelings to the next generation of partners, at least they hadn't offered them the sordid spectacle of parricide. But the very bright youngsters in the firm today, the superstars said to be beating down the doors of the partnership, claiming admission as their birthright, would have received ample instruction in that blood sport, and from front-row seats. If he lived long enough, he would have fun watching them cut off the balls of the self-satisfied bastards who had been after his. Perhaps even Jon Riker's—he didn't care that it would be unseemly to sit there and laugh while one's son-in-law was neutered.

Enough sun. One more dive into the pool, five minutes of laps. Down, anger. He should learn to laugh and get rid of the scowl that etched the bitter lines framing his mouth. How lucky he was, in the end. He had plenty of money. Not for him one of those mail-order second marriages with a classmate's widow or some divorcée with a surgically renewed face—certainly not the sourness of celibacy. "Black, but comely" his wild girl, his lily of the valley; each night he lies betwixt her perfumed breasts. But how long would it be before that wild girl told him she had had it with her old and limp lover?

The telephone again. He was at the door of the screened porch. For Pete's sake, Schmidtie, stop the doddering crackpot routine; cross the porch, go into the living room, and answer. Ah, it's Charlotte. So rare that she called. Calling was his job. Stilted conversations; Schmidt timed them so that there was something he could do immediately afterward—take a stiff drink at the very least—to deaden the sense of desolation.

The weather nice out there? she inquired. That's good. The city's miserable. Perfectly awful.

A couple of similar observations later, Schmidt understood she was calling for a reason but needed to circle around before getting to the point. He waited for the "by the way."

Dad, do you have people coming out for this weekend?

No, I don't, nobody.

I think I might want to come.

The old but not yet forgotten feeling that he might melt, like a snowball, from complete happiness, leaving in the place where he stood only a wet puddle on the gleaming painted wood floor.

That's simply wonderful, he answered, I think I've heard on the radio that the weather will be fine. You and Jon aren't going to Claverack?

I'm not. I don't know what he's doing. If it's OK, I'll come alone.

Sweetie, is something the matter?

Plenty. I need to talk to you, but not from the office.

All right, baby. Do you really want to wait until Friday evening? You could take Friday off and come out Thursday afternoon. Or I could go into the city tomorrow and have lunch with you.

Thanks, Dad, it's too complicated. Friday's OK. I'll take the six o'clock jitney after work. Is that girl still living there?

Carrie. Yes, of course.

Then I'd like to stay in the pool house.

As you wish.

Silence on the other end of the line. What to do?

Sweetie, he ventured. Do let me know if you change your mind and want to come earlier. By the way, Carrie and I are going out to lunch on Saturday. At the house of a man called Mansour. Michael Mansour. You know, the financier who's always in the papers. Of all things, he's bought the old Crussel place. Shall I tell him you will come too?

I don't think so, Dad. I'll skip your activities. All I want is to get some sun and have a talk with you. OK?

Aha! The problem between her and Jon, whatever it was, hadn't put a dent in her standards. Wouldn't have Papa's Puerto Rican tootsie at her wedding, won't stay with her under the parental roof now. Let it be. Hadn't poor Mary and he fitted out the pool house expressly to make young people's weekend visits to the country easier?

Absolutely. Be good!

He went upstairs to shave. Across the landing from the room he shared with Carrie was Charlotte's old room, which, after Mary died, Charlotte had shared with Jon on weekends. Until she and Schmidt quarreled. They had never returned, except when they came to see him in the hospital. Or had their primary motive been to get hold of the VW sitting in the garage, which he had given to Charlotte, and to count the silver, the silver he had told them he didn't mean to part with while he was still alive? Schmidt threw the blade into the wastebasket and attached a new one to the razor. He went over his face another time, slowly and with care, from time to time testing the skin for smoothness with his index finger. This wasn't the moment to catalogue old insults. Granted that she had behaved badly, and the Rikers, *mère*, *père*, *et fils*, were deplorable. Wasn't it the first time that, as an adult—if there had been other occasions he couldn't remember them—she might be turning to him with a hurt? If there was something the matter—he found it difficult to imagine anything serious, probably it had to do with Jon's working too hard or "their" not having become pregnant, something that, so far as he could tell, no one did anymore. If there was a problem, it had to be the Riker in-laws nagging her. In that case, he mustn't let the least trace of satisfaction appear. An as yet unmeasurable opportunity to repair the damage between him and Charlotte: that's what possibly lay before him. If only Carrie would help. At first, the absurdity of the pretension shocked him. That was something he would have had the right to expect from Mary, not from this child mistress. But there was no one alive he knew who had finer innate tact, no one more deeply benevolent.

II

LET'S take my car.

He didn't want to tell her that a huge cloud, as yet invisible in Bridgehampton, was gathering over him. Not until he knew its shape better, not until he had had another talk with Charlotte. He was going to the beach with Carrie for their daily walk. She kept the little BMW so clean that ordinarily she preferred to take his car. What's a station wagon for if not to be full of sand. And beach toys, he might have added. But the evening was so deliciously soft that she wanted to drive with the top down.

Hey, don't forget to get the sand off your feet before you get in when we go home. Use the towel.

Promise.

Carrie the waif, Carrie attached to her one possession like a little housewife. To see her like this gave him a sad shot of pleasure, similar to the feeling in the old days when some action or gesture of Charlotte's vividly showed that she was such a splendid girl, that Mary and he, although they were only children, and Mary an orphan to boot, had done well bringing her up. Carrie's driving way too fast once she got behind the wheel of the little convertible was another matter; had they used his car she would have rolled along sedately, as behooved a lady behind the wheel of a big fat Volvo. One balanced the other. Therefore, Schmidtie, avoid remarks about people in little red cars zipping over country roads at fifty. The tires protested when she hit the brakes in full view of the ocean. It waited there, blue and black, regular small breakers lining it near the beach like the furrows that once lined the potato fields reaching all the way to the dune before the farmers sold out to make room for rich men's beach houses.

Perfect day, I'm glad you got back early.

The sand was soft and rutted. He trotted awkwardly to the water to test its temperature.

It's not cold, he called out. We'll have a swim after the walk. This is too good to be missed.

You swim. I think I'd drown.

You won't. I'll hold on to you.

No way José.

She made a neat pile of their towels, wiggled out of her sweatshirt, and took him by the hand.

Hey, what are you waiting for, how about a kiss?

She wore the smallest of bikinis. Strings around her waist and between her legs that held in place a triangle of red cloth. Two smaller triangles of the same cloth attached to strings covered her nipples. Unbroken, luxurious tan; a salacious invitation to dream of the hours she spent lying in the sun naked. He took her in proudly, noting that even her feet were brown. A savage virgin goddess: no, a temple whore, ministering to adepts of Eastern mysteries. When she untied the cotton kerchief she had put over her head to drive in the open car, her hair, a mass of tiny curls, became a black halo surrounding her face.

Feasting locals, two couples of Schmidt's age, the others younger, probably their progeny accompanied by wives and husbands, comfortably installed in folding chairs, drink beer out of bottles. The older men are big, no taller than Schmidt but heavier, with comfortable paunches under their T-shirts and dull blond faces. Retired telephone repairmen or managers in one of the supermarkets at the mall. Wives apt to work at the checkout counter as supervisors, correcting the black teenage girls when they screw up on the cash register. Sour looking, but they're the last generation to have learned how to count. Bags of Fritos and a bowl of green dip pass from hand to hand. Does the younger set aspire to the same lives, to longevity in a society that has less and less use for the old? Have they thought up new ways of making it in the information age? Beside them, a cooler with more beer on ice and a barbecue grill. The charcoal briquettes have fine white ash on them. They are ready to receive the halved chickens and coils of Italian sausage spread out on a table covered with a sheet of plastic. These good people have brought their mountain of stuff in the pickup truck and two minivans parked steps away, too close to the dune and the once plentiful sandpipers nesting in it. Men Schmidt knows, upright denizens of the Georgica Association, would bellow stentorian reproof at these yokels. Schmidt doesn't feel up to the insults they might yell back. There was a middle way: he intensified his stare. As though rehearsed, the heads turned to stare at Carrie and him. Let them. This is about class warfare, not protection of the environment. Thank you for your interest, Mrs. Mahoney and Mr. O'Toole, please enjoy your front-seat view of the father out at the beach with a daughter who doesn't look much like him. Wait for the surprise. All I need to do is rotate her forty-five degrees and stick my tongue in her mouth. Then watch closely: she'll glue her body to mine while I'm running my hand over her back and buttocks and, yes, even down the crack between them.

He reaches for Carrie. Rising on exquisite toes, she deposits a chaste kiss on his lips.

Come on Schmidtie, that's all for now, these guys are watching. Let's get away.

I love you with all my heart.

I've got a secret for you. I love you too.

Just beyond where the tide reached, the sand was better: smooth, cool, and very hard. They walked fast, holding hands. That was where one might have wanted to run. Far ahead, at what seemed a great distance, were little human figures with animated black dots, their dogs, circling around them.

Charlotte called. Right after you left. She's coming out this weekend.

No kidding.

Yes. Do you mind? She said she would stay in the pool house.

I don't mind. Boy, that's really something. Their first time. Is this an anniversary or something?

No, no. And it's not they. She's coming alone. I think there's trouble between her and Jon. She didn't want to talk about it on the telephone.

Gee, Schmidtie, maybe I should move out while she's here. Huh? That'll be one thing less to worry about.

Without breaking her stride she raised his hand to her lips. Oh, how he adored her.

Where would you go?

I could ask the Blackmans, she ventured cautiously. I don't know about my friend.

That was the waitress at O'Henry's who lived in Springs. Perhaps the boyfriend, who had made unwelcome passes at Carrie, had moved on. How true it was that they really had no one they could turn to.

The Blackmans will be thrilled to have you, but if you don't mind I wish you'd stay. You know, keep me company, make sure I don't blow it. She's a big girl, might as well get used to you.

Yes, and also to the mess Jon Riker had made. It was better not to think about that. Avert your eyes, hold your nose, and let it lie there. Thank God, so far no one has asked for your views or help; that too may come. Charlotte must know everything. If it were only a question of Jon's having an affair, it would be tempting to advise her to shrug it off. Something on the order of, Look, Charlotte, Jon is an idiot, an idiot with a big legal brain, that's all. It isn't a world premiere for a fellow like him to have a fling with an attractive female lawyer—after they've spent hundreds of hours working on a deal together, evenings and nights included. Was that in fact the case? Had this woman and Riker been thrown together irresistibly, or was he always on the make and incapable of discretion? Did postfeminist young women like Charlotte shrug off a husband's peccadilloes? An idiot, a moral imbecile, who may have also brought the roof down on himself and damaged the firm! Unforgivable. Where did that conclusion fit, in a marriage made for better and for worse? Schmidt wasn't sure whether in fact that old-fashioned promise had been made in the bizarre Jewish ceremony Charlotte and Jon had cooked up, which he had observed from the enormous distance the painkillers had put between him, the bride and groom, and the groom's parents. Killing which pain? The leftover ache from the accident or his rage at those proceedings?

It is said that until the Last Judgment, when their understanding will be wholly extinguished, the souls of sinners consigned to hell will make out dimly the shape of the distant future, peering at it as though at dusk. Afterward, no more cognition. That is why hell swarms with gossips, shadows pitifully eager to extract the news of the day from recent arrivals. So it is with parents of grown sons and daughters: children's lives become opaque, closed to them, and they scavenge for every clue, desperate to understand, oblivious of their impotence. There was an unaccustomed hoarseness in the voice of Jack DeForrest, Schmidt's law school classmate and once-upon-a-time partner and best friend, now serving out his last year as the presiding partner of Wood & King—a signal of mounting though still-contained rage. Schmidt had called the great man, thinking he would ask how the firm was doing and let anything that might relate to the trouble between Charlotte and Jon Riker float to the surface naturally and spontaneously. True, the chances of learning anything helpful by snooping around at W & K were small. At the same time, old habits of not leaving a stone unturned when a client's welfare was at stake kept him from doing nothing; he simply couldn't wait until the talk he and Charlotte might have on Saturday—and he supposed that no such a conversation, however hard he tried, would take place on Friday evening. Not right after the jitney ride from the city, without giving her first a chance to take a dip in the pool, not when they sat down for a late dinner with Carrie at the table.

That's a fine son-in-law you got yourself, Schmidtie, roared the potentate. Congratulations! What is it you said about him when he was up for partnership? Luminous intelligence? Never a false move on the checkerboard? Killer instincts? That last sound bite was right on the beam—he's killing the goddamn firm and he's killing me! You know we keep the written reviews of candidates who are admitted. To be accurate, I should say that I keep them. Presiding partner's privilege, you know. They come in handy at times like this. I assume you're calling to apologize to me and the firm.

What are you talking about? I called to say hello, because it's been a month of Sundays since we last spoke. I don't keep up with Jon's work, but you, and Lew Brenner, everybody I'm in touch with, have always said he's doing a great job, building a real practice.

Ah, yes. I let it slip my mind that Charlotte, the model daughter, and you aren't on the best of terms. That makes two strikes against you, Schmidtie. You're running out of margin for error.

Jack, you are talking to me in a way I find offensive and mystifying. That's a bad combination. What have you got to reproach Jon with?

You really don't know? Well, it doesn't matter. Just wait until Monday. You're still getting the *Wall Street Journal*? There was a little squib about the Wilco litigation ten days ago that might have alerted you. The article they'll be running on Monday will tell you all you need to know.

I buy the *Journal* from time to time, at the candy-store counter. I'll certainly buy it on Monday. Now will you please tell me what you are talking about.

A trifle, Schmidtie, a mere trifle. Nothing to ruffle the feathers of a retired millionaire, who knew how to leave the firm while the going was good. We were—I use the past tense advisedly—counsel to the Balser family, the controlling shareholders of Wilco. You do realize who the Balsers are? Excuse me, of course, in your new life you're likely to have lunch with them twice a week! They're clients of Lew Brenner's, own everything in sight in Canada. They were clients when you were still on board. Suntech, the folks who last year sold Wilco their navigational systems company in exchange for Wilco stock, have sued the Balsers and all the former management of Wilco. Usual stuff you'd expect from an outfit like Suntech. Claims of fraud, manipulation of the stock price, and rape and incest for good measure, just because the stock is down. Way down, to tell you the truth. They also got the SEC riled up enough to start an investigation of its own. We put your Jon Riker in charge of the case. The bankruptcy business is dead, so we're using him as an all-purpose commercial litigator. Remember? You wrote he was fully qualified! In fact, I've got to hand it to you; there was no problem with the quality of the work. He wrote a great brief demolishing most of Suntech's claims and got permission from the court to file it with the supporting affidavits under seal, on the ground that they contained trade secrets and compromising statements about unrelated third parties. The court's decision on confidentiality was, of course, published. But your son-in-law had a thing going with a lady lawyer representing another, unrelated company that's being sued by Suntech, where Suntech is making pretty similar claims. She's a senior associate at Wolff & Wolff. That much is clear.

If only I could make him stop, thought Schmidt, if only I could go back to the moment before I began to hear this story.

DeForrest continued: Rather presentable, I gather. Jewish girl. Miss Vogel. You know, birds of a feather! You'll get to read about this too in the *Journal*. Seems he gave her a copy of the sealed brief and affidavits, violating—you see what I'm saying, Schmidtie, don't you?—violating the very same court order he'd gotten the court to issue. No one would have been any the wiser if this had ended right there, on the pillow. But Miss Vogel cooked up a brief of her own, making arguments straight out of the brief Riker had filed under seal, and filed her brief in her client's case with Suntech. The Suntech lawyers—the Crumfeld firm, no less, representing Suntech in the Wilco case and Miss Vogel's as well—read her brief, and the shit hit the fan. You do get it, Schmidtie? Those arguments simply couldn't have been made without knowledge of Riker's brief and affidavits. The predicates wouldn't have been there. Where Miss Vogel's information came from was so obvious to the Crumfeld lawyers that they moved to have the court appoint a special master to investigate the leak. Guess what! Your son-in-law had the gall to stand up before the master and deny he'd given the broad his brief! But Miss Vogel's a better lawyer than he. She told the master, yes, she'd had the opportunity to study the brief and the affidavits but didn't think there was anything confidential about them. There was nothing on their covers that said so. And you know what? The master believed her. So do I. That fathead Riker must have given her the papers without the stamp FILED UNDER SEAL on them!

Oh!

Yes. The Balsers have fired W & K from the federal court case Riker was handling—that was a no-brainer—and from all of Lew's other matters, companies that are in fine shape. Quite a chunk of business we lost, not to mention the professional embarrassment. Lew is apoplectic. The Balsers have told us they will make a claim against Wood & King, the amount depending on what happens in the Suntech lawsuit against them. We've already returned the fees they paid thus far, we've written off all the unbilled time, and we've offered to pay the cost of bringing replacement counsel up to speed.

The district court has yet to rule on Riker. If you ask me, the judge will hold him in contempt. And the partners are meeting next week to throw him out of the firm.

Shouldn't you get someone outside the firm to look at this first? A retired judge, like Tony Dixon?

Thanks for your suggestion. You always were naive, Schmidtie, and you haven't changed. Buzz Williams has been advising us. This is an assignment for a former prosecutor. He doesn't think much of Riker's story. You've got to put two and two together: He's sleeping with Miss Vogel, and Miss Vogel gets to study the brief. A prima facie case, if there ever was one. That's how Buzz sees it.

I am awfully, awfully sorry.

Well you might be. I never liked that fellow myself. Wrong background, wrong values, I never felt comfortable with him.

That was that. If DeForrest and enough of the boys made up their minds, and they had someone like Williams to lean on, Riker was a dead duck in the firm. Nothing this naive retired partner said could help. Besides, for all he knew Buzz Williams had done a good job and they were right.

Look, Schmidt said to Carrie. They've taken away the crane.

For weeks the gracile machine had labored, piling Mycenaean boulder upon boulder, erecting a barrier between the Jackson house, at the edge of Georgica Pond, and the breakers that gouged the beach and the dune on which the house was dangerously perched. Under them, vast sheets of black plastic, the corners of which had been tucked absurdly into crevasses between the boulders and secured by smaller rocks. In a few days it would be the bulldozer's turn to shovel the mountain of sand that had been brought in from Lord knows where until the boulders were out of sight under a smooth surface ready to be planted with sea grass. The barrier would hold forever or until the next big storm.

Hey, that guy is spending a fortune. What a jerk! Why doesn't he move his house or something.

He can't. Not enough room on his plot of land. He has no choice.

Shit, Schmidtie. You mean he will just keep doing this over and over, like a kid making sand pies?

Unless he gives up and lets the house fall down. What would you do?

Move into your house, dummy.

And what if my house falls down?

Hey, what's with you? I'm falling down, not your house. We're going to walk all the way to Montauk?

They had reached the jetty made of stones as huge as Mr. Jackson's, which had been flung into the ocean before Schmidt first knew this beach. The storms had let them be, perhaps because they were useless. So many endeavors with little to show for them. He put his arm around Carrie's waist and, suddenly tired himself, whispered, Let's go home. We'll swim another day. And mindful that change is said to keep sorrow at bay, he added, Let me take you out to dinner.

She orders shrimp in hot sauce, steak au poivre, and a raspberry tart. Schmidt likes to watch her eat. Where did she get those easy and natural manners, such complete elegance? Observing the merry revelers at O'Henry's? Not likely. Except for a few oddballs, including himself, of course, they are a repulsive lot, with no manners at all. Perhaps a crash course in old movies about old money, with focus on the two Hepburns, Katharine and Audrey, Leslie Caron, and Ingrid Bergman. Or is it something God given, like perfect pitch or a slum kid's knack for booting the soccer ball? Her fabulous, healthy appetite is another gift of nature: she has no food manias and no worries about excess calories. They will be burned off as though in a flame, for instance when she makes love. Schmidt leans back. Seize the moment. He wishes he could smoke in this place, but even though the hour is late, and the room half empty, the old biddies at the table on the other side would jump him. A brandy? She might have a sip from his glass. When Charlotte was at college, yes, already then, when he took her out to a restaurant in Boston, alone or with her friends, there were intimations of conflict. Did she really have to dress up? Was she going to get back to the dormitory by ten, so she could get her paper done for tomorrow, and why did he order that third cup of coffee when no one else was having any? All insignificant and easily resolved, if he had kept his mouth shut, or had at least kept smiling. Why couldn't he have done just that? After all, these conflicts didn't involve matters of high principle; they were about her refusal to be affable. Could he lay a sincere claim to being always imperturbably pleasant? He would have liked her to be kittenish with him, like certain daughters he had seen in the old movies he had studied, like Carrie without the sex. Charlotte managed it occasionally, and then at once they would become very good friends. Mostly, though, she gave the impression that he got on her nerves. Isn't it the truth that she got on his as well?

Right then, the Puerto Rican kitten piped up: Schmidtie, you want me to cook on Friday or you want to bring Charlotte here or the Automat?

"Here" was the hotel in Sag Harbor with a wine cellar Schmidt envied and a supply of first-class cigars that he wished he could smoke on the premises. A plague on tobacco abolitionists. Can't those cranks stay at home or wear gas masks when they go out? For two centuries, cigar smoke had accompanied the end of a meal. Where had they learned that it spoiled the taste of food? The Automat was another ball game, a temple of undercooked tuna, black on the outside, not quite raw when you got past the crust of pepper, and of dubious room temperature—Schmidt's bête noire, given his conviction that tuna should be eaten raw or out of a Bumble Bee can—shiitake mushrooms on spinach leaves, and fifteen varieties of bottled water. Clientele fat or anorexic: living reminders that it's all in the genes, baby. If you haven't the right metabolism, give up. Don't bother wrecking your knees as you pound the highway under the noonday sun in your three-hundred-dollar professional running shoes.

This place will be mobbed and noisy, he replied. The Automat and everywhere else too. Why don't we have something easy at home? I'll get a roast chicken or a duck and some cheese. Once upon a time she liked cheese. Who knows? Perhaps she still does. If she doesn't, you and I will eat it.

That wouldn't be right. Not for her first evening with us. I'll make the dinner. I don't have classes on Friday afternoon so I can shop on the way home. Like a surprise party.

You're my love. Don't let it hurt your feelings if it turns out that she can't eat this or that. She's always been picky. God knows what kind of diet she's on.

Don't worry. Hey Schmidtie, I haven't ever seen you so sad. It's because of the trouble between them?

It has to be. There is no other reason.

They've got no kids and you aren't crazy about him. Maybe they should split. It's heavy, but you'll get her back.

I don't want to think like that. Besides, somehow I don't believe it. I'm afraid that everything—good or bad—will just put more distance between us. She'll think that deep inside me I'm gloating, because once more I have told her so. She may be right. Perhaps she's got my number. There is another thing: if I get her back, what do I do with her? All the time, I rub her wrong. She doesn't want to be on the telephone with me, telling me how she's doing, what she's thinking, day-to-day kind of stuff. That's what she did with her mother. With me it's usually to pick a fight. You haven't seen her take the trouble to come out here to see whether the old man is doing all right.

That's because of me. She knows I'm here. She'll do it if I go.

Never. You're my love. If you leave me, it will have to be because you've stopped loving me or you love someone else better.

Hey, remember? When I asked you to tell me that you want me to be faithful, and you wouldn't? That really hurt my feelings. Schmidtie, there won't be anybody. Not as long as you want me.

Then don't worry about what Charlotte thinks.

C'est moi pour lui, lui pour moi pour la vie. . . . His own unhoped-for sparrow. He took the long hand that lay close to his on the table and kissed the palm. Rather than wipe a tear that was perhaps forming, he blinked and blew his nose. He was desperately happy at her side, in such fabulous luck.

The waiter, profile of a Sioux warrior, thick black hair tied in a ponytail, brought the check and gave Carrie the once-over while Schmidt counted out twenty-dollar bills. Flesh calls to flesh. Will this fine, loyal girl think Schmidt wants her when all he has to offer are geriatric caresses? Unless tedium, living alongside a fuddy-duddy retired gent shuffling among memories, does it first. Count your blessings, Schmidtie: it won't be long before you are really alone.

III

HEY, you want to see what I've cooked?

She had stuck her head out of the kitchen door to get him to come in from the garden, where he was busy giving Jim Bogard a hard time about the job his men had done edging the flower beds. He wanted clean, straight lines. Instead, he had gotten gentle curves, as though they'd been plotting bond yields during a week of market doldrums. And why hadn't they mulched, when he had especially explained that he wanted the place to look trim and fresh? Not that it mattered: Charlotte wouldn't be in a mood to notice. Still, getting things right was important to him, for the pleasure afforded to the eye, and as proof that he hadn't let himself or the place slide. Schmidt left Bogard scribbling in his notebook, promising that the work would be corrected that very afternoon. What a strange way to write for such a gritty and wiry little man: huge capital letters that ended in manic curlicues, followed by script too small for Schmidt to make out without his reading glasses. But at least Bogard didn't belong to the insupportable genus of handymen and gardeners who refuse to take notes on what the client wants, claiming they will remember. During his entire professional life, Schmidt had not tolerated a young lawyer coming into his office without a yellow pad and pencil. Why bother explaining a problem or giving instructions if in the next five minutes what he said would be forgotten or distorted? Or not taking notes during a meeting? Idle hands, idle hands.

The menu was fish lasagna, followed by a green salad and raspberry mousse. She had a small portion of the lasagna ready on a dessert plate and handed it to him.

Here, taste. But careful, it's real hot.

Carrie, that's a great dish. If you made it you are a great cook. Where did you get the idea for this?

It was, in fact, extraordinarily good, with a light taste of nutmeg. Nothing about the way he had seen her grill hamburgers or lamb chops on the kitchen stove—which was all he ever let her prepare, and at that only rarely, suspicious of what she might do to food and preferring the known and reliable quality of his own limited repertoire—had given him a hint that she might be a full-blown chef.

Surprise, surprise! You want to try the mousse?

He did. There was a separate portion of that waiting for him as well.

Fantastic! Why haven't you been whipping up these dishes for us every evening? How come you know how to make them?

Mrs. Gorchuck. My mom.

And she?

Haven't I told you, Schmidtie? Until she retired, she was a cook in an Italian restaurant off Atlantic Avenue. Boy, she can make anything.

But why have you kept your light under a bushel?

You dodo, I haven't cooked for you because you're always there in your apron cooking for me. Plus you do the dishes. It's a good deal. Why should I mess with it?

Well, that's over. The new deal is I stick to washing dishes and you do the rest. We'll never go to a restaurant again.

I'll stick to the deal I have. Schmidtie, you think she'll like it? Maybe you should tell her the food was catered. If she knows a dumb Puerto Rican waitress cooked it she'll think it can't be good. Also she'll think I'm like all over everything here. She'll freak out.

No, Carrie hadn't learned manners watching old movies. Mrs. Gorchuck had taught them to her, as well as recipes and skills that Brillat-Savarin would have found worthy of note, on her days off from that restaurant located on a street corner somewhere in the mythic Hispanic and black slum, once full of Jews, that stretches to infinity past Brooklyn Heights, the only part of Carrie's native borough Schmidt had visited, or late in the evenings, after the trip home on the graffiti-covered subway, dead tired though she was from the heat of the stove, her forearms covered by burns all the way to the elbows. Also true modesty and tact of a princess, precious matters of heart, more valuable than deportment, if indeed they could be taught. Or had these been the contribution Mr. Gorchuck, the retired board of education employee, whose former functions there were a mystery, had made to his only daughter's remarkable upbringing? Schmidt had on occasion imagined, during higher flights of his idiosyncratic humor, that Mr. Gorchuck, descended from Muscovite princes and czarist generals, had been guilty of his own misalliance, so that in the veins delicately lining Carrie's dusky skin the bluest blood of the steppes mixed with the cocktail of Puerto Rico. Less fanciful but appealing was the notion that Carrie might be a foster child, if not a foundling, whose native grace this pair had tenderly allowed to flower. Views as to the relative importance of nurture and genes were shifting anyway; the meaning of nurture was itself in question. Carrie's case, it seemed to Schmidt, called out loud for scientific study. His personal research had not progressed far. Occasional suggestions, both veiled and explicit, that he should really meet the parents and that he would enjoy going to their house (that is how he put it, from persistent habit of speech, although he realized that home might be a walk-up apartment) or receiving them in his own house—the latter prospect being, of course, one that filled him with dread—had been pushed off with a vague, Jesus, Schmidtie, they're doing OK, which he took to be another way of saying, Lay off. All right. That was her business. He supposed she had let Mr. and Mrs. Gorchuck know she was living with a man in the Hamptons and no longer working at O'Henry's, but not necessarily that he was a rich fellow, older than her own father. That had to be the simple explanation for her refusal. He couldn't believe that she, his brave and passionate Carrie, was ashamed of them. But he didn't know much, not even the father's age or whether he was, in fact, retired. Retired! Of course, he was. New York City employees could retire with full pay practically the day they started work. This was a subject better to avoid with Schmidt unless one wanted to get an earful.

Sweetie, I've told you, you really can't be sure with Charlotte. I haven't had a meal with her in so long I don't know what's on her approved list these days. Fish and pasta used to be right up there. Don't worry about it. I'll finish anything she doesn't eat.

Jeez, Schmidtie, you don't need to do that. I'm a big girl. I can take it.

He pulled her over to him, put his hands on her breasts, waited till the nipples hardened, and squeezed. Holy God. The stirrings of an erection. He rubbed it against her hip.

Later, Schmidtie. Keep the little guy in your pants until tonight, when we're in bed. Hey, let me put the mousse in the refrigerator. The pasta I'll let cool on the counter and then reheat real slow so you can eat anytime you want. Unless you want the food at room temperature? Mom likes that, like when she cooks for a party or whatever.

That evening, waiting for Charlotte at the bus stop, Schmidt tried to keep his mind on that conversation and the way Carrie had set the table for dinner in the kitchen, because that would be cozy with just the three of them. Lurking nearby were taxi drivers ordered in advance or hoping for a passenger no one was picking up, a man with hairy legs in shorts and dirty running shoes, two oversize secretaries with New York voices and fluffed-up hair, and other indistinguishable summer-rental types he preferred not to examine. His nerve had failed him. He hadn't agreed with Charlotte that she should call when she arrived so he wouldn't have to wait at the stop until the jitney pulled in. Since there was no telling whether the bus would be on time, that was what local residents did—except, perhaps, the most ardent lovers and anyone expecting a child or a passenger too infirm to get to the phone and wait for a ride. But suppose she had forgotten the custom and took amiss his not standing there at attention to welcome the returning prodigal daughter. It was not a risk worth taking.

Just then a bus from New York arrived, the vision causing great disturbance in Schmidt's feelings. Ceiling lights turned on by the driver revealed indistinct figures, standing up, gathering their belongings, reaching for overhead racks. Avidly, he scrutinized them one by one. Such a long time ago—could it really be twenty years?—waiting in a group of Brearley School parents for the bus that brought the whole class back from a field trip, and, as the girls filed out, he realized that he could not summon Charlotte's face before his eyes. It was as though he had forgotten it. At that very moment she appeared at his side and threw her arms around him. He knew that not being able to make her out in the dim light, through tinted windows of the jitney, with the summer people milling around, was different, perfectly understandable, but the anxiety that he had disastrously lost the memory of her silhouette, possibly even of her face, was the same. The last passenger got off. No Charlotte.

Is this the six o'clock bus? he asked the driver.

Nah, five-thirty. The traffic's real bad.

When do you think the six o'clock will get in?

You tell me. Could be fifteen minutes, could be more.

This was the worst of all worlds. If he went home, intending to return in half an hour, assuming the man's estimate was realistic, he'd be wasting fifteen to twenty minutes on the round-trip. Besides, the bus might have traveled fast, so that it would arrive in Bridgehampton before he returned, in which case Charlotte would be waiting on the sidewalk, fuming. Unless she called the house. Then she and Carrie were bound to have the first of what was apt to be a series of testy conversations. The advantage of going home, though, was that he could hug Carrie and be hugged by her and drink a large bourbon. The image of Carrie's embrace was in itself so immediately comforting that he found himself able to postpone, for a brief while, its physical realization. A bourbon could be had at O'Henry's. He would get his drinks at the end of the bar and every few minutes take a step or two toward the sidewalk to keep an eye on the bus stop and the road beyond it. But he had better call Carrie and tell her the jitney was late.

The hoarse voice responded: That's cool. Say hi to Pete. I'm going to wash my hair. Don't worry, silly, I'll be ready. I won't bother drying it, that's all.

Pete the bartender winks at Schmidt. The old-timers at O'Henry's are given to winking at him—when he walks into the restaurant, when they run into him on the street. Why not? He is the old geezer who walked off with the big prize. Does Schmidt want the usual? Yes, a double sour mash, with lots of ice. The liquor relieves his tension, like diving into a wave. Forgiveness and absolution. Knot after knot dissolves. The place is packed and unbearably noisy; a chorus gone mad, singing crescendo. The roar invades the sidewalk outside. Pete has another question for Schmidt, but there is no way he can be heard. Schmidt smiles back and shrugs his shoulders. Gestures do work. Pete pours him a single. It has just made it down the hatch when Schmidt registers the huge shape of the jitney slowing down, then drawing up at the curb.

There was no mistaking his daughter; how could he have thought otherwise even for a moment. Her strong and open face, a little tired but so beautiful, rich blond hair gathered in a knot at the back of her head, an Amazon's gait, even though she is carrying a duffel bag and a heavy briefcase, both of which he takes from her hands in the prolongation of a gesture that began with kissing her. A quick, surreptitious look at her clothes. Deplorable: a parody, possibly self-conscious, of a man's charcoal-gray pinstriped double-breasted suit, the jacket ridiculously long, aggravating the disgrace of the skirt that ends a good five inches below the knee, the shoulders heavily padded and too wide. Clunky black shoes with thick high heels. Why would one dress like that, and especially on the most beautiful summer day, at the end of which one was leaving town for the beach? Mysteries of fashion and unfulfilled aspirations. Her business and none of yours, Schmidtie.

I am so very happy to see you, sweetie. Welcome. The car is across the street.

It's good to get out of the city. You know, you didn't have to come to get me yourself. A taxi would have been just fine.

The thought didn't cross my mind.

It certainly hadn't, and, if it had, Schmidt would have rejected it indignantly. Is she giving signs of a new considerateness that borders queerly on humility? Or firing a first salvo intended to rattle the old guy, put him in his place? If so, for what purpose? Most likely it's nothing of the sort: she just doesn't give a damn. She took the bus because she has something she wants to talk to him about in person, that's all there is to it, nothing to make her heart go pitter-patter. Irritated by the silence, but unwilling to be the first to speak, he turns on the car radio. *Rigoletto* comes on, his favorite moment, when the old clown begs Marullo and his accomplices to say what they have done with the kidnapped Gilda.

Can you turn that off, Dad?

Sure.

Her name is Carrie. Right? Will she be there?

Carrie Gorchuck. Yes, she's at home. In point of fact, she has prepared a rather nice dinner for us.

I'm not sure I want to eat.

Suit yourself. If I were you I'd have a dip in the pool, get out of this Al Capone outfit, and come to dinner—whether you eat or not. Otherwise you will make me very annoyed. And, above all, please don't talk back.

Sure, Dad. Thanks for the nice compliment about my clothes.

They're fine, baby. I was just trying to be funny. You know me and my sense of humor.

Don't bother.

That was to stop him from carrying her bags. He nodded, although she did not turn back to look, and waited beside the car. Such a beautiful night! With the moon lost somewhere in a sky that had finally turned black, the stars had no competition. Every constellation known to Schmidt was on parade. Not a mosquito, and yet the breeze off the ocean was so light that he hardly felt it. A screen door slammed. That would be the pool house. Such wretched waste—why hadn't he for once resisted making a crack? It was no use following her to plead for peace; she wouldn't listen. He had better be patient. Unless she had gorged on peanuts and pretzels aboard the jitney—which would be unlike her—he could count on hunger after that ride. It would bring her to the table. Luckily, he hadn't stocked the pool-house refrigerator. And if she proved malevolent enough to hold out anyway, he would send her packing to New York first thing in the morning. Would Carrie tell him he'd gone crazy in the head or congratulate him on his strength of character?

I'm here.

By the time Charlotte thus announced her presence in the kitchen they had started dinner. Her place was still set, Carrie having stopped Schmidt when he had made a move to clear it. Why do you want to spook her, she said. So what if she's taking a bath or feeling upset or whatever. The food's cold anyway.

That's nice. Now sit down and help yourself. I'll pour you some wine. You know Carrie, I believe.

Hi, Charlotte.

Oh, yes.

She put her hand over the wineglass, reached for the water pitcher, and reconsidered.

You have any Perrier or other bottled water?

In the icebox. You know the water is still from our own well.

OK, I'll drink the tap water. Since when do you eat dinner in the kitchen?

Since whenever we aren't numerous and no one's waiting on table. Do you mind? I thought you liked this kitchen.

Sure, sure. What's this in the ovenware dish? Some kind of pasta?

Fish lasagna, Charlotte.

Is that rice over there? I'll just have the rice. Pasta and rice together. Isn't that rather odd? Another innovation?

Unusual, but it tastes good.

Oh, I believe you.

What was he to do? Hit her? Leave the table? First call a taxi to take her to New York, and then slug her? Carrie's expression was one he knew well from the restaurant: a dreamy, disconnected smile that illuminated her face when she took orders from a party of boors or when an impatient diner snapped his fingers for the check. When she was like that, nothing short of an irresistible fit of the giggles could break down her composure. He thought the giggles were about to start, when, instead, she addressed Charlotte: Gee, that's one of my mom's ideas. They serve lasagna with rice on the side in the restaurant where she cooked. It's like an Italian specialty.

Really? Is your mother a chef?

Chef? No. She cooked for a neighborhood restaurant in Brooklyn. A lot of Italians eat there. Nothing fancy, not like O'Henry's. Yeah, she worked until the veins in her legs got real bad. Also her blood pressure. That's why I quit college. When she stopped working, Mom and Dad couldn't afford it.

He needn't have worried. Carrie could take care of herself. That was how she had told him her short life story too, in flat, matter-of-fact statements, leaning on the backrest of an empty chair while he ate the hamburger and French fries she put before him. Not a hint of self-pity or desire to appear other than she was. She knew what she considered her place and, without fuss, calculated the position of others in relation to it. Only she was worth far more than her modesty allowed her to take into account.

I'm sorry to hear it. And is that why you came to Bridgehampton?

That's right. I left Brooklyn College after a year and got the job at O'Henry's to make enough money to go back to school. Maybe in a couple of years. But now Schmidtie's helping me so I'm going to Southampton College. I'm majoring in social work, but someday I want to study film.

Having said that, she blushed. In a moment, Schmidt felt her naked foot, which had traveled under the table, insert itself into his trouser leg and rub against his calf. Cautiously, he reciprocated the caress.

Maybe I should have studied film too. Sometimes it seems that half my college class is in Hollywood, doing something or other. Mostly writing scripts. I think it's too late for me.

Dad's friend Gil Blackman should be able to help you. If they're still friends.

Yeah, he's talked about it. I think I should finish school first. That way, maybe I can get a job on my own. Wouldn't that be something!

Never happens in my father's circles. Remember, Dad? When you sent me to meet Mr. Ogglethorpe—the man who would help me enter the workforce. It seems it was impossible to believe that any PR firm would even dream of hiring me unless my father, the great Mr. Schmidt of Wood & King, pulled the right strings! God, I hated it. The same way Mom would never leave me alone. Every summer job I took had to be something she cooked up. Basically another intern slot at some la-di-da country newspaper.

She looked drearily sad but also triumphant.

You loved those jobs, Charlotte.

Sure, tagged from the word "go" as the kid of the publisher's friend. Someone you better not mess with, if you know which side your bread is buttered on. Like living at the publisher's house, with one of Mom's pre-Alzheimer authors.

Hah! An unkind cut, one that Schmidt hadn't expected. That was the job in Pittsfield, at a first-rate paper, liberal then, owned by Jay Kane. Jay became known when he threw himself into Ed Brooke's Senate campaign and antiwar protests. The little snake had stayed with Jay and his wife, Sue, who had been Mary's roommate at Milton. Mary published Jay's *Dangerous Games* a couple of years before Charlotte's summer at the newspaper, when it was still on the best-seller list, making Jay even richer. Coals to Newcastle. He remembered Charlotte's telephone calls—a little too breathless, he had worried—commenting on the glamorous doings in the Kane household. He would have sworn then that she was having the time of her life.

Carrie spoke. Man, I wish I'd had those problems. So this guy Oggle-something handed you a job.

No way. I could just see myself stuck forever as his assistant in charge of sending birthday cards to members of Congress and their wives. What else would Miss Schmidt, who couldn't get a job on her own, be good for? Thanks a lot! I got my job all by myself, through the college placement office, just like everybody else. Only Dad thinks it's shit, because I do public relations for tobacco! Lobbying for tax breaks, like Dick Ogglethorpe, that's OK.

Oh, I've pulled in my horns, believe me. Anyway, now that all your clients' chairmen have told Congress they don't believe cigarettes are addictive, you may be out of work. Everybody will recognize they're just lovable businessmen. They won't need public relations help at all!

Very funny. You think all I can do is tobacco. Well, you've always been supportive.

Not at all. I can see you just as easily fighting for the cause of snack foods—or the Sierra Club. It's all the same. Just working on a case, representing a client.

That's what you thought too about your clients, when you still had them. Hey, this lasagna is great. You really made it from scratch?

Just the filling, not the pasta itself. I got that from the Italian guy at the mall. But I could have made the pasta if I'd had more time. Mom showed me.

That's cool.

She helped herself to another serving, without bothering to pass the dish to Carrie or to Schmidt, and held up her glass.

Carrie filled it. You like it? Your dad got it. He said we should have Italian wine.

He would. Always saving his good wine for a special occasion. Actually, it's OK.

That too was a low blow. Since French red wine in the year of her birth was not up to the mark, he had laid down cases of the next great vintage to drink the night before her wedding, at the rehearsal dinner, and when she had her first child. The former occasion he had missed. Either the Rikers, who had taken over all the arrangements, had not given such a dinner, or he hadn't been invited. One could hope the wine would hold up until time came for the latter event.

I consider this is a special occasion, Charlotte, he told her, and the wine is a great Chianti, not just an OK wine. We can cook some lamb on the grill tomorrow evening and break out a burgundy.

If I'm still here.

It was time for Carrie's foot to visit Schmidt's leg again. It remained there, gentle but busy, until she got up to clear the dishes.

I'm going to make coffee. You guys want to talk in the library while I clean up? I'll serve the coffee to you.

Thanks, Carrie, I'm beat. No coffee and no talk with my father tonight. Can't do that unless I'm rested. Tomorrow morning, if that's convenient.

You're sure, Charlotte? Won't you sleep better if we have a chat before you go to bed?

Dad, it can wait.

He came down early, careful not to interrupt Carrie's sleep. The sheet on his side of the bed confirmed his recollection, entwined with dreams, of how the evening ended. The most exposed, vulnerable flank of his position was for the moment secure; he thought he could face anything. Charlotte must have gotten up even earlier. He had run his morning errands and was starting to read the *Times* when she walked into the kitchen in her running clothes. Sweat stains, hair tied back, tall and fit. That was how he remembered her when he thought of the morning, in his distant earlier life, when she told him she was going to marry Jon Riker.

I've been running.

I see that. I've made orange juice for you. It's still in the juicer. Tea or coffee? The tea is right here on the table. If you want coffee, the machine is all set to go. Just flip the switch.

I'll take the tea.

A croissant?

Is there any yogurt?

In the icebox. Do try the croissants. They're quite good.

I don't eat them.

Ah. Try lying low. Listen without making a noise. Back to the article he was reading in the paper. It was pure rot to pick on him and claim he was an anti-Semite. There were some Jews he liked and others, including selected members of the Riker family, he didn't. Mostly, he didn't notice them, one way or another. He certainly wished Jews in general and the state of Israel the best of luck. Right now, his hat went off to Rabin—maybe that wasn't the right metaphor—for being willing to get physically close to Arafat, an unshaved, probably ill-smelling, loudmouth with bad teeth. It must be hard to tolerate being in the same room with him, never mind performing those Levantine embraces. Even when it came to Arabs, his dislikes were individualized; they weren't racial prejudice. He had absolutely nothing against King Hussein. Arabs should be looked at one by one, just like Jews and everybody else. That didn't mean one had to ignore group characteristics, such as Arabs'—and Jews'—odious rhetoric. Always exaggerating. Unable to stop themselves.

Dad, can we talk?

Of course.

When is she going to come down?

Carrie? I don't know. When I last saw her she was sound asleep.

Sure. I mean could we talk somewhere else?

As you wish. In fact Carrie is very discreet. She'll probably stay out of the kitchen if she sees that we're having a conversation. Anyway, she won't mind. Let's move to the back porch.

The old rosebush at the edge of the lawn had never looked better. Schmidt decided he would keep his eyes fixed on it, to stay grounded.

So look, I want to talk about some business matters. I suppose your investments are doing well in this market. Is that right?

I think so.

She fell silent, so he babbled on: The Romberg people still look after them, and they do a good job. I try to see Herb Stein over there once every few months, just to make sure he hasn't lost his marbles or hit the bottle. Other than that, I don't pay much attention. In fact, I've sold those two little funds I'd invested in on my own. Remember? I was always looking them up in the business section. They appreciated nicely, and that's how I paid for the little convertible I gave Carrie.

Nice for her. Then you haven't lost all your money—or the money you got from your stepmother.

Bonnie's money? Oh, no. Not at all. Though I have given a good chunk of what she left to me to the hospital in Palm Beach. Including the house.

He wished he hadn't thought of the house. It was his lawyer Murphy who had urged him to transfer it to a charity, and as a business matter the advice was good. Disliking Palm Beach, he'd never use it, and the cost of upkeep, if you included the salary he paid as tribute to Bryan, was ridiculous. As part of the deal, he did get the president of the hospital to agree that Bryan would go on the payroll as a handyman at the conference center into which Bonnie's house would be transformed. But when he announced the news to Bryan on the telephone, the little creep didn't seem pleased. Working for the hospital wasn't what he had in mind. What was he thinking and what could he be up to? If Schmidt only had one of his yellow pads at hand, he would make a note to himself to check into the situation.

Oh yeah? How much did you give away?

Basically I kept what my father had left to her, which was everything he had when he died, plus the average return she had on her investments. It seemed to me I was entitled to that. But the money that came to her from Sozon—her first husband—that was another matter. I didn't feel right about keeping it, so I gave it to the hospital.

That's pretty grand, Dad. I didn't know you had become a philanthropist.

Not at all. It just seemed the right thing to do, to honor her for what she had done for me, which she wasn't under any obligation to do.

I sure hope you didn't give away too much, because I have to ask you for money.

You mean to tide you and Jon over until he sorts things out?

This has nothing to do with Jon. I guess if we have to we can talk about him later. Gee, you really have Jon on your mind or something. Dad, the thing is that I'm plain tired of working for other people. Marden Bush is OK, I'm still on the learning curve, and, believe me, representing tobacco clients isn't a dead end, like representing some other kinds of institutions.

Were these gratuitous digs ever going to stop? This one, Schmidt tended to think, had been prepared in advance. On the other hand, it might have just popped out. Having lived five—or was it six?—years with Jon Riker, she must have heard plenty about how Schmidt's clientele, insurance companies acting as lenders to corporations, had melted away until he became, in Riker's estimation and that of his cohorts, one of those older partners who burden the firm, siphoning off income from others who are more deserving, especially the Young Turks. Considering that she was apparently about to ask him for something—something big, he was willing to bet—she might see the wisdom of holding her tongue just once. But then she knew him well enough to realize that in the end it wouldn't matter how much she hurt his feelings. It was possible that she felt she was striking out as an independent, real grown-up by getting what was due to her without being nice or grateful.

I see.

She continued, There is this great guy at the firm I work with a lot on a bunch of campaigns. He's very good, they just made him managing director. We've been talking how we could go out on our own. You know, set up our own shop. Start small and grow the business or whatever. You never did that, but lots of people do. It's no longer standard to stay in the same firm all your life.

She paused, as though to give Schmidt equal time. A grunt, somewhere between "oh" and "right," seemed to him a sufficient and prudent response.

You don't seem very interested.

Oh, I am. And what would you hope to do? Provide the same services you are providing now to the same clients? Is that possible? I would imagine Marden Bush has some sort of noncompete rules that would apply to a managing director, if not to you.

Harry's looked into this. That's the name of my future partner, Harry Polk. We want to go into organizing special events, like fund-raisers and seminars and that sort of stuff, and we're allowed to do it. That's what the lawyers have told him. We'd get a consent anyway, to cover all the bases and make the firm feel they're participating. That's good strategy if we want them to refer work to us. They might. Marden Bush doesn't have an events capability.

He smiled at her. Polk, Polk. Interesting, but let's not jump to conclusions about family and background. The name could be a short version of Polski or Pohlstein. Or whatever, if he might borrow Charlotte's and Carrie's entrancing locution. It was amusing how belonging to the same generation seemed to transcend differences of upbringing and class. Why not call a spade a spade? Schmidt knew that the expression could no longer be used in polite conversation, but he wasn't talking. Just thinking.

So we need some start-up money. For the new office and as working capital. Are you willing to help?

Hold on. I am always there to help you, but there are things I have to know. First, how much do you want from me; second, how much money you have from your savings and what your mom left you; and, third, what about your partner, Mr. Polk? Does he have the money to invest in this venture? And where does Jon fit into this? I assume you realize that he's in very serious trouble. Financial trouble, as well.

She named her figure. It was even larger than what Schmidt had expected.

This has nothing to do with Jon, she continued, you won't be giving comfort to the enemy. It turned out that the price you paid when you bought my share of this house wasn't enough to pay for the house in Claverack and the renovations there and the apartment in the city, so I spent Mom's money too and most of my savings. I have all the records and statements with me, if you want to take a look. Harry has some cash. The rest has gone into a loft he bought a couple of years ago, and fixing it up. He thinks he can borrow against it, but not very much. For the time being, I'll have to be the money partner!

I see. You realize, I hope, that when I bought your remainder interest—what you call your share in this house—I simply paid the market price. Quite frankly, it never occurred to me that what I paid was supposed to be enough to let you buy and restore that place in the country so you could be next to the Riker parents and also to pay for an apartment in the city. Weren't the Rikers going to give you and Jon the money for the apartment? I recall your telling me that was the plan.

Yeah, but he decided he didn't want to take so much money from them. You don't have to make that face. Renata thought he was right. She said if he took the money from his mother—it would have to be her money because Myron doesn't have much—it would increase his sense of dependency. So we borrowed as much as we could from the bank, and I put in Mom's money.

There were endless advantages to be found in the exercise of a psychoanalyst's profession. How it served to torment the father of the woman your son was going to marry, Schmidt had already seen. This was a new vista: you could back out of a financial commitment you made to that son and his wife and end up with them convinced you were doing them a favor. Empowering them! That was probably the fashionable expression.

I see, he told her.

Immediately, Schmidt was sorry he had repeated himself. It was time to break the habit of those automatic rejoinders. They steadied the nerves, but so would keeping his eye on the rosebush. There was no way out. However much he hated it, he had better go on with his questions.

And what did you and Jon do about title to these properties—I mean who owns what? I assume the house in Claverack is in your name, but what about the apartment? Are you both liable for the money you borrowed from the bank?

We thought we should take title in both our names, in Claverack and in the city. I think I signed on the loan. Jesus, Dad, give me a break. Isn't that what married couples do?

Not always, not when there is such a financial imbalance. That's something you will have to sort out, since I gather there is trouble between you. Is there trouble? What about you and Jon? What is Jon going to do? I don't understand your ducking a subject that really seems very urgent.

Dad, can't that wait? I'm trying to talk to you about my work and my life.

From within the house, Schmidt picked up welcome, happy noises. The whir of the juicer. The kitchen radio tuned to the Southampton University station. Carrie was up. His rosy-fingered dawn with the instincts of a grande dame. She would have understood that they were having that father-and-daughter talk on the porch and wouldn't venture near them unless it went on so long those same instincts told her it was time to come to his rescue. Impossible to count on that anytime soon, but he might just sneak out on the pretext he was getting a glass of water, and hug her, plunge his hand into the dark cleavage still warm from the bed.

I am just trying to get a full picture, and I think what has happened to you and Jon as a couple is very much at the center of it. I had a talk with Jack DeForrest a couple of days ago. What he told me wasn't just unattractive. It rocked me. Jon is in bad trouble. So I think we will have to talk about that sooner or later, and frankly I don't quite see how you can think about quitting your job and starting a new business of your own without taking him into consideration.

Later, Dad. Can I get you to understand that?

Yes, you can. I have already understood that much. What is it then that you want? A loan, or do you want me to invest in this operation? In either case, I think I should first get to meet your partner, Mr. Polk, and take a look at your business plan. I suppose you've prepared one. Certainly Mr. Polk will need one if he wants to borrow from a bank. I guess I am quite ready to go either way, if your project makes sense.

He couldn't immediately remember when she had given him a look like that. Ah yes, when he told her that Mary and he couldn't afford to buy a hunter with serious show potential, and certainly couldn't afford to keep such a horse in the city. And after that? Perhaps never; he may have shattered her illusions forever with that refusal. But this time, he wasn't saying no; he thought he was saying yes. What could be the matter?

Gee, Dad, this isn't real, I can't believe it. I didn't think I was going to see a banker. I thought I was talking to my father who's rich enough to give people BMWs as presents. Yeah, I was stupid enough to think that since my father has only one child—that's me, remember—he might just give me the money, as a present, without buying anything like my interest in a house, or making me a loan, or investing in my business. I can't figure you out. You think Harry and I want you to own our business? We'd be working for you. I don't know about Harry, but I'd rather work for Marden Bush.

Ah.

Her eyes filled with tears.

Now, now, Charlotte. Can't we discuss this calmly? It is, after all, a business matter.

Forget it. It's like Renata said. You need to control my life. If I let you, everything's peaches and cream. The moment I don't, it's Schmidtie the Hun.

Yes, Dr. Renata Riker. Why hadn't he strangled her, in plain sight of the afternoon crowd on Fifth Avenue, after their first and only lunch tête-à-tête? Help, help! Voices have told me I had better waste that shrink before she wastes me.

No American jury would have taken more than five minutes to acquit him: self-defense or in the worst case not guilty by reason of insanity. He might not even have had to stand trial. Now it was too late.

Look, he said. You are asking for a lot of money. Nevertheless, you are quite right to think I am able to give it to you and go on living as I do.

She snickered.

Easy does it, Schmidt counseled Schmidtie the Hun. Don't pay attention.

The point is that the gift tax has not yet been abolished, he told her. If I make a gift, I will have to pay the federal government and New York State a tax of more than seventy percent on top of what you want me to give you. That, too, isn't the end of the world, although when you put the two together, the gift and the tax on the gift, it means parting, all of a sudden, with a large sum I hadn't counted on spending. On the other hand, you are my only child, and I suppose no one can fault you if you expect to inherit from me. But that's when I die, not right now. There will be an estate tax too when I do kick the bucket. That's why some tax planners would say that it's smart to make gifts and pay the gift tax because then the money I've used to pay the tax will not be in my estate and won't be taxed on my death.

Wow, Dad!

No need to be sarcastic. It's good tax advice, although I am not sure it fits my case. I am in good health and seem to take after my father, who lived to be very old. I might need every cent of my money to pay for a nursing home!

There was no telling whether she was listening. The hurt in her face had turned into bored gloom. What the hell, he might as well finish his speech. Trying not to hear his own words—the speech, he admitted to himself, was tiresome—he continued: Especially if the business you and Mr. Polk start doesn't take off. If that was the case, if I made you a loan or invested, I wouldn't have paid the gift tax and might be able to write off the loss on my loan or investment. That's how sensible people plan their financial affairs.

I get it. Let's just skip the whole thing. I'll talk to Harry. Maybe we'll just stay where we are.

Do talk to him. And think over what I have said. Look, sweetie, please get it into your head that if you decide you don't want a loan and don't want me to invest in your business, but you do want me to make you a gift, the money is yours for the asking, tax or no tax. But I want to meet Harry Polk first, and I don't think it's unreasonable that I ask to see a business plan. That's for your protection. People used to pay a lot of money to get my judgment on that sort of thing. For you, it's free.

Very funny. I guess I should say thank you.

You might, and you are welcome. When is all this supposed to happen?

We thought of giving notice like next week and then going on vacation. I'm beat.

Would you come here? I'd love it.

Dad!

It was just an idea.

He had really better stop the automatic speech and automatic ideas. This was a lousy one. How could he imagine that Charlotte would want to spend a couple of weeks with him and Carrie, and how could he make the offer without first asking Carrie? Probably she'd say, That's cool, but suppose she didn't, suppose she said, instead, You've got to be shitting me. What then? How does one back out without making a real mess? He had to hand it to Charlotte, she had saved the day.

All right, we were thinking of going to this tennis camp in Aspen. But Harry doesn't know if he can get away. It depends on the children.

Oh.

He's divorced and he's got these two boys, seven and five. If his wife can get some time off later this month, he'll stay with the kids in this place they share in the Berkshires. They're cute little guys. That's another reason Harry hasn't got much money. He's paying both child support and alimony.

And he's sure it makes sense for him to leave a job with a steady income for a start-up business?

Dad, this is a big chance. We know we can make it. Harry will never get out of the hole unless he makes real money and owns something.

I see.

He sure did. A divorced man with two children, obligations to his wife, and no money to speak of in the bank account, who wants the use of Charlotte's money for his new business. In the meantime, why not take a vacation together at a tennis camp! That seemed unambiguous enough, no need to probe. Who knows, she might even choose to tell him more. But she gave no sign of being about to speak.

Therefore he continued: Right, I do want to meet him. The sooner, the better. Look, Charlotte, could we talk about Jon now? I've told you that I've spoken with Jack DeForrest. I really don't know where to begin.

All right, Jon's an asshole. But he didn't give that bitch the brief, she stole it out of his briefcase, and he's too fucked up to tell on her. That's the problem in a nutshell, and it's his problem. I'm going to leave him. What would you suggest instead? Is there anything else you want to know? You must sure be glad you were right about him.

No he wasn't, thank God he wasn't. He hadn't become the bad, vengeful witch. He had cast no evil spells, hadn't hoped for vindication of this sort. That part of Renata the shrink's warning, delivered during the presumptuous, inexcusably familiar lecture she gave him upon their first meeting, directly after the Riker family Thanksgiving lunch his daughter and the imbecile fiancé had blackmailed him into attending, he had taken seriously. Yes, he had grown to loathe Jon Riker. Furthermore, Renata may have been right, and Jon too, if she was repeating faithfully what Jon had told her, to claim that deep inside he had always disliked that boy—even when he worked with him so closely at Wood & King and pushed hard to have him made a partner. Their decision to be married in an odious restaurant in SoHo rather than in the family house, Charlotte's refusal to wear her mother's wedding dress, the way she had taunted him—how else could one describe telling him that only a rabbi would officiate at the wedding and she planned to convert to Judaism?—Jon's calumny, which she had dared to throw in her father's face, that he was known throughout his firm as an anti-Semite, all this and more rankled. But none of it could make him rejoice to hear Charlotte, cool as a cucumber, make light of her marriage and dismiss her husband with a vulgar epithet. Nothing had prepared him for such disgrace. He must have been blind.

I am so terribly sorry. Poor Charlotte. Have you told Jon what you plan to do?

You're sorry? You couldn't stand him. You should be saying good riddance. No, I didn't have to tell him. He's an asshole, but he's not dumb. The thing is that he won't move out of the apartment. And I have to sleep in the guest room, because he won't get out of my bedroom either. Harry says I need to get a lawyer real soon. Do you think W & K would take the case, since they're throwing him out of the firm anyhow? He's already got a lawyer, a guy with an Italian name—Cacciatore or something.

Schmidt sighed. I should think it would be very awkward for any of the lawyers at the firm to represent you against him, he told her. From the way you've just talked, and the way you own the apartment and the house in Claverack jointly, I don't believe this is going to be a friendly separation, in which all you need is a lawyer to advise on taxes and write up what the parties agreed on. If you like, I'll call Murphy and ask him for a recommendation. You must remember him, he's the partner at the firm who has done Mom's and my wills. He knows a lot of divorce lawyers.

I remember Mr. Murphy. He's not what I want anyway. I want a real tough Jew, so Jon and Cacciatore don't run circles around him. I'd use Harry's lawyer, but Harry doesn't think he did such a hot job for him. You think I can move in with Harry? I'm sick and tired of having Jon around, but I don't want him to be able to say it's my fault if I leave the apartment and live with Harry.

These days I don't think it matters. You had better check though. Murphy will know. I'll ask him when I talk to him about a lawyer for you. Charlotte, I began to wonder when you mentioned the tennis camp, but now it seems crystal clear. I take it you're having an affair with Mr. Polk. Did it begin before Jon started seeing this woman?

You mean Debbie Vogel?

The lady lawyer. The one who's at the center of the trouble about the brief.

It started before, but who cares? Jon was screwing one of the paralegals after hours, in his own office, on the floor or on the desk. Dennis's wife told me. Everybody knew about it.

He heard Carrie's footsteps in the front hall. Honey, he called out. Charlotte and I have almost finished. Do you want to make some coffee? We could have coffee out here.

Not for me, said Charlotte.

My poor baby. You've been married for such a short time, you and Jon knew each other so well, you'd been together for years, why marry only to go with other people?

You've got to be kidding. Don't you admit to yourself that people have sex? You of all people, living with this girl! Let me ask you some questions. Why did you cheat on Mom? You think I didn't know you were laying my Vietnamese babysitter, right in this house, under Mom's nose? Please explain that one to me. Jesus, you even made a pass at Renata. Couldn't resist it, could you? If you ask me, men are shits. Oh great, you look like your eyes are going to pop. I get it. I guess I just blew my chances of getting that money. Stupid me.

Her voice was reaching him from a great distance. Another voice, much smaller and closer to him, whispered, Don't worry, stop counting your money, it will all be hers pretty soon anyway. It was extraordinary how tired she made him. He shook his head, as though to get water out of his ear, and reassured her: The money's at your disposal. Charlotte, just tell me into what account I should have it transferred.

And seeing that she had brightened and was going to speak, presumably thank him, he raised his hand and added, Please no more speeches.

A man is stuck with his bad nose, eyes, hair, teeth, and texture of skin—curses of heredity, always there to remind him where he began. Schmidt was not far from believing that he had taken from his parents their worst traits of character as well. He watched for them in his own behavior, wondering when he was about to do this or that, whether, for once, he might shake free of the recurring nightmare. Usually, he failed. Just as in his teens he had been on the alert for pimples around his mouth, ready to squeeze them between the nails of his two index fingers until the pus had been extruded ahead of a drop of fresh blood. The "look what you have done to me" treatment had been his mother's specialty, directed as easily against Schmidt's father as against himself. Grave, pale, and trembling, since she was always recovering from one illness or another, hands ice cold and red at the joints, she glided from room to room sighing and shaking her head in unexpressed wonder. People get used to continuous background noise—the dripping of a faucet, a neighbor listening to the ball game—and soon stop hearing it. Therefore, at irregular intervals, the mother's sighs became louder, more like stifled sobbing. Oh, she would get out of bed and dress as usual in one of the housecoats she wore to spare her better clothes, and in this garb she came to meals, but it wasn't to eat or speak. The wound—one or the other culprit sitting at the table with her, Schmidt or his father, knew all too well which wound it was and how it had been opened—was too deep. And this could go on for days, until Schmidt's father, deliberate and implacable, would commit a larger offense, for instance crushing a crystal wineglass in his hand, red wine all over the white linen tablecloth—an admirable trick, since he never cut himself—or coming to the table with a legal brief or a ship mortgage he corrected all the while he ate, pausing only when he was served. As though out of the blue, the trance she was under was dispelled. They would return to speech as gray and mean as the silence that had preceded it.

To have his own offenses forgiven, Schmidt had to grovel. With his haughty and normally impassive father, it was the onsets of rage that stung: absurd in their unpredictability, the violence of the insults he hurled, and the way he had of forgetting almost immediately what he had said and done. Whereas his mother never forgot and never forgave. Every hurt was planted and nursed tenderly like a seedling until it bore its venomous fruit. And what could he say for himself? Had he dealt in good faith with Charlotte about money, had he not mistreated her? The stuff about the funds he had given her when he bought out her remainder interest in this house, the money she spent on the house in Claverack and the apartment in the city, the payment to her that stuck with such stubbornness in his craw, after all, it was entirely his own invention, born out of anger and a grudge quite worthy of his parents. It was never a necessary transaction: he entered into it because he disliked his son-in-law-to-be. If that Jew lawyer and he were going to spend weekends and holidays under the same roof, he wanted at least to be able to lord it over him—an ambition difficult to fulfill completely so long as the Jew's wife, his daughter, was a part owner of this house. The wasteful, needless strategem had turned against its inventor. Who knows? If he had kept his mouth shut, had not pushed for a change, Charlotte and Jon might have used this place as their weekend house. Then perhaps he could have helped them be more prudent. After all, he knew W & K so well. But there too he had allowed resentment over all-too-real slights get in the way of friendships, however tepid, old tics that might have moved a Lew Brenner or Mike Woolsey, or even DeForrest himself, to phone or take him aside after a firm lunch—in fact he hadn't taken the trouble to attend a single one since he left, slamming the door behind him—and say, Schmidtie, I know it's none of my business, it's bad to meddle, but Jon should be more careful, people are whispering, you might just want to look into it. A word to the wise. Had he seen the handwriting on the wall, he would have surely read it. Anyway, it hardly mattered what he read or what he knew: the skill and patience needed to help weren't his. He had thrown his daughter to the dogs.

IV

No, there hadn't been many changes in the Crussels' house Schmidt could point to after the visits to Mr. Mansour that for over a month had been recurring with such regularity, and yet the impression was one of difference. For all the effort the old couple's decorator had expended to restrain them, somehow Jean and Olga had always gotten their way, so that their arrangements held a mysterious potential for recalling both the five-and-ten-cent store of years gone by and the most up-to-date mail-order catalogues. No such hobgoblins' ears peeked out under Mr. Mansour's regime. The deck Schmidt stood on was in itself the same vast rectangle of pure burning white, with not a grain of sand, not a scratch to mar its surface, perching above a dune overgrown by rugosa roses and green and silvery grasses. The trick, the distinction, may have been simply in the way the swarm of chairs of every size and description, settees, tables, and parasols were disposed: at first, these masterworks of steel, aluminum, canvas, and linen gave an impression of randomness, as though they had been set down carelessly by movers who might return in a moment to carry them off to another location. After a longer look, they revealed self-assured, calculated refinement. And so it was throughout the house and its whimsical dependencies.

The beach, of course, endures and yet changes every day, showing itself at this lunch hour as brutally gnawed by the week's storm and tides. Schmidt removed his sunglasses and peered at the ocean again, wanting to see its true colors. A man dressed in baggy black clothes, his naked feet sometimes licked by the water, was still standing there, his attitude unvaried since Schmidt had arrived a good while before. Perhaps he too was intent on the struggle of the faraway sailboat, hardly more than a nervous white brush stroke at the edge of the horizon, almost immobile, beating its way against a west wind. What could be its destination? The marina at nearby humble Shinnecock, where Indians, before white men came, had already dug a passage to link the ocean to the bay? New Jersey? The Pillars of Hercules? All of a sudden, as though having decided to abandon the distant craft to its fate, perhaps wanting to make up for the time he had lost, the man shrugged his shoulders and started to walk very briskly eastward. A longing, perhaps related to the man's abrupt action, came over Schmidt: for absence, for a life that wasn't seeded with mistakes of his own making. He recognized it as childish and drank what was left of his gin and tonic. According to Manuel, the houseman with a Mediterranean accent, Mr. Mansour was on a conference call with London, had been for hours. And Carrie had stood him up. They had agreed that she would come directly to this house after her last class.

Instead she left a message for Schmidt with one of Mr. Mansour's ubiquitous security men. She was on her way to Brooklyn to see her parents and wasn't sure when she'd be back. But it wasn't an emergency and he shouldn't worry. She would telephone him at home at the end of the afternoon. Schmidt understood that to mean that she was probably spending the night. There had been no discussion of anything of the sort. Why hadn't it been possible to tell him in advance if this wasn't an emergency, why hadn't she caught him before he left home, during a break between classes?

He wasn't sure he was up to lunching alone with Mr. Mansour. In any case, he had been kept waiting longer than was decent. That this might also be Manuel's opinion occurred to Schmidt when the former brought him a second drink and said he would hand to Mr. Mansour another note about lunch. The concern of this nice servant was almost embarrassing, and Schmidt wondered whether he hadn't better refuse the gin and tonic and depart—perhaps leaving his own note to the effect that they should try to get together another day, when Mr. Mansour was less busy. He didn't doubt that it was awkward to interrupt a telephone conference with London, where it was already close to seven in the evening, and, by the time Mr. Mansour had finished lunch, people would want to be at table eating their own dinner, but Schmidt had seen enough of his host's dealings with his colleagues to be sure that no such considerations would stand in the way if Schmidt were an important guest he was keeping waiting, or if Mr. Mansour wanted from him something that required the sort of wheedling he called "making charm." In the end, Schmidt took the drink Manuel had offered. There was no other place where he particularly wished to go to just then. Nor was he willing to put at risk the entertainment that frequenting Mr. Mansour provided, in itself and as a subject for conversation with Carrie.

They had fallen into a camaraderie that Michael Mansour had been quick to call friendship. In fact, Schmidt thought he hadn't seen friends around that gentleman, not in the sense that Schmidt understood that word, and apparently there wasn't, after all, a café society of which Michael was a member. He belonged instead, Schmidt had concluded, to a less amusing but infinitely more exclusive spiritual brotherhood, the insignia and privileges of which included being on first-name basis with other billionaires in North and South America and Europe (and even those parts of the Middle East where having been born a Jew in Egypt was not a serious black mark for someone like Mr. Mansour who was as rich as a Gulf Arab sheik), possession of their unlisted and zealously guarded private telephone numbers, and eligibility for invitations—otherwise inexplicable—to the islands they owned in the Caribbean and chalets in Vail and Gstaad, as well as, of course, to their weddings and funerals. It was mid-August. Michael's helicopter took him into the city only for brief visits. The demeanor of the guests at the lunches and dinners that Schmidt and Carrie were solicited to attend almost daily—it seemed to Schmidt that a new invitation was offered following each meal they had with him by the insistent host or by the secretary who made early morning telephone calls—evoked for Schmidt more nearly clients of a colossally rich Roman, probably a freed slave such as Trimalchio, gathered in expectation of the inevitable moment when favors would be granted. Money was in the air, like the heady scent of the honeysuckle hedge that lined Mr. Mansour's driveway.

I am sorry about Carrie, he told Mr. Mansour when they finally sat down at the small table of the dining room that gave on the deck, the wind having stiffened so considerably that Manuel counseled against eating outside.

The lobster salad was served to the host with extra dollops of mayonnaise. Mr. Mansour took a second helping, reconsidered the matter, and helped himself to mayonnaise again.

Forget it. She's one great kid. Between you and me, she must be going crazy, she's so bored. That too is something I want to talk to you about. The immediate piece, he continued between bites, is what are you doing about your son-in-law? I had my people do some checking on him. I think I should meet him and your daughter and sort this thing out for you. I am probably the only person who can pull it off. You may want to be there too, so I can bring all three of you back together, but not at the first meeting.

This was not the first time that Michael had referred to Jon Riker, let alone his disgrace. Hovering over the food, Michael's perfectly oval face, perhaps a bit too large for such a compact man, was all smiles, as though he had just told or heard a first-rate joke. His bald pate gleamed. He wore white linen trousers and a white cotton shirt with long sleeves. Rolled back for comfort from the wrists and open over the chest to the fourth button, it showed off serious muscles. The resemblance to Manuel the houseman was marred only by Manuel's handlebar mustache. Perhaps Mr. Mansour had required him to grow it, just as he might have asked him to change his name from Michael to Manuel.

You are very kind to think about him.

Forget it. You're not answering my question. As I tell you all the time, I don't understand your attitude.

The man should have been a dentist. No, the lady who scrapes your teeth with one of the newfangled drills that squirt water. Who else could be so relentlessly repetitious in his investigations?

There is nothing new. Nothing to add. He had to leave my old firm. I'm afraid there is nothing to be done about it, certainly not by me, and I have no idea what other plans he has made.

Michael reached across the table and gripped Schmidt's forearm. It was a long and affectionate squeeze.

I've made it my business to know as much about you as can be found out, he said. After a pause, he added, Including from Gil Blackman. To get the context. You sure don't make it easy to give you help. That's a great friend you have there. Gil really loves you. Look, it doesn't matter. I can figure out most things about you just like that. He snapped his fingers and continued, Instinct and feeling.

Ah, Mr. Mansour and the wisdom of the East. That Gil and he should have talked about Riker was natural, Schmidt supposed. One could wonder who didn't. In its own minor way, it was a juicy story for people interested in that sort of thing, and that was just about everybody in the Hamptons except the natives who serviced the rich. Schmidt had gotten the *Wall Street Journal* and had read the dreadful article Jack DeForrest had predicted. He had forced himself to ask the firm librarian to clip and send to him anything else that appeared in the press about the case. Out of pride, so that no one could say he was hiding his shame, or because he wanted Carrie to say something, express an opinion, he would leave the clippings regularly on the kitchen counter, where she was bound to find them. He knew that she read them, although she made no comment. Small wonder. He had thanked her for having gotten him and, for that matter, his daughter through those twenty-four hours, right until that now distant Saturday afternoon when he finally put Charlotte on the bus to New York. But he had not said a word about Charlotte or Jon to her since then, except to mention, in his very best victim's voice, while he was doing the dishes and she was practically out the door on the way to class, that Charlotte was planning to leave Riker and had asked for money to start a business he had his doubts about. Money that he intended nevertheless to give. That was how he had managed, against all reason, to wall Carrie off at the time when he needed her most. And, against all reason, for the first time ever, he hadn't turned to Gil Blackman with a family catastrophe. He was, in fact, too ashamed of Jon and of Charlotte. Was that something Gil would have mentioned to Mr. Mansour as well, if he had figured it out, to give him a rounded context?

Look, Schmidtie, continued the latter, we are very different. Don't laugh, I know we look different. I mean even if we looked like twins, inside we would be very different. That doesn't stop me from understanding you. I don't believe you know how well I understand. The point is we don't think or feel the same, and you've never learned to express yourself or to get along with people. If you happen to hit it off with somebody, that's OK. You're nice. With most people you show them right away how superior you feel. Same story when they bore you or you don't like them. Oh yes, right in the face. I've watched it at this house, with the people who come here, some of whom I think are very interesting and make a real contribution. Your nose is up in the air, ten stories high. How other people feel is not your business. You treat me OK because you admire me. Ha! Ha! No kidding, you do. And you've had fabulous luck with Carrie. She's the complete package. You should study how she handles people.

You're right. I have serious faults.

Just now you're thinking, Where does this guy get the balls to come out and say he understands me? God forbid. A Jew from Cairo claims he can think and feel like Mr. Albert Schmidt. What chutzpah!

Come on, Michael. I've got good news for you. I'm beginning to like Jews.

That means you're getting smarter. All kidding aside, here is how I see it. We have the same kind of intelligence, except that overall I'm smarter and more creative. Don't let that worry you. You haven't been brought up by my mother. The real difference is you're closed up, all tight, whereas, you see, I know how to deal with people, to reach out. Maybe it's because when I started out I had to. Maybe it's because I am who I am. In Egypt, in Morocco, even here, when we arrived, yes in the good old days, let me tell you, Jews didn't deal from strength. There's one way you resemble me. You're not satisfied with yourself.

Schmidt nodded.

See? I should be satisfied with what I achieved—just like you say I've achieved plenty—but I'm not satisfied inside. That's the key fact. Believe me, when I came to this country I didn't have much to be satisfied about.

The essential elements of the Mansour family legend were not unknown to Schmidt. During the walk on the beach Michael proposed after Carrie and Schmidt's first visit to his house, Michael had exposed them quite dryly. Their completeness, certain areas of shade and perhaps improbability, were another matter. It appeared that, from their great prosperity in Cairo, where the family had, like all Egyptian Jews whose stories were worth telling, dealt in cotton, with shipping as a sideline, the ascent of Nasser propelled the Mansour parents, little Michael, and *toute la smala* to a refuge in Morocco, under the protection of cousins of the mother. This branch of the family was confidential suppliers of jewelry to the court, and therefore hardly less grand. A sojourn in Paris followed, the length and financing of which Michael glided over. The reason for the move to America from the city of such linguistic and cultural affinity for an Egyptian Jew, and more specifically to the Bronx, where the parents were reduced to sewing and selling curtains, was the treachery of two uncles, which went undescribed. Chastened, the Mansour parents saved every penny and mounted a curtain and upholstery business. The pennies accumulated rapidly enough, but in this alien land neither parents nor son grasped that someone of Michael's talent was suited to attend Harvard, Princeton, or Yale. Instead, *comme un con*, he went to NYU. If only we had known, mused Mr. Mansour. I can tell you it would have had to be Harvard or Princeton. As it was, he took the subway from Forest Hills—the family had moved—to Washington Square and studied accounting. And that was a good thing, for by the time he graduated, Mansour Curtains had become a big business, ready to be diversified. The rest of the story he absolutely didn't need to tell. The rise, first of the Mansour parents and then of Michael himself, was part of American business history, recorded in case studies and magazine articles, and, insofar as it concerned more specifically Michael, also in testimony before courts and regulatory agencies. Ever since the car crash on the corniche, along which they were being driven to their new house in Cannes, killed the mother and put the father into a coma from which he would never recover, the son's activities had been garnished by more than one man's share of controversy, investigations, and lawsuits, all of them ultimately resolved, one way or another, pretty much in his favor. Oh, he was no Ivan Boesky—just eerily brutal and bright. Reporting on Mr. Mansour's recent divorce, and on the settlement obtained by the Mrs. Mansour who now occupied his former East Hampton mansion near the Maidstone Club, had also kept reporters busy and, one hoped, content.

The heart-to-heart talk Mr. Mansour was having with Schmidt had quickly become part of their routine. There was no foreplay. Mr. Mansour had a penchant for having you know that he worked behind the scene. In the coulisses. The display of his insights, claimed variously to derive from Gil Blackman's confidences, his own intuition, and even research performed by his staff, was part of establishing the principle that he always held the stronger hand. He was, Schmidt believed, the only man he had ever met who wanted everyone around him to feel manipulated. Likewise the superiority of his intelligence was a subject to which Mr. Mansour returned fondly and with some frequency, and not only in relation to Schmidt. In fact, it appeared that there was nothing Mr. Mansour wanted to do in business that he couldn't accomplish, a judgment with which Schmidt was ready to concur. The question was, as Mr. Mansour liked to explain, How do I allocate my energy? How do I use my power? I've taken time to build a business; I'm worth between six and eight billion; if I go on building my business, in ten years I could multiply that by a factor of *x*. You name it. *Pas de problème.* I think that's enough. I don't want to give all my time to business, and I don't want to own assets unless I give them the attention they deserve. The question is, What do I do with my wealth? That's the big puzzle. My foundation will get most of it and I must give it more leadership. That too is no problem.

Mr. Mansour might have added excruciating persistence to the list of his principal qualities. Oh, for a shot of novocaine! He asked again: What are you going to do about them, your daughter and son-in-law?

Well, nothing. My daughter says she wants to leave Jon. That's not an irrational decision.

It's unfeeling.

Is it? Perhaps you're not taking into account her feelings. Anyway, she has to make the decisions about her life. What would you suggest I do one way or another?

I'll tell you what my father would have said. Make them feel you're on their side. You are one family. Riker never gave the brief to the woman lawyer. That's bullshit. Please believe my instincts. Your firm screwed him. Maybe it's because he's a Jew. Have you thought of that?

What nonsense! Lew Brenner's a Jew, he is one of the most powerful partners, and Jon was working for him. Why would Brenner let a thing like that be done to Riker if it wasn't right?

No problem. I know Lew and his wife. They're at every fund-raising dinner. From my point of view, that guy is about as Jewish as you. Who knows? Do you have enemies there? They could be getting at you through your son-in-law. It doesn't matter. The question is what you do next. You should give them your support and enough money so they'll be all right until he clears his name and gets his career going.

You can't clear your name from being thrown out by Wood & King. Believe me, he's a knave or a fool. Anyway, I think it's over between Charlotte and him. There is a man with whom she wants to start a new business. They're together in other ways too. I am giving her money for that, more than I can afford.

He described the arrangements with Charlotte and Mr. Polk.

Tell them to talk to Larry Klein at my office. If he thinks it makes sense, I can help them. You know, having me as a client is like a guaranty of success. Maybe I can't straighten out your family, but I can make sure you don't lose money!

It will be her money, but thank you. I'll ask Charlotte to call for an appointment. But don't be surprised if you don't hear from her.

What are you talking about? I'm trying to help.

Charlotte wants money, she doesn't want help. I mean my help. If I ask her to call you, she'll think I'm meddling, and she doesn't want me anywhere near her projects. It's been like that since before she got married to Jon Riker. Maybe earlier. Since her mother died.

Then you met Carrie and started living with her. That made it worse.

Yes, she's been unpleasant about it, but the trouble started, and got bad, before she found out about Carrie. Actually, Carrie was terrific with Charlotte when she came here last month.

So now you've got a problem with your kid and you've got a problem with Carrie. *Que c'est bête.* What are you doing about Carrie?

The houseman served key lime pie, which Schmidt recognized as coming from the establishment where he got his daily croissants. It was delicious. He wasn't going to let Mansour's questions interfere with his enjoyment. He pointed to his wineglass. Wine was poured. One good thing could be said of Michael: he drank red wine with meat and fish alike and did not skimp on quality or quantity. But that habit went together with other, less attractive ways with money, which were not unrelated to Schmidt's doubts about the man's fundamental generosity. Were his gifts freely given, or were they purchases of kudos and useful allies? He squinted at his host through the beautiful and precious liquid. The filter improved the face. Perhaps it came down to this: Mr. Mansour was a busy man, with many things on his mind and countless claims on his attention. One couldn't expect him to make fine distinctions, for instance between an ally and a parasite.

These matters having been weighed, Schmidt lit a cigarillo and asked whether his host was remaining in Water Mill for the balance of the week. The watchful Manuel appeared, bringing an ashtray. A harsh judgment had been reached by that paragon, surmised Schmidt: Why does this guest take it upon himself to smoke at table when no ashtray has been provided? Well, that was just too bad.

I'm going into the city this afternoon, but I'll be back on Sunday. I want you to come to lunch. No, make it dinner. I'll get Hillel to play before we eat. You'll see, we'll have an interesting group of people. You like the idea?

Michael had taken to flying Hillel in his jet to and from cities across the country, and in Canada as well, where the great cellist had engagements, often sending along Jason, the security man with a gift for shiatsu massage. Sometimes, he traveled with the artist himself. I help him relax, he would explain. We go over his schedule. Half the time, we don't talk at all or we talk about his investments. They're on his mind quite a lot. With me he can unload. I give him advice on bookings too. Some places are key; others he shouldn't even think about. After that, when I go to the concert and hear him, it's a whole different thing.

A fantastic idea, replied Schmidt. Of course, we'll come.

Excuse me. I want to go back to Carrie. The question is, What are you willing to do to keep her? Have you got a plan?

Coffee having been served, Schmidt was prepared to be more assertive. Do I need a plan? he asked. Why?

You're kidding me. So you think you can just go on like that.

Of course. We are happy together. That's about it. Nothing to plan or discuss.

How much longer? That's the question.

As long as we are happy. What else do you have in mind?

Lots of luck to you! That girl will go nuts, she's so bored! It is no problem. I can see it from beginning to end. All right, so right now I'm here pretty much all the time. You come over. She gets to see people I work with. They're doing important things. I don't know if you've noticed, but I've had some young people over. Just for her. What do you do for her? I'll give you the answer: nothing. Zero. You don't even take her to the movies or to a restaurant. I've talked to her about the best restaurants out here. She doesn't know them, she hasn't been anywhere. And in September you expect her to go on with the college routine. Classes in the morning, homework in the afternoon, to bed with Schmidtie after an early dinner. The question is, Are you kidding yourself or her? Maybe you think you're some sort of Michael Jordan in the sack?

Schmidt hoped he wasn't really changing color. This oaf and his sensitivity! To paraphrase Mr. Mansour, the problem was the proportion, in his prodigious rudeness, of sadism to well-intentioned meddling. No, it was not well intentioned; the force behind it was vanity, the need to show off. Of course, he was saying nothing Schmidt had not said to himself over and over. But Schmidt wanted to keep those dirty little secrets hidden under the layers of his habitual self-deprecation and scoffing. Thanks to Mr. Mansour it turned out that they weren't secrets at all. Obvious to Mr. Mansour. Therefore to his herd of clients as well. To the Polish brigade. To Gil and Elaine Blackman. Of one thing he could be sure: Carrie had not been disloyal. Because she would never, never have complained to Mansour. It might be that she did not look inside herself skeptically enough—although what was her refusal to marry him but proof of self-knowledge. Nonetheless, he thought he could be sure that for the time being—even if possibly not for very long—the life they led, whatever Mansour might think of it, was the life she wanted. His Carrie among jocund derivatives traders and with cocained-faced models they brought out for weekend partying at the new clubs in Southampton? Never! Were those the entertainments Mansour had in mind? Schmidt's vision of such establishments derived from local press accounts mixing in his mind with memories of brothel scenes by Degas. Consequently, he was convinced he could imagine the requisite little black dresses cut in back so low as to invite the most obscene of caresses, unbearably long legs intertwining with the legs of hirsute men, their hairy hands and thick fingers. Never! Really, Schmidtie, never? Why not?

You insist on talking about things I would rather not discuss, he told Mansour. This has been a delicious but very long lunch. I think I'll go now.

Somewhere on his person Mr. Mansour surely wore an electronic device that enabled him to summon a security man or, indeed, Manuel without pressing any visible call button. Faster than one would have thought possible—but perhaps he had been waiting all the while in the passage leading to Mr. Mansour's study, the door to which was open—Jason was behind Schmidt's chair, kneading his shoulders.

Schmidtie, said Mr. Mansour, I'm trying to give you advice, like a brother. Stop wiggling. You can't get away from Jason until he lets you, so don't try. And don't be like that, all tense. That's right, relax, or he will hurt you. You should take an apartment in New York and let the kid have a life. She should meet people. I'm willing to arrange it.

Like claws, the fingers were getting right at the pain.

Michael, please tell Jason to stop. Jason, stop it. I know it's very effective but please stop.

A movement of Mr. Mansour's eyelids. Jason gave Schmidt's neck a parting squeeze and was gone.

Thank you, Michael. Jason's a good masseur, but I don't want a massage just now. Look, Carrie doesn't want us to have an apartment. I've already offered it and she said no.

You're kidding yourself. Here is the problem: Does she want some dark two-bedroom apartment on Park Avenue, with you and your former law partners and their wives for company, or does she want a life? A life where things happen? You want to bet?

Michael, Carrie is living with me, not you. I am me, not someone else, not you. I can only offer things I have.

It's no problem, I hear you. But I'm telling you she needs something more. That's why I said to her, Look, I'd like to take you to a couple of places, introduce you to some friends. She's no dummy. She understood what I meant right away. By the way, you know she's gone to New York, don't you?

To Brooklyn, to see her parents.

That too. But I said she should call me in the city anytime. I wouldn't be surprised if she called me. No problem. I'm going in for meetings where I'm the only person who can make the deal. It's nothing Eric can do in my place, but I won't be busy all the time. Come on, don't make that face. We're friends, all three of us. If you like, come with me.

Mansour stopped to wet his fingers in the finger bowl and pass a finger over his lips, before carefully drying lips and fingers. Satisfied, he began to play with his worry beads. Click click. And he continued: Anytime you're in the city when I'm there, I expect you to call me too. Get serious, Schmidtie. Wouldn't you call me? Hey, come to New York with me. I'll send Fred or Manuel over to your house. They'll pick up anything you need and drive it in.

I couldn't possibly. Carrie will be back tonight.

He didn't necessarily believe what he said and saw that he had made a gigantic blunder he should at once repair. He should get on that helicopter in his pajamas, if necessary. But he had missed his chance. Mansour spoke first.

Suit yourself. I'll see you here on Sunday night.

Beyond the garage, where cars parked, the less blond security man, a giant, a mountain in human image, stepped out into the sunlight and opened the door of Schmidt's Volvo.

Schmidt noted that the car had been moved so that it would be in the shade. Apparently, he had almost overstayed his welcome. Jason, the massage giver and message taker, could be seen placing Mr. Mansour's paraphernalia in the trunk of the Rolls-Royce. The scheduled moment for the fifteen-minute drive to the airport and the flight to the city was at hand. To the rendezvous with Carrie. Just as well to admit what it was, since Michael had felt the need to announce it. Meanwhile, he, Schmidt, had fallen into a trap so large he could not see its confines, although he heard the door snap. He drove out of the concealed driveway onto the road and then very slowly toward Route 27, not sure which direction to take. Surely not toward Southampton. Eastward, home, that was the idea. Surely nowhere else, unless he was to break a lifelong habit and stop by at Gil Blackman's without having first telephoned. He went to parties and meals at the Blackmans' when asked, he met Gil for lunch by prearrangement, but there were no spur-of-the-moment visits in the middle of gorgeous, golden afternoons. Home then, to his azaleas and roses and apple trees, to the pond shimmering beyond the now overgrown hedge, to his and Carrie's bedroom.

A pickup truck in his own driveway. One of Jim Bogard's men was deadheading the flower beds. That and pruning the smaller trees and planting annuals had been things Schmidt had once liked to do himself. Did Carrie like better the touch of his hands on her skin, and inside her, now that he kept them so smooth? There were three messages for him on the answering machine. One from her. Hey Schmidtie, everything's OK, I'm spending the night. He wondered whether the Gorchucks' number was written down someplace he could find it, but why would it be, since she knew it by heart. If he really wanted to call he would get it from information—it's not as though there could be that many Gorchucks in Brooklyn. Another from Gil Blackman, Please call. And a simple one from Bryan: I'll get you later. Schmidt dialed the Blackmans' number.

How are you doing?

Could be worse.

No better than that? Got any time for lunch, drink, or dinner? How about tonight? Can you and Carrie come over this evening? Elaine's in the city with darling Lilly, spending the night.

So is Carrie. With her folks.

Then come over at eight. Don't worry, no chow mein and flied noodles tonight.

Mr. Blackman never tired of imitating the accent of his Chinese cook, or making fun of the blue slippers she wore when waiting on table. I'll get a roast duck, he continued. Felt Slippers will serve it. We'll get drunk.

It was a long time until eight. A Maker's Mark and then another, drunk more slowly, on the back porch. Bogard's man finished and waved good-bye. Schmidt waved back. No, he shouldn't offer him a drink. A nap was out of the question. His skin was ice cold and itched. Walking on the beach was out of the question too. He might miss Bryan. In the pantry there was a cordless phone Charlotte had given him for Father's Day, when Mary was dying. He had hardly used it since, but it seemed to work; the dial tone was there. Information, which he called not to find the Gorchucks but to make doubly sure one could still use this antique, answered. Immediately, he hung up. It didn't matter; the lady on the other end of the line was no lady, just a nice, forgiving computer.

No one was going to drop in on him. He undressed in the kitchen, leaving his clothes in a pile on a counter, and, the bottle of bourbon and glass in one hand, the telephone in the other, went to the pool. The deck chair burned his skin when he lay down on it. So much the better, he had to get warm somehow.

V

THE PHONE finally rang while he was still doing laps, trying to shake off the last of the sleep that had overcome him. Six-thirty! He pulled himself out of the water. The burnt skin really hurt. It would be worse when he put clothes on. A collect call. It was Bryan, all right, the simpering voice, the diction of a horrible twelve-year-old who hadn't managed to grow up, all quite unchanged.

Jeez, Albert, thanks a lot for taking the call.

Schmidt remains silent.

Albert, you still there? You got a minute?

Just about.

Albert, you're mad at me or something? What have I done? Hey, I'm sorry if I've upset you. Come on, tell me you're not mad.

Silence.

Albert, I'm calling from the Miami airport. I got this real cheap flight. I'll be in New York tonight. I think I can get over there to see you tomorrow.

What for?

Jeez, you are mad. I'm sorry. I really want to see you. I want to see Carrie too. Will you let me stay at the house until I work things out? Just a couple of nights?

As a general matter, I want to remind you that except in an emergency I have asked you to write when there is something you want to tell me. Work out what?

He was beginning to shiver and got the towel from the changing cabin to put over his shoulders.

Man, that was when I was fixing the house and wanted you to give me an OK on what I was doing. This is different. I got to have someplace to live until I get settled. You know how I want to come back. This hospital is heavy, Albert, real heavy. You wouldn't believe it. It's oppressive.

You mean you got fired from the job I got for you?

Albert, I knew you'd be mad. I had to leave. I'm sorry. It was unreal. I got to tell you about it. You won't believe the shit.

So you did get yourself fired. That wasn't very smart. Anyway, get it into your head that you can't stay in this house. Don't even try to argue with me. It's out of the question.

Schmidt says that last sentence very slowly, as though he were trying to put Bryan to sleep. Then he continues: I can't talk now. You may call once you're here.

Can you get Carrie to the phone?

Good-bye.

Click. Immediately Schmidt was sorry. Why not hear this punk out? Once Bryan got to Bridgehampton, making him leave wouldn't be all that simple. There might have been a way to stop him from coming. What way? He shrugged his smarting shoulders. Offer money right off the bat? Something along the line of Listen, you had a good job out there, you were doing well, I don't want you to give up so fast, I'm sending you a thousand dollars care of the hospital, so if you want the money you just go right to Palm Beach. I'll help you get that job back. Or maybe he hadn't been canned. Then the speech should be, Give it a real try, kid, make an effort, exactly, make a real big effort the way you know how. Nonsense, it wouldn't have worked, and if by some miracle it had worked it wouldn't have worked for long. There would be another collect call soon. Therefore, Schmidtie, we might as well face the music. How could he possibly have guessed that Carrie's absence would seem providential, a real miracle. A miracle he was now obliged to hope would continue for the time he needed, just a few days, to make sure the old triangle would never form again.

He went into the house and in the folder in his desk drawer, where he had filed the correspondence with the hospital, found the personal telephone number of the director. Office closed. Of course, why would anyone work after six? But you can't get rid of Albert Schmidt, Esq., that easily. He had the home number too. Gotcha. Ah, what a pleasure to hear from Mr. Schmidt! The charitable Mr. Schmidt forbore from saying, I'm about to spoil your pleasure, there isn't a single peso or dollar more coming your way. Instead, in dulcet tones, he inquired about the young man he had recommended for the handyman job at the new conference center. Was he fitting in well? Audible consternation. How should the deeply embarrassed director put it? There had been a distinct problem, perhaps Mr. Schmidt could call again in the morning and speak to human resources, the director not being sure he had details at his fingertips or was allowed to disclose them. No, not even to Mr. Schmidt. Ah, Schmidt could tell the poor man wished he had let the phone ring off the wall, never touched the goddamn thing. The police department? Yes, there had been some involvement. He wasn't sure how the problem was resolved.

By jumping bail, that's how, whispered Mr. Schmidt to Mr. Schmidt. Yes, he might call human resources. He might call the cops too, but that the director didn't need to know. The cops! The bulwark of the civil society! The law-and-order jurist inside Schmidt rejoiced. But was there enough in it for them to travel all the way to Bridgehampton to get their little old Bryan back? That's all right. He'd offer to pay their airfare. And if they came to get him, how long would they keep him? Just long enough for that very handy fellow to figure out how to get even with his pal Schmidtie the moment he was sprung. Work him over, real good. He might even get some of his Bonaker chums to assist!

The phone rang again. Could it be Bryan? In that case, he would speak to him calmly and wisely. Irascibility: these uncontrolled fits of ill-timed anger. They were the portents of his ruin. Of course! Carrie, calling to explain. She would make everything all right. Just as when, waking from a nightmare with her right beside him, he was at once able to laugh at how afraid he had been. Only it was Charlotte's voice, and not his sallow sorceress.

Dad, I've been calling and calling.

No message from you though.

I didn't leave one. It's so horrible.

Here she began to cry. He hadn't heard her cry like that since when? Not Mary's funeral; they hadn't cried then, either of them: it was the afternoon when he told her it was time to let Mary go. Four medium-size pills, out of eight prescribed by David Kendall, the prescription filled by the pharmacy in East Hampton. He hadn't been able to bring himself to go to the pharmacy in Bridgehampton, where all these years they had bought nostrums against poison ivy, pinkeye, and the cold sores that regularly afflicted Charlotte. The pharmacist in the mall where he went instead made him wait while he called poor Dr. Kendall to confirm and then took on a consoling look, a look he recognized the next day on the face of the man in the business office of the funeral home.

Honey, what is it?

Oh, Dad, I feel so horrible. It's Harry Polk.

What's happened?

He's left me. Just like that. He went to Egremont for his weekend with the kids, and their mother was supposed to be away as usual, only that bitch hadn't left, so they all spent the weekend together in the house. Then he took this week off to stay up there, and today, just as I was going to the gym, he called to say the divorce had been a mistake, they were getting back together. The bastard! He told me I should be happy for him. Dad, I love him. I did everything he wanted, and he still made me feel I was some kind of a goddess. And now he tells me he's happy with her!

I'm so very sorry. Do you think he means it?

Yes, he means it. You know what he said to me? You'll get over it, and you should be glad for the boys too. You always said you liked them. Now they've got their dad back. See you at the office next week.

That's very hard, sweetie. But you will get over it. I promise.

Dad, I'm all messed up. Really messed up. Everybody in the office knows about us. What do I look like?

Like a lady who has been wronged.

You mean dumped. What do I do about the new business? I signed the office lease. And all that money!

Isn't that the last thing to worry about right now? I'll help you sort it out. You haven't quit your job yet?

No, we were going to give notice next week.

If I were you I'd stay put. Anyway, for the moment. Do you want to come out here? I'd like to have you. Very much.

I'll call you. Maybe this weekend. If I can pull myself together.

Come tonight. Or tomorrow. You need to be babied.

I can't, Dad. I'm still working. Remember? I'll call you about the weekend.

So much for Mr. Polk of Virginia or wherever in truth he came from. This did not seem to be a very good day for what was left of the Schmidt family, but at least in Charlotte's case the hateful old saws seemed to apply: It's better to have it happen now than later, good riddance, and on and on. Dreary mantra of idiot wisdom to recite while the heart breaks. Examined in the light of that consummated wrong, Carrie's unexplained trip to New York could be said to call for a stay of judgment; one might assert that nothing had happened. Except that wasn't true. She had planned to go long enough in advance to have made a date with Michael Mansour. That would have been at least two nights ago, when they dined at his house with the cellist—unless, of course, Carrie and Michael were in telephone contact. And she made that date. Whose idea had it been? His—When you will be in New York, *chérie*, there are some things I could show you. Hers—Hey, I'm thinking of seeing my parents, I don't know, gee, maybe this week. Could I see you too? Wow! Mike, you're putting me on, you mean we could really do that? What manner of sights would Mr. Mansour be showing to Miss Gorchuck in the big city? What entertainments? Why, the usual, perhaps with an Egyptian flavor. It was Jim Morgan, a veteran still hanging around Harvard Square when Schmidt was a freshman, having served on some staff in Algeria, who told him how Arabs like to sew up their women's labia to make them tighter, or, anyway, used alum to pucker up the inside. Ah, Schmidt can see it, all the way from Bridgehampton. There they are in the Fifth Avenue penthouse. One security man has scurried off to get the lox and bagels that the housekeeper forgot to stock in the fridge. His partner lurks downstairs, perhaps in the kitchen that's somewhere off the marble foyer. He looks up from the newspaper to chuckle at the louder noises (Mansour the swine will have left the bedroom door open, and Jesus God she does shriek). Before Carrie and the boss finally descend, he will have clued in the bearer of postcoital delicacies, and they will each let just enough of a smirk float over their dutiful straight face to make sure she'll know they've heard more than enough. Welcome to the team!

He waited until almost eight o'clock, hoping the phone would ring. There were ways of forwarding telephone calls from your home to whatever number you were going to be at. He wished he subscribed to such a service or owned a cell phone she could try if there was no answer at home and she really wanted to reach him. Another solution was to stay at home. He could call Gil and break the date, or get him to come to his house. Never mind Blue Felt Slippers and whatever Gil had prepared. Let him bring the food over. They could eat and drink right here. Then Gil would be driving home dead drunk instead of Schmidt. But he didn't want to tell Gil the reason for changing their plan and didn't want to lie to him either. He rushed out of the house and into the car the way you plunge a needle into your foot to dig out a stubborn splinter, not slowly but with a sudden, quick thrust before your nerve fails.

Forget the champagne, Gil told him. Elaine pushes that stuff. I am against it. A lot of volume and calories and what do you get out of it? Gas. That's all. So far as the central nervous system and the higher spheres of your brain are concerned it's a washout.

Majestic and soigné in a black silk shirt, black trousers that could be silk or one of those new fabrics, soft to touch as a mole—assuming you can bring yourself to touch the mole your dog has just killed—and black sandals, Mr. Blackman was mixing martinis. Schmidt has been drinking his martinis, composed, stirred, and then shaken with unchanged attention, since their first meeting, almost half a century ago, in the living room of the suite they were to share in a Harvard freshman dormitory. A day as brilliant as the one that had just ended and, for mid-September, very warm. Their suite was on the ground floor, the living room facing the Memorial Chapel. They stood at the open window giving the once-over to Radcliffe girls, of whom there were so many you'd think the Yard had been invaded by Amazons in kilts and Shetland-wool cardigans. A Jew from one of the better parts of Brooklyn and a public high school that was the incubator of little Jewish geniuses, mixing drinks, in principle a WASP specialty, for an Episcopal chump educated on the cheap by Park Avenue Jesuit fathers. This was the first Jew Schmidt had ever met. There hadn't been any at school or at summer camp. When they hear the news in their small but historic house in the West Village, the parents will have a fit. What better reason to be friends with this garrulous roommate the university housing office had bestowed upon him!

When Mr. Blackman and Mr. Schmidt meet, it is not unusual that inquiries about the children are the first order of business. Thus Schmidt rapidly learns that Lisa has left her latest small-magazine job to write copy for a mail-order catalogue, and Nina and the Greek Orthodox priest's son with whom she has lived longer than Gil wishes to remember plan to be married. The time has come because, at last, the erstwhile baritone's voice has been repositioned; he's now a forty-year-old tenor without discernible prospects of displaying his gift to the public. Except at the wedding itself:

the girls' mother has taken charge of the ceremony and, after the Orthodox priest has pronounced his son and Nina man and wife, the newly minted tenor will sing Schubert lieder in the large barn on her property.

I don't suppose she will invite me, Schmidt ventured. You know, after the divorce she never said one word to Mary or to me. The last time we saw her, at the ballet, she didn't even pretend not to recognize us. A cut, pure and simple.

You may be right. She'll have to have me, I suppose, since I'll pay for the wedding, but my lawyer! The snake who handled my divorce! Unforgiven and unforgivable. You're paying for loyalty, Schmidtie. Wait. I'll tell her no Schmidtie, no champagne. As an opening move. We'll see where it gets us.

Nowhere. I'll look at the wedding pictures. And the beautiful and much maligned Lilly?

Gil chuckled. That's right, you are my stepdaughter's fan. Getting fitted for a bridesmaid's dress. Her father's getting married to a chick who's actually a full ten years older than Lilly. That's progress. Her predecessor was Carrie's age, for Chrissake. I can tell you Elaine is relieved. I think she's going to give them a wedding present!

Ah, yes.

Speaking of which, how is Carrie?

This was not a subject Schmidt wished to take up. To tell Gil what he thought was to burn her bridges. Gil would not keep the secret, he would talk to Elaine, then Carrie would never again be on the same footing with the Blackmans. And Charlotte, he realized, was in the same situation. He would not betray Carrie, and he would not betray his daughter, not to Gil. Gil would recognize a betrayal. In self-defense, he pointed to his empty glass and kept silent while Mr. Blackman concentrated on the preparation of a second round of martinis.

Splendid!

Not too bad.

This was said frowning, after a pause, possibly a sign that Gil's thoughts were running in a different direction.

I am concerned about you, he said when they sat down to eat the beef stew of a provenance entirely familiar to Schmidt, which was actually preferable to the promised duck. I have been concerned for some time. You are leading the most bizarre life. Really, you see no one except Carrie. Brother Mansour, of course, and that's something I want to talk to you about too. The girl goes to her classes, that's all well and good, and then she comes home to do her homework. I bet half the time you help her!

No, no.

It doesn't matter. You haven't lost your marbles—not yet—but your horizon is shrinking. Every day. Just when you should be making every effort to widen it.

I do read, you know.

That's lovely. The newspaper, every morning, I suppose, and you watch the news and the Yankees. Oh yes, and the Giants when the season starts. But what do you and Carrie talk about? What can you talk about?

She's very intelligent, you know.

Please, Schmidtie. She's also gorgeous and you're an old goat. And you know I like her a lot—sometimes maybe too much for your comfort? Right? That's not the point. How long were you and Mary married? Just short of thirty years, by my count. Don't you feel the difference, don't you understand it?

Schmidt blew his nose.

Really, Gil. My life with Mary was just that. Life with her. It ended when she died. It can't be reproduced. I am happy with Carrie. It so happens that we don't miss seeing people. Anyway, what do you suggest we do about it? Join the seniors' bridge club at the community house? Or should I take up Rollerblading? I think there's a group that Rollerblades in some parking lot in Southampton. Perhaps they even do field trips.

Schmidtie, you're full of shit. Instead of facing where you're at, you fence with me. That's all right—for the time being—but sooner or later it will all come to a head. Let's talk about Mike Mansour. You do realize that I have known him for years. He's backed all of my movies—since *The Raven*—mostly making good money. How many years is that? At least twenty. That's how long I've known Judith too—the alimony queen. I've never met the first Mrs. Mansour, but she belongs to prehistory, before the triumph of the House of Mansour. A nice Sephardic girl from Brooklyn he just pushed aside. Repudiated by Mansour Pasha. She got married again pretty fast—a skin doctor in Israel! That was a smart move. As Mike will tell anyone who'll listen, the alimony he was paying her was like the minimum wage.

Really!

Oh, yes. Judith is a different story. For one thing, she was rich and she let Mike invest her money. That's something he doesn't talk about, although he did very well with her money and in the end gave it back, with a nice slice of the profits. The guy is not a crook. He's something else!

For instance, what?

I'm about to explain. I introduced you, and I take responsibility for it, and I don't mind your having fun and games in Water Mill. But you should know more about him than I think you do. Carrie, too.

It was a windless night without a moon. They went out on the back lawn sloping down to Georgica Pond and, following an old, shared habit, urinated ponderously, aiming at the mulch under the rhododendron, away from the grass.

One of the great underrated pleasures available to man, observed Mr. Blackman.

Schmidt did not disagree. Although the hour of mosquitoes might well have passed, he proposed they sit on the screened porch. To hell with taking chances. He had always been sensitive to bites; of late they turned into small infected sores. The golden, sunset years, and the underrated humiliations they hold in store. There was clearly more to be learned about them.

I've gotten greater insight into Mike Mansour, said Mr. Blackman, since he developed artistic ambitions. That goes with re-creating the family's Egyptian past. This cotton-merchant stuff is bullshit. They were poor. Besides, ever since that guy read *The Alexandria Quartet*, you know, he resents it being known that he's from Cairo. Can you imagine the past he could have invented in Alexandria? Holy Moses! Anyway, it used to be, when he backed a film, he'd put up *x* hundred thousand toward development costs and, say, *y* million more when we went into production. The lawyers worked out his take—I should say that this guy Holbein who does numbers for him would regularly butt in with new ideas about the split and how we should realign the backers' interests—and the deals were tough but fair. I had no complaints, and Mike didn't give me any grief when we struck out. Take *Beauty of the Hemlocks*. That was one huge mistake. I was just getting over Katerina—my version of Carrie, *n'est-ce pas*, Schmidtie—and her having dumped me, otherwise I wouldn't have filmed that monstrosity for all the tea in China. From the start, it creaked like a cheap bed, and dealing with Martin Quine was a disaster. All right, he wrote the book, but let me tell you every time he touched the script I could have murdered him. I wasn't myself—that's the only reason I agreed to let him consult on the movie. By the way, can you believe it, Katerina and that imbecile Papachristou have divorced. She called me about it last week. Only one kid. A boy.

This could be your big chance, observed Schmidt.

Never, replied Gil. I will never be unfaithful to Elaine again. We've always had a good marriage, but now when I'm with her I feel actively happy. There is no other way to put it. My heart ached though when I heard Kat on the telephone. The woman won or the woman lost—nothing changes in that department. Let's get back to your new best friend.

Please, he isn't.

We will see. Anyway, when we did my last movie, he asked to be named as coproducer. That was a bombshell. I must admit Eric Holbein was a big help because all he cares about is money so that he can be objective about this kind of nonsense. He also saw the risk for Mike—for his Life Centers. Hey, you know about that foundation shit? Actually he does a good job with it. Also the threat to his vanity, and so forth, because the film was bound to be controversial. Of course, Eric was proved right. For a while, we thought the ACLU, Anti-Defamation League, and Jerry Falwell were all going to come out against us. So Eric and I found a formula that I thought made everybody happy.

You know, I hardly read movie credits.

That's all right, nobody expects you to. The film I'm about to make—he doesn't only want to have a production credit. He wants to be an executive producer! My first instinct was to tell him on the spot to take his money and stick it up you know what. I restrained myself, naturally, because it's really quite a lot of money and we can use it, and besides we've done business together for such a long time. So I asked what this was all about. He had the nerve to say he feels he is ready to give me real creative input. To move my work to a higher plane! The first thing I was supposed to do was to hire Omar Sharif as a consultant. I was eating a chef's salad and almost choked. Really, I asked. He replied, Really, really. To make a long story short, he laid out for me how he had never failed at anything he really wanted to do and had already accomplished everything that could be accomplished in business—by the way I stopped myself from asking whether he had measured himself against Microsoft—but he still doesn't feel he's reached his potential. He wants to fulfill himself through art. Cinematography! At that point I could no longer hold back and asked whether he had ever considered the need for talent in making art. What makes you think you have any, I added, just in case he hadn't gotten it. In all honesty, I thought he would slug me—you've probably noticed there is muscle under that envelope of fat—or anyway get up from the table and leave. Not at all. *Pas de problème.* He said he had always felt he could have been an artist, it was only the need to rescue the family business when his parents got into that accident that put a crimp in his style, and he had already proved himself by backing me and giving me advice. And he went on to recite, in detail, all the suggestions he had made over the years that I had followed. Nine times out of ten: utter rubbish.

Extraordinary! Where do you stand?

I'm talking to Holbein—he's my new best friend. That's also where you come in. You have to realize that Mansour is one of the real world-class—ugh! why did I use that expression?—manipulators of people, not only money. I wouldn't put it past him to think that if he lures you in with his entertainments and flattery (the subtext being you're a WASP idiot, but he sees in you something special he loves)—I know he's feeding you that stuff—you may just possibly agree to lobby me. Because he knows what you mean to me, he probably thinks it's not impossible that I'd give in. You have to understand that he wants me to do this for him very badly. He knows he can't make me do it by threatening to withhold the money if I say no, because he knows I can get financing elsewhere. Anytime. The thing is he believes there is no other place he can go. Got it? I have an alternative, and he doesn't! He's determined to be an executive producer for me, and not for just any schmuck he can buy in Hollywood. He wants class. In this money is secondary to him, though not to Holbein.

No, it wasn't a dream. Gil had actually said, quite naturally, as though the words had simply slipped out, and perhaps they had, that he, Schmidt, was important to him, had a meaning, therefore, a value in those regions where Gil's real life was played out, regions from which Schmidt had always thought he had been excluded, dwelling but in the suburbs of affection that Gil visited when the desire to gossip with an old roommate about the times gone by, children, and sex overcame him. Like a sudden yearning for a pastrami sandwich.

I would never do such a thing, Gil. To tell you the truth, I can't imagine his asking. It's inconsistent with the way he has behaved—quite recently.

Aha, he's made a pass at Carrie!

No, not quite.

You don't have to tell me. Let me tell you something. I don't know what went on between him and Judith—in these matters I am always in agreement with the last speaker. The husband tells me *A:* fine, it's *A*. The wife tells me *B:* all right, it's *B*. But I've seen enough of Mike in New York and in L.A. to have a pretty clear idea that he's a one-night-stand mechanic—though of a rather unusual sort. He zeros in on some woman, and bingo she thinks she's Cleopatra. He will give her a kingdom, make her wonky kid a satrap. What goes with the goodies, I've often wondered. Something, I suppose. Maybe nothing much. It seems to end no sooner than it has begun, and yet it doesn't end. There are these curious re-appearances of women you think have dropped into a black hole. They show up in the restaurant where you're meeting him for a meal; he calls you up to get their sister a walk-on part in some sitcom series; you get on his plane because he's offered to take you to Paris or London, and there is one of them playing gin rummy with the security man. It happened to me once when I brought Elaine along. You should have seen her face. She was good friends with Judith, you know. The point is that there's nothing simple or wholesome about the way this guy operates with women. A kid like Carrie is vulnerable. I've got to say though that usually he goes for married women—some of whose husbands hang around his place! Come to think of it, that almost fits your situation. Shit, Schmidtie, I hope I didn't go too far.

Don't worry about it. Carrie's strong. Stronger than you think.

Perhaps.

Schmidt listened to his messages the moment he got home, too impatient to go to the bathroom first. Hey, I've eaten with Mike. In a Japanese restaurant. They give you twenty little dishes and you have to guess what you're eating. The way they treat him he's got to own that place. Surely, thought Schmidt, in a private room, no shoes, tatami mat, feet and legs meeting under the table. My folks are real glad to see me. I'll call you tomorrow. Fuck it, Schmidtie, I love you and I'm thinking about you. You know what I mean? She laughed. The other voice on the answering machine was Bryan's, whining, promising to visit tomorrow, as early as he could make it.

VI

EARLY in the morning, between sleep and waking, he understood how it would have to be. Unbearably familiar, Bryan puts his backpack and the tube in which he transported his paintings on the square table in the poolhouse kitchen—in Florida he had taken again, with wild hunger, to covering four-by-six sheets of wrapping paper with poison green, magenta, purple, and pink acrylic paint, the colors he had liked the most back when he painted at his buddy's place in Springs, yes, he has decided to work on paper, canvas and stretchers being a real hassle—and also a tool kit made of shiny metal, the contents of which, although unknown, fill Schmidt with dread. The boy has changed. A yellow goatee complements the long yellow ponytail, and he is fatter and dirtier, particularly the hands, and those horrid fingers that end in nails he has chewed off. In fact, they end in suppurating scabs. But, under the fat, the same marine boot camp muscles, only he has never been a Marine; he's the kind of guy who can twist your arm out of the socket while puffing on a joint, without giving it a thought. Stronger than

Michael Mansour. You bet he is, this is the real McCoy. Sure, he says, he's staying. He's come home. Home is where if you have to go there they have to take you in, isn't that right, Albert? Holy cow, thinks Schmidt, let me out of here, the son of a bitch is quoting poetry, I've got to call someone. But it's difficult for Schmidt to get to the telephone, because Bryan sticks very close to him, first in the house and then in the garden, and probably the only way to shake him loose is to say he's calling to order pizza. Then when the pizza truck is already in the driveway he'll go out to pay with his credit card and plead with the driver to get him out of here, straight to the Southampton police station, that is if Bryan hasn't followed him to the truck, which he will certainly do if he isn't in the john. Definitely, Schmidt should have called the police the moment he heard Bryan was on his way, but how would that work, since he doesn't know the date and number of the warrant that is out for him in Florida, so it's all the hospital director's fault unless it's Schmidt's fault because he hadn't asked him. Only nothing's been lost, it isn't too late because Bryan will never take a taxi from the bus stop; he will call to ask Schmidt for a ride, and that will give Schmidt his big chance.

Then Schmidt remembers that he is in his bed and Bryan for the moment is God knows where, although, as sure as eggs is eggs, he'll be turning up here, but later in the day, it being only six in the morning according to the alarm clock on the night table. So it isn't too late to call the Florida state troopers, find out whether there is a warrant out for him, and, if the news is good, if the little prick has jumped bail, put the Florida cops in touch with the Southampton cops and have him picked up before he knows what hit him. So long, it's been nice to know you! Except it's Bryan who's got to be moving along. Mr. Schmidt will stay right here, in his comfortable house, everything going tick-tock like a Swiss cuckoo clock. Such are the rewards of virtue when it combines with wealth and impeccable standing in the community. He gives his name and address. The police dispatcher connects him to a Sergeant Smith or Sergeant Jones. Thank you, sir, for bringing this annoying matter to our attention. We will have a cruiser on standby, just give us a call. Yes, sir, no reason at all for you to worry. That's what we are here for!

As always, there is a catch. Short-term, everything depended on there being a drug offense, jumped bail, an outstanding warrant, and so forth. Otherwise there wouldn't be any Southampton or Suffolk County officers cuffing Bryan and handing him over to their Florida colleagues who have arrived here on the big fat airplane to return their fugitive to southern justice. What if Bryan has been fired simply because he was lazy or rude or because a telephone operator complained that he had felt her up. But long-term, even if Bryan is indeed carted off to Palm Beach, how long will he stay in jail? Not very long. He will cop a plea and be back here, on a plane or bus to Bridgehampton, within the year—all right, within eighteen months. For one purpose only: to kill Schmidt or hurt him so bad he would wish he had never been born. That is what the aluminum toolbox was for. The man who has made a specialty of detailing cars would know ways to detail his old pal Albert, with some of those pliers, cutters, and gouges he always carries with him just in case. The present visit isn't for that. All he wants now is money. Then give it to him, give it to him in installments payable somewhere far away. Or maybe he wants something kinky that has to do with Carrie. No problem! She'll know how to deal with that, unless she wants it. Like with Mansour. How base! Once he had taken its measure, disgust with the ignominous thought, with its origin in his brain, drove Schmidt out of bed. He went to the bathroom, urinated, blew out the wind that had turned his stomach into a soccer ball, brushed his teeth, and went down to the kitchen. It was too early for the newspaper, hours before a croissant could be bought, so he had better make himself tea.

This business isn't for the police, and it won't be settled by his going down on his knees before Bryan. There must be bars, perhaps in Hampton Bays, perhaps in Riverhead, where certain locals hang out. Not those "fuck me I'll never smile again" fatalistic jerks who are only too happy to pump out septic tanks, haul garbage to the dump, and hand dig with shovels holes for the foundations of rich men's houses so that bulldozers don't mess up the vegetation on their land. Killers. Guys with balls who own handguns. He'll find one of those joints and be there, evening after evening, talking to the bartender confidentially but loud enough. It won't be long before they get used to him. An old codger with money, stooped but still pretty big. Fancy car. Chain-smokes little cigars he'll pass to you right away if you seem interested. By now the bartender has the old codger's story down pat and thinks Schmidt's been screwed. So do some of the other guys who paid attention. One evening, pretty soon, when it's slow, the bartender will have one of those bourbons Schmidt is always pressing on him and say, Al, believe me, you don't need to take shit from this fuckhead. Be here tomorrow evening and talk to Vince.

At the appointed hour, Schmidt is there. The bartender greets him—The usual, Al?—and points with his chin toward a booth. Vince over there has the job figured out. It's a pleasure to see that he's the strong and silent type, neatly dressed, polite, in fact you wouldn't be surprised if he were Michael Mansour's security man. He explains the concept. Two guys I know will come in specially from the city, get into your house when you tell me you're going to be out late, whack this fucker, and make it look like a regular burglary. All you've got to do is to make sure he's there and it's better if he's alone. It gets complicated when there are other people. Like you tell him you've got a guest coming to spend the night and he had better be there to open the door and do the honors. Then the guys drive back to the city and that's that. How much? Vince shrugs his shoulders and says, Hey, Al, you've got real class. Let's say that I'll let you decide. Only one thing: remember, it's like when you go with a girl, you pay up front.

That won't be a problem. Schmidt has figured out how to get the money for Vince and his friends. No big cash withdrawals the bank has to report or phony transactions on which you're bound to lose money, like buying a big diamond ring in New York in order to sell it for cash in Amsterdam or Geneva, which leaves you anyway having to bring the cash back through customs without a declaration. Instead, he will buy gold coins—nice and simple—and pay the boys in gold. Good as gold, that's it. Vince is a smart operator. He'll know the value of the Krugerrand to the penny, and if he doesn't he will know where to look it up. Actually, Schmidt will make a sizable investment in gold, which will please the man who looks after his money and improve the appearance of the operation if anyone cares to inquire. A question of asset allocation and prudence, carried out exactly when the stock market seems frothy, rather than a small purchase matching some specific need.

The more Schmidt thinks about his plan, the better he likes it. These fellows are professionals. Once he's paid them and Bryan has been whacked, they won't be in touch again unless he needs them for another job. But he doesn't think using them a second time would be a smart idea. Really, this is quite different from trying to buy Bryan, because Bryan will never stay bought. You bet. The difference is that he'll stay dead. It's a pity that he can't ask Vince to take Mike Mansour out too. They'd need a guerrilla commando to get past the security. That's a job for Schmidt alone, when it becomes necessary to perform it. While that jerk is standing there with a big grin waving good-bye, shove the car into reverse, gun the engine, and crush the bastard against his own garage wall. Yes sir, accidents will happen.

VII

JESUS, SCHMIDTIE, said Carrie, after he had given her, all during lunch, and even before, while they were putting the cold chicken and the tomato salad on the table, the polite silent treatment that had been, while Mary lived, part of his ingrained behavior. What's the matter with you? I get up early to be out here in time so we can eat and then take a nap, and you treat me like a piece of shit. I don't have to take this.

He wasn't only sulking. He felt dead inside.

You're right. You don't. I don't suppose you will.

Thanks a lot. I want to shower. You can do the dishes by yourself. You're so good at it.

He hadn't heard the car on the driveway or the door being slammed. She took him, therefore, altogether by surprise, tiptoeing into the library and putting her arms around him as though nothing at all had happened, licking the inside of his ear and blowing in it. At first, he remained seated at the desk, before the stack of unpaid bills, careful—no, unable—to respond. She shook him by the shoulders.

Hey Schmidtie, guess what, it's me, your Puerto Rican broad. I'm back.

He had prepared himself for the worst. There wouldn't even be a phone call; she'd give him no news at all. Instead, Jason or his colleague, the human mountain, or, more likely, Manuel would come and say, Miss Gorchuck—or would he call her Carrie?—asked me to pack a few of her things and bring them over. He'd point to an unfamiliar overnight bag in his left hand. I guess they're upstairs, in the master bedroom? Then, on his way out, Have a nice day, Mr. Schmidt. Or she might, in fact, telephone and lie, between fits of giggling. He was sure she had not lied to him in the past, and that, were she to begin, he would know it at once. But to return like this! It was only with the greatest difficulty that he managed to stand up and croak out, So I notice, so I notice, and to add, preposterously, Please, make yourself comfortable. Then he pretended to go on with his bills although his hands trembled and his eyes began to smart. Perhaps this being the second surprise of the morning accounted for his utter stupidity—no, it was worse than stupidity, for the numbness of mind, feelings, and body that had overwhelmed him.

The first surprise had come as soon as he returned home with the newspaper. There was Bryan, at the kitchen table, his right thumb in his mouth. Working on what was left of the nail, just as in the old days. The Melitta pot was half empty, because, having made coffee, Bryan quite sensibly had poured himself a big mug. His duffel bag was on the counter. That was all: no tube holding tantric paintings, no toolbox.

Don't jump to conclusions, Schmidtie, they might be in the pantry, merely out of sight. And no trace of a beard. Just your regular local, whom you have let become too free and easy, having taken the plane all the way from Florida to JFK, and who knows the means of transportation to your house, ready to start the blackmail before you've had a chance to eat your breakfast. The ponytail was missing, too. But Bryan had shaved his head, revealing a nasty scar right down the middle of a knobby skull. Souvenir of an empty beer bottle? Always well mannered. As soon as he saw Schmidt, he stood up, gave the nail an embarrassed look, dried the thumb on the seat of his blue jeans, and held his hand out to Schmidt. Not so fast, kiddo. Schmidt preferred to wave a distant greeting with the newspaper he held in his own right hand. Because this was really unfair. He wasn't ready for Bryan. The thought that there might be a bus or train capable of delivering him at this hour had not crossed his mind.

Hi, Albert, I'm here. Sure feels good to be back.

Fancy that: Bryan had become really thin. Since there had never been any fat on him, not when Schmidt knew him, he must have been losing muscle. He was pale too, with yellow circles around those disappointing, uncertain eyes. Florida couldn't have agreed with him. He might have already been in jail. Somehow, the way he looked made it worse. Therefore, without responding to Bryan's greeting, Schmidt put the *Times* on the table and sat down. The tea he wanted so badly would have to wait. He poured the rest of the coffee into the clean mug Bryan had set down.

Albert, what's wrong? I don't get it. Aren't you going to say anything, not even hello? I told you I was coming. I need a place to stay. You've never been like this before.

Should he let him have it right then and there, no matter what, even if it made the little prick go crazy? Ha! According to Carrie, she used to let him bang her on demand, just so that he wouldn't freak out. For instance, just for openers: Well, I get it, even if you don't. I told you to keep away from this house and to telephone to ask whether you might see me. Instead, you've barged into my kitchen. It's a big mistake. This is not your home. Get that into your head and clear out. Whereupon, he would hear the insufferable whine: Gee, Albert, I can't deal with this. You're so angry. Why? Remember me? I'm Bryan. I nursed you all that summer—bathed you, brought you food, everything. Why are you acting like this? Where's Carrie? Somebody's got to explain to me what's going on. What to do then? Admit he didn't know where Carrie was or when she'd be back? Impossible. He might as well go all the way. Say to him: Listen carefully, you little shit. You'll never see Carrie again. Not if I can help it. That's why I sent you to work on my house in Florida. That's why I got you a soft deal with the hospital after I gave away the house. Your sin is that you fucked her. That's the whole point. Now clear out before I call the police. First they'll work you over, because that's how it is. In the Hamptons, rich guys aren't to be bothered by trash like you. Then they'll put you back on the plane, send you back to those people you left behind in Florida. I bet they can't wait to see you.

He didn't do that. Keeping quiet, he drank the lukewarm coffee.

Albert, aren't you going to talk to me? Don't treat me like this. Can I see Carrie? Somebody's got to talk to me.

You're not seeing Carrie. This Schmidt blurted out.

Holy shit, Albert, is that what's eating you? Carrie's my friend. You know it's over between her and me. Finished, dead. Hey man, be a human being, you've got nothing to worry about. I'm in deep shit. I need help.

Who doesn't, Schmidt might have answered. But he didn't need to. Bryan's gift for monologue proved sufficient for the telling of a banal story, the punch line of which Schmidt had guessed. It was, first of all, about how he had hurt Bryan's feelings by coming to see the house, after Bryan had restored it to 1930s splendor, only once, without Carrie, walking through it with a lawyer and spending the night in a hotel when everything was ready for him at home! Didn't even take Bryan out for a meal. Was that the way to show a guy appreciation for two years of work, all of it wasted? And when Schmidt gave the house to the hospital Bryan couldn't believe it. Then some secretary told him to get himself and his stuff out of his own room and move to the dormitory for male nurses. That he refused to do. Next thing he knew, the security guards hassled him, threw his personal possessions, even his tools, on the floor in the corridor, and, big surprise, discovered the treasure trove. This provoked his fabled fury. Nazi assholes! He pointed to the top of his head. It was they who did it, and then called the police, accusing Bryan of disorderly conduct and directing them to the stuff which was in his smaller toolbox! It was really nothing, Bryan assured Schmidt, he wasn't dealing, Schmidt paid him enough so he didn't need to. It was just a reserve he had on hand for himself and for Bonnie's former neighbors, in case they called on a weekend to see whether he could help out. Jesus, the way they wrote him up you'd think he'd mined the fucking Hialeah racetrack. That's when one of the big guys who was following the case got him out on bail and dropped the hint that Bryan maybe wanted a lift to the Miami airport. I got the point, Bryan concluded. It was adios, man, get lost. So there he was. He'd gone straight to his one friend, the guy who had sent him to Florida, for Chrissake.

I'm sorry I never used the house, replied Schmidt. It's in the wrong place. I don't like Florida.

Fuck Florida. Where's Carrie?

In the city.

With her folks?

Something like that.

When's she coming back?

I'm not quite sure. Maybe today. Maybe later.

Hey Albert, let me stay here, will you? Until she comes back, I mean. Like I told you, you don't need to worry about me.

I've already told you I don't know when she's coming back. While she's away, I prefer to be alone. When she returns, I'd rather not have you hanging around.

You've got it all wrong, man. I'd help with the house, like before, whatever needs fixing. Hey, I'll keep an eye on her for you too. That's one full-time job, believe me! Maybe with you it's different, maybe you're like such a great lover that's all she needs. Shit, that would have to be something else!

What do you mean?

What do I mean? With me, it was like every time I turned my back! Even my buddy Hollis, in Springs. You know Debbie, the red-haired girl works at O'Henry's Carrie was such great friends with—she almost scratched Carrie's eyes out. That's why Carrie had to move out. It was tense, let me tell you, until I helped her find the apartment in Sag Harbor. Man, I couldn't believe it.

That security man in Florida who hit you on the head must have hit you very hard—assuming that story is true. You know perfectly well that Carrie moved out of Springs because your friend Hollis tried to rape her. She never wanted to go back there. And now I think it's time for you to move on. I won't hear such nonsense about Carrie.

Wow, Albert, have you got it all wrong. What do you think Carrie is? A fucking nun? All the time we were together, she screwed every waiter and busboy at O'Henry's. Ask anybody, they'll tell you. You know the closet behind the kitchen? She'd let her pants down, lean over, and take it doggie style. The owner didn't use the closet. He fucked her standing up against the wall in his office. Or he'd sit down in a chair, open his fly, and she'd get on top. It was like a joke. Sometimes after work she was so sore she'd just give me a blow job. I got to hand it to you, Albert, once she started with you she slowed down, it was like she was too proud for everybody else or something, except Hank Wilson. That bum dicked her anytime and any way he wanted.

Mr. Wilson?

Yeah, the guy you ran over. He'd come to the apartment and stink like a piece of dead meat. Jeez, Carrie was always after me to sell her shit so he could get hard when they fucked. Most of the time, I'd give it to her free. All I asked was that they do it on the floor. You sure wouldn't want that guy's cock in your bed.

The kitchen knives hung neatly on the magnetized holder to the left of the stove, the edges all turned in the same direction. The long fancy Sabatier knife Schmidt had bought when he still lived in New York and kept watching over like a mother lest it be nicked, saving it to carve lamb or the occasional roast beef; the short knives made of soft steel with unvarnished handles that came from Mr. Johnson's hardware store, two doors down from O'Henry's, which were really better and easier to keep razor sharp, although they cost far less; the real shorties for use on vegetables and fruit, some of them serrated. Which one should he leap for and plunge into this monster's belly, right above the low-slung belt? Stick it in and turn, then slash the face. Flood the floor with blood. Soak in it himself: shirt sleeves, socks, shoes. Then call the police. If possible, bring matters to an end before they arrived. He'd manage it, with the pills upstairs. Spill blood on this accursed house that Charlotte doesn't want. She'll sell it, take the money, take the other money he has—so much more than she supposes. So long as she remakes her life.

You goddamn monster.

This was surely some other man talking. Schmidt had never heard such a voice. It couldn't be he. Must be an incubus or the herald of apoplexy. Like his father. He had never asked Bonnie what it had sounded like, what noise the old man had made before he fell, face right into the black bean soup, at the dinner table in Grove Street. Perhaps he had made no noise at all, self-possessed and distant to the last. By the time Schmidt had gotten there, the butler and the cook had him lying down on the leather sofa in the study, but they had all forgotten to wipe the little bit of brown foam off his mouth.

Gee, Albert, you really thought Carrie was a virgin? Get with it, man. She told me how she came on to you. Why do you think she did that? You don't know? I'll explain it to you. She laid you because you're old. She wanted to see what you'd do. Stuff like that. That's no crime. Sure she loves you, Albert, but it's not exclusive. Nothing is. What do you say? Do we have a deal?

It was too late. The moment to kill had passed.

The police will get you, Schmidt said inconsequentially. Around here is the first place they'll look. You had better go. Far away. Somewhere you've never been.

Nah. This Florida business is chickenshit. How about it, Albert? Are we friends? I'll be your watchdog. Believe me, I don't miss a thing.

I really wish you'd go. And then he added, stupidly, She never told me she was sleeping with the waiters at O'Henry's. Or the owner.

You ever ask her?

No.

Albert! Why should she tell you if you didn't ask? What do you think she was doing after work? Soaking her feet? She's still a kid, don't forget that. Hey, will you drive me over to Springs? There's no way I can get there. I walked all the way here from the bus.

That was beyond Schmidt's strength. Should he offer to lend him Mary's Toyota, assuming it would start? Call a taxi? No, Bryan had better walk back to the town and take a taxi from there. He will need money for the fare. Of course. Then give him money; it's better to give it to him before he asks.

But Bryan refused, shaking his head. I've got money, he said. Fuck it, man, I thought you were my friend.

So that was that. Bryan had certainly put things in perspective. There weren't all that many dishes to wash after the ghastly, silent lunch. Sooner or later, she would come down, and she wouldn't use the back stairs or fly out the window. Of course, nothing stopped him from getting into his car and driving off—to the beach, to Montauk, to the airport. Men disappear all the time, for no reason at all. Instead, he dried the two crystal wineglasses, put them away, and went back to the library to work on the bills.

She always moved soundlessly, even when she wasn't barefoot, and it was not because he heard her steps that he became aware of her presence. She stood in the door, wearing the white terry-cloth bathrobe she liked. Her wet hair glistened. Darling, she said, you're real mad at me. I've never seen you like this. Why?

You left me—without any warning.

Schmidtie, I went to see my parents. I called from school, between classes, and my mom wasn't feeling good. Then I called Mike Mansour's house and told Manuel to give the message. There wasn't anyplace I could reach you. Why is that bad?

You didn't call me from the city.

I did. I left a message on the machine.

Yes, a message that you had gone out on the town with Michael Mansour. Was that part of taking care of your mom?

I drove her to the hospital for her leg and then drove her back home. There was nothing she needed. Yeah, I called Michael. So what's wrong with that?

Nothing, if you're going on dates with other men. I didn't know you were.

I'm not. Whoa, Schmidtie, we see him all the time. He's your friend. I wanted to see his apartment. I've never been to a fancy place like that. Then he asked if I like to eat Japanese. So we went to that restaurant. I told you that in the message.

And later?

What do you mean later?

I mean what did you do later, after dinner.

We went to a club in Tribeca and danced.

Mansour danced?

Yeah, he danced. He dances pretty good. Hey, he showed me how to belly dance! I danced with Jason too. Jeez, that guy really knows how to move.

I see. Security all the way, even on the dance floor. That's nice. And what else? I mean what happened after that.

Michael asked if he should drive me home or if I wanted to stay at his place.

And what did you decide?

Boy, Schmidtie, you're a real lawyer. I said I'd stay in his apartment. Here are the reasons: I left my car in his garage, so I would have to get it and drive all the way to Canarsie at three in the morning, which I didn't feel like doing.

Aha! Mr. and Mrs. Gorchuck lived in Canarsie. That was an interesting, and someday possibly useful, fact, heretofore unknown to Schmidt. The precise situation of Canarsie in relation to Brooklyn, likewise unknown to him, merited investigation.

Second, I didn't want to wake my dad up. When mom's sick like this he sleeps in the living room.

Then where did Carrie sleep? Also in the living room? On the floor or on a second couch? Was there not a second bedroom, however small, or did she sleep in the kitchen on a folding bed? Sharp pain in Schmidt's heart: Why didn't this poor child trust him enough to have let him see how the parents lived, why didn't she let him lift them above such sordidness?

I see, he said. But you didn't think they would be unable to get back to sleep if one of them woke up in the middle of the night and saw that you hadn't returned? I might have thought that was worse.

You've got to be kidding. They think I'm a grown-up.

True enough. And what happened once you got to the Mansour residence?

What do you mean?

I think it's clear what I mean. Did he make a pass at you? Did you sleep with him?

You really want to know?

He didn't, but he nodded his head.

Guess what! He raped me. Yeah, and Jason held me down. You happy now?

Carrie, Bryan was here this morning.

No shit.

Right. Back from Florida. I got his message, right after I got yours. He screwed it up there. It's the old Bryan, only different. He talked a lot. About you.

Like what?

Like you slept with every waiter at O'Henry's. The owner too. A full-service waitress, that's what.

And what's that to you? You thought you were the first, Schmidtie?

No, you told me the man—excuse me, Mr. Wilson—was the first. But I didn't know that, to take Bridgehampton alone, you had serviced every waiter and busboy at your place of work, in addition to the owner, Bryan, and Mr. Wilson.

You mean like if you had known you wouldn't have fucked me? Is that it? Up yours, Schmidtie. Mr. Wilson sure had your number. You're a shithead, that's what he said, a hoity-toity shithead. I should've believed him.

She cried, the way she always did when the subject of the man came up.

I am sorry, Schmidt said. You want my handkerchief?

Wipe yourself, you bastard. What's your problem? When you're in my pussy, it doesn't feel right? Not clean enough for you? You don't like what you get when you eat it because you're not the first? How about me? Do I ask you where you've stuck your dick? Remember, I asked you if you wanted me to be faithful. You blew me off. And now you're jealous!

I am. I love you, Carrie. I've asked you to marry me, over and over. We've been together. I don't know how I would live without you. When you asked me that question, at the very beginning, it was different.

Shit.

No, it's the truth. Please come over here.

He couldn't believe it, but he had somehow managed: he had, perhaps for the first time in his life, actually broken out of the box he had put himself into, had made a gesture of peace. She took a step toward him, then two. Trembling, he drew her onto his lap and caressed her hair. It was still wet, like a young dog's just in from the rain.

Please, Carrie.

Don't.

He had put his hand on her knee, where she allowed it to rest, and then tried to move it higher, toward the center, where he imagined she was wet too.

Carrie, this isn't about the waiters or the busboys. That was Bryan talking, wanting to humiliate me. By the way, he did a good job. This is about now, about you and Michael Mansour. I can't just let it go, I have to know. It's not just some guy who thinks he is my friend. He's someone we see all the time, together. What happened?

You really want to know? she repeated.

He nodded his head and took his hand off her knee, finding a neutral ground on the terry cloth.

OK. He's got this triplex. His bedroom and a kind of living room with a big fireplace are on the second floor, and also a room with mats and machines—treadmill, bicycles, and a cage for weights. All kinds of stuff. He has a trainer come in every morning. You won't believe it. At six. The guest rooms are on the third floor. He showed me into my room, and where the lights were and everything, and the bathroom, and I thought he was like going to kiss me and say goodnight. Instead, all of a sudden, he drops his arms and says, I want to see your breasts. I look at him surprised, and this time he says, Please show me your tits. I was like let me out, man! I had on this black blouse you gave me, you know, short, with little shoulder straps, that doesn't button, so I just lift it up and tell him, Here they are. Say hello. I think he's going to grab me or lick them, but no, he asks me, What's Schmidtie going to say? I couldn't believe it, so I say he's going to try to break your stupid face. I'll tell you, it was like he threw cold water over me. I closed up. So he says it's all right, Schmidtie doesn't need to know and other kinds of shit, and I tell him forget it, I'm going to sleep.

And then?

In the morning, he comes into my room again and says he's sorry, he couldn't sleep all night, he was jerking off thinking about me, and he'll give me a million dollars if I fuck him. I ask, Right now? So he says, No, not now, I can't get it up, I'm too worn out, but please soon. Don't make me wait too long.

Oh, Carrie.

Some friend you've got there. You want to hear the best? On my way out of there, I was saying good-bye to Jason, and

Mike rushes out from somewhere, I don't know where he was, and says, Don't forget the dinner on Sunday. Hillel's going to play. I expect you and Schmidtie. It'll be a fabulous party.

Carrie, I'll give you a million dollars if you don't let that man get near you.

She looked at him very carefully and replied, It's no good, Schmidtie. If I take your money, I'll never sleep with you again. Then she took his hand, put it back on the inside of her knee, guided it upward, and whispered: Hey, you haven't written that check for one million dollars yet, have you? Come on, dopey, we're wasting time. Let's go upstairs.

VIII

BEFORE Carrie left for school the next morning, he gave her a gold pin in the form of a scarab. It had been his present to Mary to mark the date old Dexter King told him that the firm had taken him into the partnership. It was a beautiful piece, although perhaps a bit strong—some might say too elaborate—in the manner of jewelry made in Boston at the turn of the century. To his surprise, Mary never wore it. That wasn't the sort of thing that Schmidt would mention, let alone inquire about, but it occurred to him subsequently that she might have seen the bill, which he had put on top of his chest of drawers, together with other papers, to take to the office and send to the insurance broker. The price was high, well beyond Schmidt's means. Not wanting to sell any of the few stocks he owned, he had borrowed to pay for it. She disliked—as in fact did he—his anomalous outbursts of extravagance, and, since they could bring themselves to talk about money only with the greatest difficulty, and then always stiffly, as though the subject made their flesh crawl, putting this object away would have been her way of annulling an action she reproved. She could count on him to understand and to keep silent. This circumstance was probably the reason he had not offered the pin to Charlotte along with the rest of Mary's trinkets, the bittersweet chronicle of his devotion and sense of circumstance reposing in leather boxes of various shapes and sizes as though in miniature tombs. Mary's mother had died very young, her father, cut down by machine-gun fire while he waded toward a Normandy beach, even earlier; there was nothing she had inherited from them except their wedding bands and an engagement ring, all of which Schmidt had also withheld: the former because they made him uneasy, the latter because it was such a pitiful thing that he thought it best not to expose it to view and comment. The good jewelry in Mary's family had belonged to Aunt Martha, and that Mary put in a safety box for Charlotte directly after the old lady died. Most of what Schmidt offered to Charlotte she accepted. The rest he sold for more money than he would have thought likely to a merchant he had dealt with over the years. But not the Boston scarab; he liked him far too much. He had made the right decision, to keep him and to give him the second time: when Carrie saw it—he had held out his fist enclosing the jewel and said, Quick, go knock, knock to see what's inside—she asked him in her little voice, Darling, is this for me, and, when he nodded, she kissed his hand, called him darling once more, and then Bebop, and, after she had attached the pin to her shirt, offered to skip school and spend the day with him, because he had made her so happy. But he said, Go on, be sure that you're not late and that you drive carefully, held open the door of the little car for her, and remained in the driveway a long time after it disappeared. Bebop. The diminutive of his godfather's name, and the only pet name Schmidt's mother ever used. She had a way of saying, when one of his friends telephoned and he was sitting in the same room as she, and she happened not to be in one of her crankier moods, You want Bebop no doubt, I'll get him for you, he must be somewhere in the house. It made him cringe. Spoken by Carrie, the color of the word changed. It was as gay as the rainbow.

She wouldn't be back until late in the afternoon. There was nothing, literally nothing, he needed to do. It was pointless to make the bed or clear the dishes because the Polish women would arrive later that morning. Carrie had said she would pick up sausages and fruit and vegetables for their dinner on her way home. There were enough cans of tuna and sardines in the pantry to withstand a siege, and he had bought bread and cheese when he got the breakfast croissants. Lunch, therefore, was taken care of. The soft but steady rain that began to fall almost as soon as Carrie left—he was glad she had put up the roof of her car—did not rule out doing laps in the pool but made the prospect unattractive. Gil Blackman had left for the West Coast. Schmidt wasn't sure he would have risked telephoning and being told by Gil that he couldn't take time off from work to have lunch, even if Gil had been in Bridgehampton, or that he was ready to see him if that implied resuming their last conversation, and probably it did. He could always invite Elaine to lunch in his place. This was, however, something he had never done before or even contemplated. Did Elaine go out to lunch when it was not a social obligation involving Gil? Schmidt doubted it; she had told him she was in the thick of research for her book on colonial orphanages. She had not mentioned how that was accomplished, given the limited resources of the Bridgehampton library. Presumably, she had books sent to her from the Society Library in New York or got them on some interlibrary loan, and, now that Gil was a Harvard overseer, perhaps even from the Widener. At any rate, why would he ask her to lunch? Whatever turn the conversation took, it would only lead to trouble. Carrie was not a safe subject, and neither was Charlotte or, for that matter, Gil, of whose secret sentimental life Elaine was convinced Schmidt knew the ins and outs. Was it worth the collateral risk that Elaine might see in his initiative some sort of absurd romantic overture? It wasn't, and there was nobody else he considered even remotely possible.

That left Trollope—he had embarked recently on the project of rereading his favorites—paying bills, and waiting for Charlotte to telephone. It seemed to him that she really should let him know whether she was coming for the weekend. If for any reason she couldn't or didn't want to, he would go to the city to see her. But he had decided he must above all avoid making her feel she was being ushered back into the nursery, that he was somehow "taking over." It was best to wait. Eventually, she would call. The thought of sitting down with a book first thing in the morning was not appealing. To that extent, it was clear that he had given Gil Blackman a touched-up version of his hours of solitary leisure. The bills—there weren't all that many of them—had to be paid. But first he was going to shave. Of late, especially on days when Carrie had classes, he found himself putting off his toilette until later and later, and that was surely the slippery slope on the way to becoming a neglected—yes, why not say it—a dirty old man. He had seen it happen. A literary agent, one of the few whose taste and principles Mary had respected, in fact she had thought he should have been an editor with his own imprint in a major house, whom they used to see regularly, retired. Soon afterward, his much younger wife divorced him for no apparent reason; certainly they knew of no other man in the picture. Perhaps the reason was that he insisted on spending most of his time at their house in Georgica, while her work as a partner in another agency required her to be in New York during the week. In any event, she had made no pretense of liking the country or her husband's retirement. Soon after she left, one began to see Jake doing his errands at the local markets with two days' growth of beard, shuffling about in sneakers from which he had removed the laces he apparently found superfluous, and preternaturally stooped. At some point, he lost two of his lower front teeth. There was no reason to suppose that he had been in a brawl; more likely he had bitten down too hungrily on the bone of a lamb chop. The teeth went unreplaced, and, within months, Jake was dead, of a stroke, leaving a complicated estate, with not enough liquid assets to pay taxes on it, to be divided among hard-up nephews, nieces, and stepchildren. That was not the sort of end Schmidt wished for himself. Not shaving, he recognized, does not inevitably bring on apoplexy, but it might be a harbinger!

Upstairs then, to the bathroom. He could not recall how often he had used the blade clamped to his razor. There were two alternatives: try the blade again, with the possibility of switching to a new one in midstream if the shave wasn't smooth, or insert a new one. Halfheartedly, because the not-inconsiderable price of top-of-the-line razor blades had become something to reckon with, he settled on the latter course, applied the shaving cream, and started to scrape. Hello! Through the open window Schmidt heard a car on the driveway going faster and breaking harder than he thought appropriate. It was not yet the hour of the Polish cleaning brigade. He looked out and saw Mr. Mansour's little Rolls-Royce. The door opened on the driver's side and that gentleman got out. Another figure—Jason, Schmidt supposed—remained in the passenger's seat. Mike Mansour strode toward the front door, mounted the steps, and rang the bell. Aha, he was on his best behavior. His usual form, and, for that matter, the form of most people Schmidt knew, was to walk in and shout, Anybody home?

This time Schmidt faced three possibilities. He could go down and open the door; he could shout, Come in, I'll be right down! through the open window; or he could pretend he wasn't at home. He'd be damned if he was going to depart from his normal habits because of that lout. Therefore, he emitted the normal yell and heard Mike Mansour's even louder reply, Take your time, I'll wait on the back porch. Well said: Schmidt wasn't about to rush. He took his time, twenty minutes by his watch, before joining his guest, who stood up solemnly and held out his hand. Schmidt walked past him and leaned against the arm of the chintz sofa. He did not ask Mansour to sit down.

Carrie has told you?

About her evening—I should say night—with you in New York?

Oh, intoned Mr. Mansour, forgive me, Schmidtie, please forgive me, do you think you can forgive me? I behaved so badly and didn't mean to. Can you forgive me, can we go back to the way we were?

I think the question is whether I can continue to know you. I haven't got the answer.

Even after I said I'm sorry? I lost my head. Look, she's a fabulous, sexy kid. You'd have to be a saint to keep your hands off her. Come on, Schmidtie, you know this better than anybody.

Nonsense. This wasn't like kissing a friend's wife at a party. You set it up. Planned it in your head. You asked her to spend the night in your apartment. Then you made a pass. Then in the morning you offered her money for sex. How dare you ask me to forgive you?

Because I'm sorry. Schmidtie, be reasonable. Haven't you ever fucked up and been caught?

What has that got to do with you and me?

Because we're both human, so we can both fuck up. Then life goes on. Look, Schmidtie, we've talked for hours. You know how I am. I'm not all bad. Go on, Schmidtie, say you're not mad at me. If you don't, I'll get Jason to break your arms and legs. He'll do a good job, I'm telling you. It is no problem. By the way, I'm just kidding. OK. Have you ever fucked up?

If you mean to ask whether I have betrayed friends, the answer is no.

Jesus, Schmidtie. I haven't betrayed you. I made a pass at your girl. You're Sicilian or something? You've never cheated on your wife?

Schmidt had been waiting for that question. The way Mary had found out about Corinne, Charlotte's having known and remembered with such bitterness that he was carrying on with Corinne in the room off the kitchen while she was supposed to be asleep in her nice white bed in her nice room, the women he'd pick up at bars on business trips—what kind of Tartuffe was he? Hating Mansour was fair game, except that he didn't hate him but the high moral tone!

Michael, where is this conversation supposed to lead?

To your saying, It's all right, I have forgiven you, and here is my hand. Don't you understand, you boob, that you're the best friend I have? Can't you get that into your head?

Then I feel sorry for you.

You should. I am very lonely, and this really hurts. I screwed up—when I tried to be so good and to be your friend. I told you over and over: Carrie needs to have a life. The question is, How can you give it to her, if you keep her here cooped up with you? What about the next guy who's after her and doesn't fuck it up? Answer me that one.

How I live with Carrie is my own business.

How can you say that? It's my business, because I'm talking of your good now. Don't you understand that? You're more important to me than Carrie.

I think you had better leave now.

I'm not. I'm not going anywhere until this is settled. When it's settled, we'll be even better friends, because you'll stop being so distant. You don't realize it, but that's your big problem. You don't let anyone get near you, except maybe Gil Blackman. That's why you're so lonely, even lonelier than me, because at least I have all these zeros you see at my house waiting to lick my ass. By the way, I don't want you to talk to Gil about any of this. Promise?

I believe Gil has gone to L.A. No, I'm not going to call him there to discuss you or your behavior.

That's right, I know he's out there.

For the first time, Mr. Mansour sounded discouraged and sat down. He chose the settee that was also a swing and set it in motion.

I don't suppose you realize this, he continued, after a pause, but I'm having a major influence on Gil's career. I don't mean just my money and investing in his films. It's my artistic input. He needs my judgment on a number of issues. The money is important too. I give him freedom he wouldn't have otherwise. Those meetings he's gone to, I set them up. I was going to fly out today to join him, but sitting with you was more important to me. I don't want this business about Carrie to interfere with Gil. You have to promise me that.

I don't see how I can.

You can. Don't tell him, or if you tell him, say you understand how it happened and that we're better friends now than before. You know, that could just help him work through some problems. Schmidtie, I know you realize that I'm a very exceptional person. I don't want to boast, but there is really no one like me.

Mr. Mansour leaned back, looked up at the ceiling, and rolled off the names of other notable takeover artists and raiders, his colleagues and peers.

My question is how I should use my power and my wealth. That's what I'm working on now. One plan I have is to let you take over my foundation. I'd still give it the intellectual leadership, but you would run it and get exposure to a new world: social issues, science, really large people. With Gil, I know what to do. I've decided I and he are going to work as partners. Then the sky is the limit. *Pas de problème.* What do you think of that!

Nothing at all.

That's because you're still confused. I want you to come to lunch. That's the reason I came over. Come just as you are. It'll be just the two of us. Manuel will make something special. You'll see.

It's out of the question.

Goddamn it Schmidtie, I'm not taking no for an answer. I've begged you to forgive me. I know that in your heart you have forgiven me. So stop sulking. Jason will pick you up at one and drive you home after lunch.

The rain had turned into the sort of drizzle that could go on all day and then the next. Was Charlotte going to call? The voices he could hear on the other side of the house told Schmidt that the cleaning women had arrived. Mansour had tired him to the point that the prospect of paying bills had become a longed-for relief, and yet he made no move to leave. In fact, Mansour had sat down and put his feet up on the glass coffee table. Tiny feet in some sort of white loafers. Like all his clothes, they looked as though they had never been worn before. Yellow linen trousers and a red silk shirt. That was something you'd expect to see on Gil. Did Mansour buy Gil's shirts, or was it the other way around? Mansour's ankles were tanned, or perhaps he used artificial coloring. To hell with him, his yellow trousers, his worry beads, and his yellow Rolls.

Look, said Schmidt. My mind, my feelings, don't work like yours. The way I've been taught to behave is different. Until now, I haven't known people like you. I mean socially. I am expecting someone to telephone. Someone important to me. I don't want you around when I take that call. Why don't you leave?

Because we haven't finished talking. You wouldn't treat me like this if I was one of your old friends. That's the truth, isn't it? Let me tell you, I wish I had old friends, but I was thrown out of my country. I had no time to make friends. I had to take over from my mother and father and build the business. My first wife was a mistake—not a big mistake like my second wife but still a mistake. You don't know I have two kids, do you? They're about the age of your daughter. I had them right away. They live in Israel, can you believe it? With all the opportunities I can give them! They don't care about what I've accomplished. Can you believe it, they could go right to the top and they still refuse to work with me. So I've no family life. I can tell you one thing: in the next life, no children. Then there's Judy, second wife. With her, it was dinner out every night. With the same queers. Without exception! Queers putting on Off Broadway plays for queers! Queers who photograph road kill! In my position, I don't need that. I don't mind having dinner with Gil Blackman and his crowd, or even people like you, but that was too dull for Judy. You've been to the parties at my house. What do you think of that? Except for you and Hillel, it's the schmucks who work for me or want to work for me or want me to give them money without working for me. It's all the same thing. Do I need it? Now you understand how I could lose my head and behave badly? Don't look like that, I know you do. By the way, these things about me, I've never told them to you before. You see? We're better friends already. I'll see you at lunch.

There is no chance of my having any sort of relations with you, never mind going to your house, before I've talked about it with Carrie. That won't be before this evening. Lunch is out of the question.

Schmidtie, you're wrong if you think I'll give up. I'm going to change you—all the way inside. Letting you run my foundation may do it. All right, be good. You are both coming to my dinner on Sunday and I want you to come to lunch tomorrow. Talk to Carrie. She's a smart girl. We'll drink good wine and clear the air.

He held out his hand.

Come on, pal. Shake my hand.

What was he to do? He took the hand, whereupon Mansour enveloped him in a big embrace. You're a great guy, he cried out. You don't even begin to know how much you mean to me.

The Polish ladies had left in a profusion of farewells. Schmidt licked the last envelope. As usual, he hadn't enough stamps. The rain had stopped. If he was going to the post office, shouldn't he have a bite at the counter of the candy store? Sit down between two sets of grandfathers and grandmothers feeding kids in jodhpurs their grilled-cheese sandwiches and chocolate milk shakes? He didn't think he could bear that. The checks could be mailed the next day or the day after or next week for all he cared. At the rate Charlotte's life was falling apart, there would never be a grandchild for him to take to lunch. Sardines and bourbon in the kitchen were going to be just fine, and then a nap until just before Carrie returned. He wasn't going to sleep all that hard. If Charlotte called, she wouldn't realize that she had awakened him. He was still working on his second drink when the telephone rang. Two-thirty. She was at the office, unless she had quit her job or simply not gone to work. Pray God she hadn't rushed into anything foolish. He picked up the receiver and said, I've been waiting for you.

This was the wrong way to begin the conversation, he realized immediately, but he hadn't intended any sort of reproach. Fortunately, she didn't take it too hard.

Gosh Dad, I don't think I said what time I'd call.

I know, I know. It's perfectly all right. We've had rain, so I've been hanging around the house, that's all. How are you?

How do you suppose? Rotten. I go to the office this morning and he gets into the elevator with me. He had the nerve to kiss me. I almost hauled off and punched him.

I'm glad you didn't. Will you be here on Friday? I'm all excited about it.

Dad, I don't think so. Something's come up. Renata wants to see me. She and Myron are on vacation in Claverack, so she's coming into the city specially. I guess it's important.

Oh.

Why it was important for Charlotte to see the mother of the husband she was in the process of divorcing, more important in any event than to see her own father, was not immediately clear to Schmidt, but he didn't think he would gain much by asking. Realizing once more how little he knew, he ventured, Come to think of it, where are you staying? I suppose you're no longer in Mr. Polk's apartment?

Are you kidding? I got out of there the day he told me the great news.

To where, sweetie? I don't believe you've told me.

I'm staying with a girl who works here. Marcia Schwartz. You don't know her.

I see. Not in your own apartment.

Dad, are you kidding? Jon's living in it.

Goodness, he said. I take it then you haven't agreed on the financial settlement, and so forth. But the lawyers are working on it?

We haven't gotten anywhere. I don't want alimony from Jon or stuff like that, so that's no problem, but he doesn't want to sign over the place in the country and still doesn't want to leave the apartment. His parents are right next door to the place in Claverack. That's why he says we should share it. I don't get it. I've filed for divorce, whatever that means.

I don't get it either. And these loans you signed together with Jon. Who's paying them?

He says he can't just now. So I guess I am. I was going to ask you to help.

I see. What does your lawyer think of all that?

Joe Black? He says we should go to court. That's why he filed those papers. I think that's what Renata wants to see me about.

Have you talked to Mr. Black about seeing her? Does he think it's a good idea? Normally, one would leave negotiations of this sort to one's lawyer.

Dad, it's my life, remember? Renata's always been a good friend to me. The best I've ever had. When I told her how Harry dumped me, the first thing she said was I should move back to the apartment.

To live there with Jon?

I guess so. She said it was his idea. He always said I should move in anytime I wanted. Anyway, I've got to go now. Have a good weekend.

It seemed to Schmidt that she was about to hang up before he had had a chance to reply. Perhaps that would be just as well. The words on the tip of his tongue—For God's sake, haven't you had enough of the Rikers?—were of no use. Even he knew that. But he wouldn't let go.

Not so fast, Charlotte, he cut in. I am not being nosy, or trying to meddle, not really, but in fact it's extraordinary, now that I think of it, that until a moment ago I didn't know where you are living. Or where you stand with your divorce. You can't say the divorce is none of my business, and that's not just because you are my only child. The divorce is tied to financial issues, to the money your mother left you and to the money you got from me.

You haven't given me any money. Gee, I'm wrong. Excuse me, Dad, I beg your pardon, how could I forget the allowance you used to give me before my salary was raised and the Christmas and birthday checks! I'm really stupid.

Oh!

He should have let her slam down the receiver. Now it was too late. If he said, as he was tempted to, All right, all right, let's not quarrel, and took it upon himself to end this odious conversation, there was no telling when they could talk again. He would be leaving her in the hands of the Rikers, mother and son.

Look, Charlotte, he continued, you're getting this all wrong. Either cool down so we can talk now or find time to see me tomorrow. I'll come to the city to see you.

Tomorrow is no good. I'm in client meetings.

Then shut the door to your office and listen to me now.

A grunt of assent, a pause, and another grunt that sounded like OK.

Thank you. I wanted to give you my share of this house, so it would be all yours, yours and Jon's. Your mother would have wanted me to. You decided you wanted money instead. That is why I bought your share. If I had given you the money, I would have paid almost the same amount on top of the gift in taxes. At the time, you understood this. Certainly

Jon did. I was happy to give you that money, and I will be happy to leave to you whatever I can when I die, including this house. The house I live in, where you spent every weekend and holiday until you married Jon.

You mean you might if I play my cards right leave to me what you don't give to Carrie or whoever else you pick up!

It's quite possible that I will leave money to Carrie or to Harvard or to whomever else I choose, but it's my intention to make sure that you are more than all right. Please listen to me carefully. Just a while ago, you asked me to give you a very large amount of money so that you and Mr. Polk could start a new business. You weren't very nice about it, but never mind. I said all right. The reason I haven't sent the money is that you and Mr. Polk didn't set up the account to receive it. That's just as well, because it would have been a mess. Yesterday, you called me all broken up about Harry Polk and what you told me broke my heart too. Not because of Mr. Polk, obviously, but because of you. Yesterday, you also said you needed—or wanted, I can't remember which it was—to see me here, at home. Today, you've told me it's more important for you to stay in town to see Renata Riker.

That really ticked you off, didn't it?

It did. I wanted to see you.

So you could talk to me like this, only longer? Like two days in a row?

I've almost finished. Charlotte, you've also just told me that your lawyer has made no progress getting Jon to return what's clearly your property. That is absolutely outrageous. He has no right to the house or to the apartment you have paid for. At the most, at the very most, you might take over the loans if it's really true the money you borrowed went to pay for them. I am sure that Mr. Black has thought of that.

Yeah, he's talked about it.

To you or to Jon as well?

He's talked to Cacciatore.

And?

And nothing. Jesus, Dad, I've told you they haven't gotten anywhere.

All right, here is the conclusion of my boring speech. I think it's foolish of you to talk to Renata Riker about the terms of your separation from Jon and about your property, if that's what she wants to do. It's a setup. They're going behind your lawyer's back and that's outrageous as well.

Nobody's going behind anybody's back. I resent that.

I hope you're right. I also hope that you are not going to move into the apartment with Jon or, what's more important, take up with him again unless there is first a settlement of your property rights, and by that I mean that you get your property back. This is a question of basic honesty.

Thanks, Dad, and good-bye.

This time she really did hang up.

The rain had stopped altogether. In fact, the sun had come out. Schmidt opened the kitchen windows and the door outside the door of the mudroom, which lay beyond the pantry. Then, a fresh drink in hand, he went around the downstairs of the house throwing open the front and back doors. Not satisfied, he opened every window in the house, downstairs and upstairs, even in the never-used guest rooms and in Charlotte's room. The pool house deserved an airing too. He found the door locked, went back to the kitchen and got the key, opened the windows of that now useless structure, and, for good measure, opened the garage doors. His garden, he noted, looked positively jolly, every leaf, every blade of grass, glistening with raindrops. Laughing, winsome nature. It was great good fortune, he thought, to own such a fine place and to have maintained it in absolutely top condition. At the same time, he noted a weakness in his legs and arms, as though he had been running hard, in heavy clothes, on some hard surface. He also noted that his armpits felt moist. This was unusual for him, as he rarely sweated, but in fact his shirt was wet and clinging to him, under his arms and in the back. He went into the house, put on a fresh shirt and a sweater, because suddenly he felt a chill, and made coffee. Against his custom, he drank it with sugar. There was, he remembered, in the refrigerator, an open package of Hershey's chocolate kisses that Carrie had used for making a mousse. He ate a handful of them, and wrote to Charlotte:

> You may, perhaps, decide to call me in the near future, but I don't know when that will be, and I wish to tell you, before you see Renata Riker, what I would have said had you given me the opportunity.
>
> First, as I once tried to make clear, not very successfully, I would have said again that the break in your and Jon's marriage gave me no satisfaction. I wished you well. I hoped you would be happy together. I have grieved over Jon's failure at the firm—I don't know how

else to describe what happened without being unfair. Therefore, I can assure you that I would rejoice if what was broken was somehow mended in conditions that I could consider honorable. Having heard you on the subject of the financial discussions between you and Jon, that means to me one thing only. Jon has to return the property that came from your family, so that, to put it very crudely, it's crystal clear he wants to keep you, and not your money and you.

Second, so that you and the Rikers might know where you stand with respect to any inheritance from me, I would have informed you that I will take steps next week to make sure that any money or other property I may leave you will be in trust. Its conditions will entitle you only to that portion of the trust income that the trustee may in his absolute discretion decide to distribute to you, and, of course, to emergency help also at the trustee's discretion. After your death, the property will continue in trust, on the same terms, for the benefit of your children until they reach the age of thirty, at which time the trust property will be divided among them. Should you have no children, Harvard University will inherit. I will, however, quite obviously retain the power to liberalize the conditions of the trust if, before I die, your family situation and your conduct lead me to believe that such a change is appropriate.

I would like to remind you that when I married your mother, she had almost no money. That was my situation as well, except that I expected to inherit from my father. As it turned out, my father left me no money, just some odds and ends. He disinherited me. Money was never an issue between your mother and me—we took it for granted that one should be forthright and scrupulously fair, and acted accordingly. Such money as I have is money I have earned and saved, or in the end inherited indirectly from my father through my late stepmother's generosity. You know all this, but it may be of some use to repeat it. In fact, quite unexpectedly, late in life, I am rich, to be sure in a minor sort of fashion. I do not wish that circumstance to twist and denature your relations with men. Men in general, not especially Jon Riker, although that is how you and he and Renata may interpret my intention. It goes without saying that I will not make additional significant gifts of money to you, while I am still alive, if there is any reason to think that you are not the true recipient of what I give you.

He signed, Your father. Years of revising draft after draft of legal documents, whether prepared by him or his younger colleagues, had made him quite unable to fold the two sheets of paper he had covered with what his old secretary would have called Mr. Schmidt's neatest scrawl, stuff them into an envelope, and seal it. He took another turn in the garden, redolent of fresh grass now that the lawn had dried, and reread what he had written. The only changes he could think of were stylistic. They weren't worth the trouble of making another fair copy. Charlotte wouldn't care and neither would any of the Rikers. Jon's drafting had never been quite up to Schmidt's standards, a failing he thought was not significant enough to mention when he pushed for that boy's election to the partnership.

Nobody had used Mary's Toyota for a month or so. He patted it, as he might have a dog or a horse, and tried the ignition. The engine hesitated and then started vigorously, as though awakened from a light sleep. Really, her car was in excellent shape. He slammed the door shut, drove to Bridgehampton, and put the letter in overnight mail. Mary might have told him to express his intentions differently, but, like it or not, he was set in this mold; he could not break it alone. As to the substance, he had no doubt she would have approved.

Carrie asked: You feeling sick or something?

They were at table, having dinner. I'm blue, he replied. That's all.

Jeez, Schmidtie, I thought I got all that blue out of you. Your little guy was happy, that's for sure. Isn't that why I got a gold medal?

She pointed to the scarab pin. She was wearing it on his old shirt. Black tights under it. He knew how long her legs were under the table. Stocking feet touching his, toes wiggling. Her elbows on the table, she stared at him making round eyes because she knew that made him laugh. Pacts must be respected. He came through with a chortle and blew her a kiss. At once, she was in his lap.

Honey, tell me what's wrong. You're still mad at me.

I'm not, really. Promise. I have Charlotte troubles.

You said she was coming on Friday.

She isn't anymore.

Then he told her about the telephone call, leaving out what related to her because of the small lingering hope that it would be good later if she and Charlotte were able to be friends. Besides, he didn't want Carrie's feelings to be hurt. It was useless, he thought, to mention the letter. It wasn't likely that this adorable child would need to worry about trusts dreamed up by choleric fathers and their lawyers.

You're going to be mad at me if I tell you what I think?

I wish you would.

She turned his face toward hers and kissed him. It was a long kiss. When she finished, she said, I think she doesn't know where her head's at. She's mixed up. You should like let up on her. She'll figure it out.

Thank you, said Schmidt. Do you think I was wrong to make such a big point of her getting her separation agreement worked out?

No. She talks tough but I think she's kind of scared of him. I think maybe it was good.

Suddenly she jumped up. Schmidtie, you want to go dancing? There's this cool place in Southampton. Come on, you'll love it. I swear you will.

Lovey, I can't do those dances. The last new step I learned was the twist. You don't want to drag an old fool like me out on the dance floor.

He was going to add, Why don't you go with some of the kids at O'Henry's, but the memory of Bryan's words stopped him in his tracks. An almost pout appeared on Carrie's face and then changed into a smile.

Schmidtie, what do you say I go with Jason? Will that make you go crazy?

IX

Excuse me, said Mr. Mansour, that's exactly where you're wrong. You know why? I'll tell you. It's what I'm always telling you. Because deep down inside you think everybody reacts just like you—no, excuse me, I know you also think you're better than anybody else, and so forth and so forth, but your first instinct is you think they don't care about money. Just like you. Believe me, that's a mistake. Most people care a lot.

No, you excuse me. I care about money. I've always worked hard for my living. I stopped working because I had to. I don't throw my money around. I've always had a professional adviser manage my savings and everything I've inherited. I pay attention. I'm very grateful I can afford to live the way I do.

Live the way you do!

Schmidt had obviously tickled Mr. Mansour's funny bone.

Yes, exactly. I'm glad to live the way I live. The way you live, Mike, is something practically nobody can imagine. If the general population knew how you throw your money out the window, the way you burn it, they would stone you. Or they'd get little men in white coats to take you away and lock you up—for good.

You're wrong. You know who the American people like? Blonds with big tits and guys like me, with more money than they can imagine. You want to know something? Listen, my wealth grows so fast it doesn't matter how much I spend. In fact, you can make the case that if I double the amount I spend and spend like that until I'm one hundred I will still die rich—richer than I am today.

Exactly. That's why the way you live has nothing to do with me. Anyway, that's not the issue. I think the letter I wrote to Charlotte shows I do care about money. It shows I'm serious about it.

Your letter is OK. I'm glad you showed it to me, although the fact is you should have showed it to me before you sent it. What were you trying to accomplish? You and I should have discussed the whole strategy. That's the question: What is your real attitude? Excuse me—Mr. Mansour raised his hand, fearing an interruption—excuse me, that is the question. The way you described your meeting with Jon's mother, the shrink, you didn't handle her well at all. What's her name, Renata? You know why? You felt guilty you wrote that letter to Charlotte and embarrassed that Renata had read it. Period. Am I right or am I wrong? You were embarrassed even though when you wrote the letter you expected Charlotte to show it to her. You let Renata see all those feelings of guilt sticking out of you like toothpicks. So what happens? Renata doesn't take you or your letter seriously, and you confuse her, Charlotte, and Jon. You should've let me handle the whole thing. I could make them understand what you think you want—I say what you think you want, because the fact is you really don't know, you're all over the place—and make it come together. I'll tell you something. You can't get anyplace unless you know where you want to go. That's my rule number one.

I think it's clear where I want to get. Believe it or not, I'm not against Jon. I am in favor of marriage, kids, the whole thing. But they won't be able to get their hands on my money unless they first settle between them the mess they've made over the money I've already given. That's what I told Renata. That's what I think—and where I stand.

That didn't come through from the way you've told me about it. The way I heard it, you let that shrink figure out that you'll do anything she tells you will make Charlotte happy. Only you'll do it holding your nose because it's Jon. So the shrink says to herself, I don't need to worry about this big goy, he'll do anything I want, all I have to say is jump through the hoop or you'll make your daughter unhappy. I hate to tell you, she thinks you're soft. Weak. I bet they do too. Your daughter and Jon. I don't know if Renata thinks you're stupid, but she definitely thinks you're weak. So what are you left with? Strictly nothing, except, one, you're once again a bad guy, and, two, you've showed them you're still down on Jon. Why? Because you don't like Jews—that's right, don't make that face, that's what they'll be saying about you—and on top of that he embarrassed you at your old law firm. So they don't need to pay any attention to you. You need proof?

OK. Have they signed a separation agreement? No. Has she moved back into their old apartment? Yes. Has he signed over to her the property? No. Has he made any other compensation? No.

I don't know for a fact that he hasn't.

I do. You want to bet? Fifty cents? A thousand dollars? Come on, I'll give you odds. You don't want to bet? You're right, you'd lose.

And what was Mr. Schmidt to make of having Mr. Mansour in his corner, giving him big-time-tycoon-deal-maker advice on this most intimate of subjects? When Schmidt thought about his relationship with Mr. Mansour, as he had done, intermittently, over the preceding weeks, he was forced to accept the peculiar fact that he had become attached to him and that, within limits that were as yet ill defined, had come to trust him. "Attached" was perhaps the wrong word: he was attached to Gil Blackman and dared to believe that Gil was attached to him. Oh, so much more loosely, of course, for reasons among which Schmidt counted his own relatively smaller power of attraction and the richness of Gil's life. The imbalance was ancient and a source of grief. Schmidt accepted it, out of an instinct for self-preservation, and out of habit, so as not to be demoted to a position that was even more subordinate. He had learned to rein in his expectations. Gil had many friendships and attachments, but he was Schmidt's only friend. Such was in any event Schmidt's opinion. That put Gil in the same relation to Schmidt as he, Schmidt, was to Mike Mansour, if Schmidt were to believe Mike Mansour's repeated asseverations. An annoying symmetry, since Schmidt's feelings for Mr. Mansour were not those he hoped Gil had for him, one that led directly to an open question: What was the strength of Gil's feelings about his old roommate Schmidt? That was unclear. At least, Schmidt had come to understand his own feelings toward Mike Mansour. He liked Mike Mansour the way that, in the past, he had liked clients with particularly infuriating problems. The common denominator when it came to them was Schmidt's satisfaction with his own skill in managing them and the amusement he derived. Keeping the ball in play over Ping-Pong tables of varying shapes and sizes. He had to admit that Mr. Mansour held up his own end of the game pretty well. In fact, he had a mean serve and a pretty good backhand. Besides, Schmidt had not been wrong when he thought, at the outset, that Mr. Mansour might provide Carrie and him with a form of society. As for trust, and the limits of trust that had to be assumed, they could not, in Schmidt's opinion, be separated from the view one took as to why Mr. Mansour should have elected him, of all people, to be a friend in the first place—before discovering that Schmidt was much more, Mansour's "best friend." Making all due allowance for his own bent for self-denigration, Schmidt had concluded that there could be only one reason: he amused Mr. Mansour much as dwarfs had amused the Spanish court in the time of Velázquez. He was Mike Mansour's new toy! Certainly, Mr. Mansour had known and dealt closely in his business life with a dozen lawyers as good as or better than Schmidt, if you took legal ability and professional standing as the criteria of election, and, in fact, these must have played some role, since

Mr. Mansour, early in their acquaintance, undertook on more than one occasion to test Schmidt's form, putting him through tests that made Schmidt think of field trials, after each of which he wondered whether Mr. Mansour would produce a dog biscuit—or would it be a piece of halvah—on the outstretched palm of his hand and scratch him behind the ears because he had pointed so well. The trials didn't include fetching or coming to heel; for all his deep psychological insights, Mr. Mansour had no assurance that Schmidt would obey, and might be content not to put that to a test. But perhaps it was precisely this suspected tendency to be insubordinate that had distinguished him favorably from the other legal retrievers, the not-quite-Schmidts, whom Mr. Mansour was happy to keep in his kennel but not on his hearth rug. Yes, it was worth Mr. Mansour's taking trouble to have at his side, in a relation of startling intimacy, someone as respectable, maybe even presentable, as Schmidt, over whom he had no hold, who was there of his own free will. To that extent he could be trusted. As for the effect of Carrie's special attraction, on which Schmidt had placed a silent bet against himself, Mr. Mansour had proved it sufficiently. But, according to Carrie, since the fiasco in New York Mr. Mansour had decided to stay discouraged. When Schmidt asked her whether they should accept the invitations that continued to be extended, she said, Why not? He'd rather die than try that stuff again. She added, inconsequently, Can you imagine it? Jason would kill him.

Therefore, as friend to friend, Schmidt said to Mike, All right, Professor. What wonder drug do you prescribe?

Nothing. A strict diet. Don't do a thing. Let them come to you.

And then?

You hear them out and say you've got to think about it. That means you and I talk it over before you make a move.

That's the sort of advice I used to give to my clients about negotiations, Mike. You could have been a good lawyer. But this isn't a negotiation. It's about helping my daughter, about her feelings, about my relationship with her.

You mean I could be a great lawyer—the greatest. How do you think being a lawyer compares with building businesses like the ones I've built? There is no comparison. Being a lawyer would take such a tiny part of my brain you couldn't even see it and I wouldn't miss it. The question is how you get some movement. That's not law. It's life. You don't get a cat to eat by pushing food at him. You let the cat take his own time. When he's hungry he'll go for it. Same thing with your daughter. OK? Remember that. *Pas de problème.*

Good for Mr. Mansour. Schmidt had been asleep, taking a nap, when Renata called. Between her and Charlotte, he sometimes thought they must have remote perception sensors rigged somewhere in his house to alert them the moment he closed his eyes, when he would be at his most vulnerable. Sexy voice, that much he had to admit, especially for a shrink whom he thought he had learned to detest. It has been such a long time, she told him, such a breach of the promise they had made to each other to work hand in hand to make the children happy. Both Schmidtie and she had been punished for it, but it wasn't too late. The children still had their lives before them; nothing was irretrievably damaged or lost. But they could use help that only Schmidtie and she, working together, could give them. She went on like that while he huddled under the covers, on the verge of hanging up and then leaving the telephone off the hook—if upbraided for it later he could claim the line had gone dead—wondering whether she had lost her pre-Columbian looks, how those varicose veins, invisible under her wool tights, that she had massaged so attractively at their first meeting, had progressed. Ha! Two cases of varicose veins in his life: Dr. Renata and Mrs. Gorchuck. It wasn't as if he had to hang on every word. The question, when she got around to it, was no surprise: Will you come into the city to see me, Schmidtie? We need to talk. I'm back at work, but Thursdays are open, as before. Schmidtie could invite her to lunch at that nice club of his, the one where they have those little *café filtre* machines. The rejoinder was impossible to resist. You'd be disappointed, he told her, they're gone, the club has bought a big central espresso machine, no different from Starbucks. What a pity! she said. But she had only been trying to show him she remembered every pleasant detail of their last meeting while he acted so angry, so full of destructive feelings that were the opposite of what they both needed for the most important job of their lives.

I won't take no for an answer, she announced. If you won't meet me in New York I will take the morning bus to Bridgehampton. We will have our talk, and then I'll go back to the city by bus, although I can't think that is how you really wish to treat me.

Now that was an interesting assertion, especially coming from a distinguished member of the New York Psychoanalytical Society: How did he really *wish* to treat the woman who had alienated from him his daughter's affection, the woman he held, right or wrong, principally responsible for a bruise on his entire body as painful as the one that the death of his wife had left? Murder her! Dip the old bag in boiling oil—that's what his startled unconscious would blurt. But the occasion was clearly unique. Dr. Renata was actually talking about manners, not hidden motives. Since good manners required him to assume she was a lady, he had only two choices: to refuse to see her, even if she turned up on his doorstep, or to meet her in New York. He was too weak for the former, too afraid of the effect on Charlotte. Since that is what you wish, he answered, I will meet you at that club. Please try to be there at twelve-thirty. It didn't seem necessary to remind her of the address.

Most likely, that was a wrong move. He had let the Rikers once more put him on the defensive. There was no need to keep making the same mistake over and over. Not just now, not even with Mr. Mansour.

Mike, how do you explain, he asked, with all these psychological insights and negotiating skills at your fingertips, that you haven't done better with your own children and your wives?

He looked up from the broiled calf's liver to see whether he had scored. It wasn't a bull's-eye. Impassively, his host chewed, swallowed, and smiled. Then he addressed Schmidt: You really don't get the point. I haven't applied my skills in that direction. When my kids were born and growing up, I was building my businesses. My businesses are the proof of what I can do. My wives! You've got to be kidding. I told you number one was a dumb mistake. So was number two. Dumb and dumber. OK, I like sex. I don't mean I'm a good lover. I'm not. I like it, that's all. That doesn't mean I like marriage. Both times it's been a pain in my ass. Now you're beginning to understand, I can tell from your eyes. You don't care about money—listen to me, I know you don't—and at this point in your life you don't have any work, any business purpose. You care about Charlotte. In fact, that's all you care about. You see the incentive? Let me make it even clearer. You've got every reason to bust your chops and get this thing with Charlotte right.

That is God's own truth. What makes you think I don't?

It's no problem. Busting your chops includes doing a good job. The question is, How do you go about it without screwing up? You want to hear the second part of my prescription? Make a life for yourself. Right now, there's nothing there. It's scary.

A leitmotiv. Blackman on the bassoon, Mansour on the tuba. These guys must rehearse. As though Schmidt didn't want desperately to get out of the corner into which he had painted himself, stroke by stroke, over so many years.

Look, he said, I live as best I can. I love Carrie. She makes me happy. I haven't anyone else. Right now that's my life, and it's not so bad.

That's a whole other problem I'm keeping my eye on. Relax, Schmidtie, I'll never be bad again with her, you know that. Anyway, Jason says she's doing great. The question is, Does Carrie help out in the situation with Charlotte? Let me put it to you this way: When Charlotte thinks about you and Carrie, does that make her say to herself, Hey, do I ever want to spend a weekend with my father? The answer is no. Am I right?

You may be right, but she is wrong. She should be grateful I am living with someone who is good to me, who makes me happy—and keeps me off her back! There is nothing worse for an only child than a retired widowed parent with no one to turn to, to think about, except the child!

This time you're right, but you've brought Charlotte up to be selfish. She doesn't think about what's good for you. You need to impress her, make her feel you're strong. I've thought of my foundation. Do you have any idea of the work we do?

Schmidt nodded.

I do. Very generally.

You should inform yourself about it. I am thinking of handing my foundation over to you, for you to run. Don't worry. As I've said, I would still provide the vision—and the money! How is that for a good situation? No fund-raising, and I'd be at your side, like your senior partner. You're in good health, so you've got what? Another ten years to be useful? Suppose I gave you a contract for ten years. You can fix your own salary. If you help me build the foundation the way I want you to, when Charlotte looks at you she will see that you're once again important. Nothing tremendous, but one hell of a lot more attractive than looking at a sour old schmuck hanging on for all he's worth to a kid like Carrie. Am I right? You've got no risk. So do I have a deal?

An old devil, got up in his father's cut-down tweeds, glints of red in his unruly hair, bloodshot eyes staring hard, put his thick, veined hand over Schmidt's mouth, cutting off the words he was about to blurt out. What, serve this man! Tell him that he has offered all you had secretly hoped for, that seemed beyond hope? Never. Gratitude is slavery. Let the thing you want with all your heart be granted, but not as a princely favor, only on your terms, and after a struggle.

Look, he said to Mr. Mansour, I'm touched that you have thought of this. I am, really, more than you can imagine. The trouble is that I'm not sure I should work for you. I think you probably like me and we get along well because I don't. I'm afraid that would all change once I was on your payroll.

Mr. Mansour drank his wine, leaned back in his chair, and pointed to the empty glass. Manuel filled it. He drank again, had Manuel refill his own glass and Schmidt's, and began to laugh. The laughter, which at first seemed to Schmidt forced, began to seem uncontrollable, until at last Mr. Mansour wiped his eyes, rubbed his face as though to make himself look serious, and spoke.

You're telling me you don't want the job?

It's just that I'm afraid that this very generous idea could turn out to be a trap. For you and for me.

You're really something. Listen, Schmidtie, I'll worry about myself. What do you say? Am I a good friend?

Mostly.

Then cut the crap and say yes. I'll get Holbein to do the paperwork.

Don't you think you should at least run the idea past Holbein and the board of directors of your foundation before we commit to each other? I mean if you really want to have me take on the foundation you should follow the usual governance procedures, just to avoid any misunderstanding.

Mr. Mansour nodded and remained silent while the table was cleared. Then he smiled and said, Schmidtie, I've got to hand it to you. You think of everything. All right, I'll do it your way. I'll run the concept past Eric and the board of directors. Holbein talks about governance too. The question then becomes what he says and how the whole thing shapes up. Let's say I tried it on you for size. We'll talk again.

Driving home, where Carrie wouldn't be until dinnertime, because the seminar she was taking finished late and afterward the students and the professor had coffee together, Schmidt remembered he hadn't asked Mansour about Jason. Why were those two discussing her? That was a stupid question. An even better question, to which, alas, he knew the answer, was why he, Schmidt, had listened to the prompting of his old incubus when he might have jumped over the net, shaken Mansour's hand, and gotten the job. No one, not even Gil Blackman, had so far offered him such an opportunity. Instead, he had set it up so that Mansour, quite rightly, hedged something that at first was unconditional. He had positively told him how to do it, had pushed Mansour to begin to equivocate and retreat! There was no mystery about the outcome: Mansour would never offer him the job again, not in that form, not on those terms, and he, Schmidt, would never bring himself to ask Mansour what Holbein had said or whether the board—all of them Mansour's compliant hangers-on, waiting for a bone he might throw their way—had expressed any opinion. As though Mike had a wish or need to consult them! This cloud has a silver lining, butted in the old devil. The likelihood of Mansour's paying attention to governance principles of his foundation was about the same as the likelihood of Mansour's actually keeping his word whatever Schmidt's answer had been. No harm has been done to your prospects, you dummy. Mike Mansour would not make good on a promise of such generosity; he would not, to borrow that preposterous expression, give you a life, not unless you were full-time on his back, riding him like a jockey, giving him the whip. Cheer up, sop, you've kept your dignity! You've got your pride, your own money, and your father's money, all intact. You don't need that vulgarian's foundation to give you standing. As for Charlotte, let that bitch screw whom she wants.

Quick, from the overgrown patch, a sprig of mint. Add bourbon and ice. Crush the mint under the ice cubes and stir. His own mind thus eased into high gear, Schmidt ponders Old Nick's advice. The bugger's off the beam; the case isn't about whether Mansour will keep a promise once he has made it. Sure, one could make the point that Schmidt has grotesquely let the big fellow get away, but there was nothing at the end of the line to bring in, except his own misery and failure. He'd bet dollars to doughnuts that Mr. Mansour had seen right through him, and knew he risked nothing in the game he played with Schmidt. Schmidt could be counted on to let him off the hook before any offer was made and there was any promise to keep or break. One small consolation: in fact, he had handled Renata better than he had handled Mike, better than Mike made out. It could be that Mike had not bothered to listen to what Schmidt had said; more likely, he had found it amusing to construct a version of his own, with which to beat Schmidt over the head. That also made no difference. He knew his own version and could hang on to it with some satisfaction.

In the end, he had changed his mind and left a message on her answering machine asking her not to come to the club. If he was to be torn apart by the furies let it be in a place of indifference, not on that hallowed ground. He gave her the address of a North Italian restaurant, where he had been accustomed to invite insurance company businessmen and lawyers who might have thought lunch in the democratic precincts of the Harvard Club an insufficient reward for the work they brought him, while he considered that they would stand out unpleasantly in his grander club or the French restaurant to which he took Mary and clients who fit in but didn't care for club food. The headwaiter, a beefy Sicilian, was his friend. He would provide a corner table as far removed as possible from the roar of investment bankers, lawyers, and clients outshouting one another over the midday meal. Schmidt supposed that in an emergency, his Sicilian would also oblige him by throwing Renata out into the street. Afterward, he might put a manly arm around Schmidt and murmur something about the old *strega* and the evil eye. She was waiting for him. Arriving a good fifteen minutes late himself, because the first garage he tried was full and going to the second required threading his way first west and then east through side streets bursting with disorderly midday traffic, he was from the start in the wrong, although he had telephoned to the restaurant so that Dr. Riker would know he was only minutes away, had not stood her up. No matter, she took the high ground at once. It was perfectly understandable, she told him, that one would be held up by one thing if not another going to an appointment one had not wished to make. The appropriate response was to understand the motive, not to feel annoyed. His response, to which he did not give voice, was to note that, since no quarter was to be given, he might as well fortify himself with gin. She passed on that and drank tomato juice, hoping, he supposed, that gin would untie his tongue. It did: enough for him to ask about the health of the male Dr. Riker and to express satisfaction upon hearing there was nothing to complain about, but not enough to inquire further or comment on her appearance. In fact, he was struck by how she had aged. Perhaps it was the effect of her hair, now completely gray, no longer gathered in a tight bun at the back. Instead, she sported an old-fashioned pageboy of the sort one used to see on young girls. He catalogued the pockets of yellow around her large unsmiling eyes, the new thinness of the Aztec face, the way she no longer seemed quite so tall. It was possible that she stooped. There was something less fresh and attractive as well about the way she was turned out, although once again she wore a suit that he would have sworn was by Chanel, of an era before the look changed. It crossed his mind unpleasantly that the Chanel outfit was an allusion to their last lunch together, rather than what she habitually wore lunching out on Thursdays. The fingers of her right hand were stained with nicotine. She had been through a lot, rather more than he, but the observation stirred no sympathy within him.

Just as well, because no sooner had they ordered lunch than she challenged him. Have you nothing to say to me, she asked him, to which he replied, he thought reasonably, that their meeting was at her suggestion. He was there to listen.

Really, she said, I would have thought you might have some urge to comment on the way your partners at Wood & King have treated Jon. I would have thought you might have some regret that you might mention about not coming to his defense.

All I know about the matter is what I have read in the newspapers, which squared with what Jack DeForrest related. Neither you nor Jon gave me any version whatsoever of what happened, let alone any version that was different, less damning for him.

Do you always believe everything you read?

I wasn't called upon to have any opinion. My former partners, though, must have had an unusually strong opinion of Jon's conduct as a lawyer. Based on what I've been told and what I've read, it was execrable. I cannot begin to imagine how else they would have voted unanimously to exclude him.

They lynched him. Jack DeForrest and his cronies went out on a limb to condemn him. Then the rest of them closed ranks. That's all. Jon was the scapegoat.

The scapegoat for what?

The fools who manage your firm. For their bigoted and mistaken judgments. For the injustice. For that senile man with a ridiculous name—Buzz Williams!—who claimed to have made an investigation.

Schmidt didn't answer. It was no longer his job to defend the infallibility of DeForrest or the management committee of W & K. Schmidt knew that in general she was right; that was how the firm worked. In this particular case? He preferred not to think about it. It really didn't matter what he said to this woman: she would manage to turn it against him and his old firm—and tell Jon Riker. She had drunk her wine and twirled the empty glass between her fingers. This gave him the opportunity to escape from her stare. He motioned for the waiter to fill her glass. He had barely touched his own.

You won't drink with me, she remarked. That's new.

I have to drive back to Bridgehampton. It's as simple as that.

And you know I am right about what they did to Jon. That's why you are so untypically quiet.

Renata, he said, I thought you got me out here to talk about our children. By that I mean what has happened to them and Jon's shameful refusal to let go of Charlotte's property. If Jon thinks he has been wronged by the firm, he is, or anyway used to be, a good enough lawyer to know how to seek redress. It's no use badgering me.

She fell silent and tousled her hair. Then in a very low voice she said, Yes, I look like an old woman. You wouldn't think anymore of making a pass at me. This happened the week your firm threw Jon out. Sorrow and shame. My great-grandmother's hair turned white during a pogrom. They beat her father in the street, in front of the house, and pulled out his beard. She watched them from the attic, where she and the other children were hidden. Think of it: she was only nineteen!

He began a murmur about being sorry, which she immediately interrupted.

You look just fine, Schmidtie, I can see you haven't a care in the world. Such remarkable upbringing! It really never occurred to you to try to stop what they were doing to Jon? To stand up for your son-in-law? Against injustice?

No, he replied, it didn't. As I've already made clear, it seems to me the firm did what it had a right to do.

You can't get away so easily. Don't you know in your heart that Jon never gave the court papers to that woman? The judge realized it. There was no punishment, no reprimand. The case is closed.

Jon was very lucky. He must have impressed the judge by his remorse.

Well, shouldn't those men take him back? Make up for what they did?

You mean take him into the partnership? Back to Wood & King? That's preposterous. I can't think he would want it.

Why? He won his right to be there.

And then he lost it. It's a partnership, Renata. As I've said, the partners voted against him because in their judgment he had to be removed. That's a fact that can't be changed. By the way they aren't only men. We have many women in the firm now.

To have been forced to speak as though he were still a member of Wood & King annoyed him. He cleared his throat and continued: There is no going back on it. How could he and the other partners work together again? If I had known this was what you wanted to discuss I would have refused to see you.

Your partners at Wood & King have broken our children's marriage. Isn't that of interest to you? Don't we have to talk about it if we are to talk about the children?

To my knowledge, the problem in the marriage was Jon's philandering and indiscretion. That's what did it, not Wood & King. Oh, I don't mean to suggest that Charlotte is without fault.

He stopped there because it seemed to him that if he were to continue he would have to say that the marriage was also beyond fixing, like Jon Riker's broken career at the firm. Who was he to take that stand? To hell with sobriety. He drank his glass of wine, told the waiter to pour another one, and got back to his lunch. The thing to do was to eat fast and run.

She too wanted another glass of wine. Looking at him hard, she said, Very well, let's stick to the children. You have written a cruel letter to Charlotte. Of course, she has shown it to me.

Of course. Is she still taping my rare conversations with her for your benefit as well?

Schmidtie, do you ever forgive her anything? Do you ever forgive anybody? How many years ago did she make that tape?

Not nearly long enough ago for me to forget.

But I explained to you at the time she only made the tape to be sure she understood all your talk about money. This time you have laid it out in writing: it's a choice between your money and Jon.

Not at all. It's a choice between making sure her financial dealings with Jon or any other man are honest and having a trustee after I die who will make sure she isn't robbed. I believe that all three of you, excuse me, four, I forgot to count your husband, are able to understand that easily. You have such finely honed minds.

That's not what you intended. You were aiming only at Jon, working to prevent their getting back together. That was clear even to Myron.

She tousled her hair again. Of course, it's a clever letter.

There is something here I don't understand. The farm or whatever it is—the place near you in Claverack—was bought with Charlotte's money. The apartment in the city that you said would be paid for by you was in fact also bought with Charlotte's money. Because Charlotte is a romantic, title to both properties is in Charlotte's and Jon's joint names. Then they decide to separate, never mind why. Is there any justification for Jon's refusing to return to Charlotte what's clearly hers?

There is the loan, she muttered.

Right, she'll take it over—get Jon released from any obligation. I don't think there has been any question about it from her side, but if there is a question I will take it over myself.

Schmidtie, it's true, you don't understand. Jon can't sign these properties over. Not now. He can't. It would mean giving up Charlotte—definitively. Besides, it's the only property he owns. Thinks he owns.

Someone else's property!

It doesn't matter. It's all he has. He's drowning, Schmidtie. Your partners, your horrible bigoted self-righteous partners, have broken him. He is hanging on to it as though it were a raft.

Then you should straighten him out. If you can't do it as a mother, get him professional help. Or give him some money! For instance, the money you promised to give them for the apartment.

We can't—it's quite impossible. My practice has fallen off. I still do analysis, as I have been taught to, as I believe it should be done, but very few patients can afford it. Almost all of them are old. Insurance reimbursement for analysis isn't worth talking about. Myron has been doing group therapy. There are positions for clinical psychiatrists he could get if he weren't bumping against the retirement age. It all pays badly. Years ago we used to think we were more than all right. Now I'm scared.

I am truly sorry to hear this. Look, out of curiosity: The story Charlotte told me about your not putting up the money for the apartment, how that was supposed to prevent Jon from being overly dependent on you, is that just humbug you invented because already at the time you couldn't afford to give him the money?

Yes, I did invent it.

Really!

No, Schmidtie, in fact I've just told you a lie. Jon made up the story because he knew we were doing badly. He didn't want Charlotte to know it, not just then. It was foolish of him.

Not just foolish. Incomprehensible. And inexcusable. As a W & K partner he could have borrowed more. They could have put off buying the apartment. They could have talked to me. None of this alters Jon's duty. I am truly appalled. By the way, don't let him cry on your shoulder. He should be able to find a partnership in another firm in New York—not on the same level as W & K but still perfectly all right. Or a good position with a corporation. The market for experienced lawyers is quite strong.

How do you know?

She had caught him out. He was improvising and wasn't about to admit it.

That's what I'm told, he continued, many headhunters specialize in placing senior lawyers.

He should meet some.

She began picking at her ravioli, stopped, searched in her pocketbook, produced a minuscule embroidered handkerchief, seemed unable to decide what to do with it, put it back in its place.

Schmidtie, have you understood what I've just told you about Jon's position, his feelings?

Of course.

Do you admit the possibility that they love each other?

I know nothing about that.

And you still stand by your letter.

Yes. There is nothing in my letter to stop those two from getting together, if that's what they want, provided he forgets about getting hold of her money. Quite simply, I won't give Charlotte a dime in a way that would make it possible for him to get hold of it.

You mean steal it.

That's not what I said.

You are certain to make Charlotte unhappy. How can she go back and be happy in the face of your disapproval? You scorn Jon.

You have no reason to question my motives. My feelings about Jon—I mean Jon's not returning to Charlotte her property—are what they are. But I can assure you and Charlotte, since no doubt you will speak to her—if Charlotte needs assurance—that I will do everything in my power to help her, to make her happy. Of my free will. Sensibly. Without any need for coaching from you.

He beckoned to the waiter.

I hardly ever have dessert. Do you mind skipping it? No? Then I'll get the check.

He had just finished paying when she asked him, Schmidtie, you said at the beginning of this meal that Jon has behaved execrably. Could that be said of anything you have done in your career? I don't mean cheating on your wife. You know, like what you did with that Vietnamese baby-sitter. Charlotte has told me about that. I meant the sort of thing they've accused Jon of. Something for which you would like to be forgiven.

That sort of thing? Never.

X

AN UNARTFUL question artfully answered: "That sort of thing? Never." True enough. He had never given documents filed under seal to someone who wasn't entitled to have them or put himself in a position from which such execrable behavior could be inferred. But as for hideous baseness, risks taken against all reason, and needless lying! Never take no for an answer. One would have thought Dr. Riker knew enough about the human abyss to probe more deeply. Perhaps misfortune took off her edge. Speeding homeward on the Long Island Expressway, exhilaratingly empty in the early weekday afternoon, Schmidt let the subject sit there, like a letter of whose baleful content we are certain from the moment we have glimpsed the familiar handwriting on the envelope. It remained unopened as he steered his car and fiddled with the radio.

Little time passed before he resumed the weekly telephone calls to Charlotte, usually in the morning on Wednesday, to give her an opening to announce casually that she would like to come for the weekend. He could not bear to lose contact.

They talked about her work—she had received the additional responsibility of a rich Native American tribe that would soon open a casino on its land—and the weather. The latter was Schmidt's subject. Part of it was promotion of Long Island in the early fall—mild days, the air so clear on the beach you thought you could see all the way to Montauk, long lazy breakers, and an ocean still warm enough for an energetic swimmer to dive into, the late roses in his garden—and part an attempt to let her know how constantly he thought about her. This took the form of warnings about the downpour predicted for the city, let's say, on Friday, just when she had to make a presentation downtown, and concern about her being able to get a taxi at first to her office and then to the client's so she wouldn't arrive looking soaked, and, after a dry week, worries about the drought. Of course Charlotte stayed in the city on all those discreetly, longingly vaunted Long Island weekends, unless indeed she made trips, which she didn't take the trouble to mention to Schmidt, to other destinations. For instance, to Claverack. Or would it be to the Berkshires? There was no way to tell: possibly she and Mr. Polk were once again office friends, so that she might visit him and his wife at the house in Egremont. She did not mention the letter that had stirred Renata into action, or Jon Riker, or the Riker parents. The peculiar fact that he didn't know where Charlotte lived—where she slept was the way he thought of it—was uncomfortably present in Schmidt's mind. He wondered whether it was present in her consciousness. It seemed more likely that she thought she had told him. Not foreseeing any urgent need to reach her outside of office hours, he decided not to ask. As Mr. Mansour might put it, he didn't need trouble, the recriminations that an ill-timed or ill-conceived question might provoke.

The second Sunday of October, while Carrie and Jason competed as a team in the Riverhead police association triathlon, Schmidt received a telephone call from Mike Mansour. Sorry to have missed you these last couple of weeks. You're doing well? I'm in great shape, really great. I had to be in L.A. to look at rushes and talk to some boys about distribution. Right, *Chocolate Kisses*, it's the greatest yet! I've got to hand it to him. Since I became his executive producer he's been bearing down hard, really taking advice. I tell you, it shows. When's Gil coming back? At the end of the month. By the way, I'm going to visit all of my foundation's centers. That's right. All forty-two of them. That will bring me back in time for Thanksgiving. I expect you and Carrie for Thanksgiving lunch, all right? By the way, I want to have Jason with me. I let him take this weekend off to do the triathlon with her, but she'll have to make it on her own until we come back. You make sure you keep her busy in the meantime.

Mike, what are you telling me about Carrie and Jason? he asked, his throat dry, finding it impossible to let that go by.

Nothing your eyes can't see. Excuse me, it's a funny thing, Schmidtie. If you had said yes to me, if you had taken the job at my foundation when I made my offer, we'd be making this trip together. Maybe the next time!

Right. There is always another day.

What the next day in fact brought was a package, delivered by courier, from the Mansour Life Institute. It contained a "welcome kit": annual reports, a year's accumulation of press clippings, many of them in languages unfamiliar to Schmidt, and reports on betterment of living conditions commissioned from outside scholars. Also in the package Schmidt found a separate scarlet folder marked HIGHLY IMPORTANT with a letter from Eric Holbein, thanking Schmidt for his interest in the Mansour Life Institute and confirming the invitation extended by its chairman, Mr. Mansour, that Mr. Schmidt consider a significant commitment to the institute and involvement in its activities. Either the letter had been backdated to the week when Mike Mansour asked Schmidt to run the foundation or it had languished on Mr. Holbein's desk, having been placed at the bottom of a pile of even more important correspondence ready for signature. It really didn't matter, although Schmidt wondered how far Mr. Mansour would want to lead him by the nose.

Make vast promises and then let them fade against the horizon of other people's harsh and empty desert. It's a rich man's game. You might as well start by practicing on a dog. Hold high a bone with meat on it, and let the poor brute get up on his hind legs and strain—tail wagging, eyes wild, hungry tongue out, saliva splashing. You wait until he thinks he's got it made. That's when you burst out laughing and toss the object of such hot desire right over his snout, beyond the high fence that shuts in the kennel. The dog falls forward on all fours, confused and yelping. That's the time to scratch him behind his ears, tell him he's been a good dog, and move on to the next game. With your first billion stashed away, you graduate to people. They're not all that different. To one guy who thinks he's invented hot water you say you'll be partners with him to develop the business, to another that he'll run your foundation. The fun is all in making some thirsty, panting fool follow the mirage and then convincing him that it's his own fault if it's not real. If only he had gotten going earlier, before dawn, when the air was still cool and fresh, if he had rationed his strength, if he had run harder, the dream would have been realized, the prize his to take! And so it goes: billions accumulate, and with them broken promises that would have been seen at once as practical jokes if the shimmering mountain of cash hadn't dazzled the eye. Large people need large names. Time comes to worry about the billionaire's reputation. It wouldn't do to have him shown up as a jerk with a big mouth. That's where retainers like Mr. Holbein come in, circumspect operatives learned in the art of turning the dross of the boss's word of honor into prophecies of the Sybil, which, if deciphered, come down only to this: There is no such thing as a free lunch. Generosity begins and ends with gratifying the giver.

After so many years of listening, out of the supine patient's sight, for echoes of memories that spring up to give you the lie just when you think you are most unshakably in the right, after all the tapes and all the notes on what the third ear may or may not have heard—why, had he given it thought, Schmidt would not have dared to imagine that Renata would let him stop there, take the "never" he threw her way for an answer. But it had been he, not the hand of a cheap desk clock placed where it can be glimpsed out of the corner of the eye, who brought the fifty-minute hour to a close, rising from the restaurant table relentlessly and in the nick of time, propelling Renata into the street, pointing speechlessly to his garage, and then striding off without a backward look. Yes, with his cunning he had given that subtle speleologist, who previously had played with him as though with heated candle wax, no chance to follow the trail of the cloven foot into the dank cave where his shame lies hidden. Take money, which Schmidt is so beautifully stiff about. Would he have told her that there was once a shop girl in a Harvard Square haberdashery with white arms, soft breasts under a blouse of white satin, blue eyes, and black hair? She worked behind the cash register. Schmidt acquainted himself with those arms, breasts, and more in the backseat of Gil Blackman's Nash, which he'd borrow and park along Memorial Drive or off Brattle Street. One by one he'd undo the little mother-of-pearl buttons, his fingers, cold and persistent, interlaced with the Irish beauty's chubby, hot, defending, but ultimately yielding fingers. It amused Schmidt to cash a fifty-dollar check at the haberdashery, particularly when he also purchased jockey shorts, so that he could play with her fingers on the sly while she rang up the merchandise and gave him change. On one such occasion, in amorous confusion, she handed him a fifty-dollar bill and with it his own check. He saw the mistake instantly, put his free hand over the check and the money, and transferred them into his coat pocket. But what use was such a large bill?

Can you give me three tens and four fives? he asked, and let go of her hand.

She counted the change and, wonder of wonders, did not reach for the fifty, although he held it out, having meantime rolled it into something like a cigarette.

See you tonight?

I'll pick you up at seven, he whispered.

No, eight, I've got to eat with my folks.

The fifty-dollar bill was in his pocket, together with his check. He arranged the other bills carefully in his wallet and nodded agreement. This gave him time to eat at the Lowell House dining room, study for the history quiz, brush his teeth, and pick up the Nash. He knew it was available. Gil had a drama club rehearsal that evening.

She waited in the rain on a street corner two blocks from her parents' house in Somerville. We're going for ice cream? he asked.

Later.

I want you.

He saw a parking place, turned into it, cut the motor, and found her mouth. Their fingers got busy. The car windows were streaming with rain. Dim silhouettes slid past.

Then, as always, he came too quickly.

Speedy Gonzalez! she taunted, and stopped moaning, although he continued the motion of his own hand until his wrist ached, the position was so uncomfortable, and she finally pushed it away.

She turned her back to him so he could close the strap of her bra, wiggled back into her panties, rearranged her skirt, and asked the question he had waited for.

Lover boy, you crazy or something? You took the check and the fifty-dollar bill! You should've heard Mr. Jacobs when he closed the cash register. Was he mad!

What are you talking about?

I'm talking about how you took the fifty dollars in one bill, and the fifty dollars in change, and the check, and put them all in your wallet. Let's see it.

He handed it to her. Here, look.

The tens and the fives were there, except what he paid to gas up Gil's car.

She went through the wallet, taking out the money, his driver's license and draft card, a wedding photograph of his mother and father, his bursar's card, and two Trojans. That was all. He didn't believe in bulging wallets or bulging pockets.

Shit, it's not there. Bert, what have you done with the money and the check?

She used the abbreviation of his name he affected during his sophomore and junior years, before he got up enough nerve to have people call him Schmidtie, like his parents.

Nothing at all, the money's all there except what I spent.

She took hold of the lapels of his jacket and tried to shake him. Bert, you've got to give it back. That guy will fire me. He'll kill me. He'll send you to jail.

No, he won't. I'll stop by first thing in the morning and tell him I handed you the check, I got the money, and there was no problem. There's nothing to talk about.

She began to cry, then shrieked, You bastard, let me out of here! and dashed into the dark street, he supposed in the direction of her home. That was their last date. In fact, he saw her once again, the next morning, following an interview with a very angry assistant dean. He held his ground during it. He had neither the check nor any money that wasn't his. What was he to do about it?

Ask your conscience about the money, the dean told him, or your heart. I don't know. You've got to give Jacobs another check.

What if it gets cashed and my first check gets cashed too? Then I'll be out fifty dollars.

You discuss that with Mr. Jacobs.

He did as he was told. Jacobs was at the cash register, she behind a back counter, pretending not to see him.

He'd brought his checkbook with him and showed Mr. Jacobs how he had entered the transaction on the stub. He was willing to write another check, but what would happen if the check the store had lost resurfaced?

Nothing. Tell the bank not to pay the check you claim we lost, Mr. Schmidt, said Mr. Jacobs. It'll cost you a quarter. Here it is, take it, be my guest, and don't show your face here again.

He threw the coin at him and continued, That's a dumb trick, Schmidt. You stole the cash from that girl.

Yes, but they couldn't prove it. The owner's voice carried. Some students, none of whom Schmidt knew, were staring at them. Presumably, they had heard it all. On his way out, Schmidt tried to slam the door behind him. It fooled him and swung instead feebly back and forth. There was no telling what might happen next, such as some follow-up by the university police or that man Jacobs. In that case, it would look bad if he dropped the business about the check after having made a fuss. His bank, the Harvard Trust Company, was only a couple of blocks away. He went there and, after an officious explanation to a teller and then a manager sitting behind a desk on the bank floor, put in the stop order.

No question. The prospect of having the extra cash, when he understood that all he had to do was take it, had made him literally dizzy. It was like finding a fifty-dollar bill on the sidewalk. He certainly wouldn't have carried it to the police station and said, Gee, officer, look at what somebody dropped in the street. By the time he had gotten to his room, though, he understood that the disappearance of the money would be discovered, that the girl would be held responsible even though no one would believe she stole it, that she would remember the transaction between them and know he had taken the missing cash, and that taking the check was a crazy move, like redoubling at poker when all you've got in your hand is a pair of deuces. At the same time, there was an advantage in having done something so outrageous, so stupidly crazy. If he was going to get caught, it could make the whole thing seem just that: a crazy, absentminded stunt, for which he should be dressed down, perhaps slapped on the wrist, but nothing worse. He knew he should go right back to the store, give back the money, give back the check, say he didn't know what he was thinking about—get down on his knees to the girl and the owner. But he didn't want to. He wanted to keep the fifty dollars, or maybe one hundred if somehow he didn't have to write another check. In the end it would be his word against the girl's, and her word couldn't be as good. She was just a salesgirl with big tits and a big mouth who had let herself be picked up at the pinball machine at Elsie's and had played with his cock on their first date. Before the haberdashery, she had worked at Snow White, doing the university's laundry. That was why she knew all about the stains Harvard boys made on their sheets, and how the pads of those chubby, hot fingers got to be so weirdly smooth. Scalding hot water and lye had made the lines on them disappear till she had no fingerprints left. She was not someone he wanted to be seen with; the one time he had shown her to Gil had made that clear.

Well, he had kept the money, and, when he remembered the miserly allowance his mother sent him, less than half of what Gil got from his parents who weren't rich, didn't live in a fancy house like his mother and father, his anger at having been made to feel such scruffy need would surge up, sometimes blocking out the shame. Even so, it hadn't really been about money. After all, he had never picked Gil's pockets or stolen the books he needed for classes instead of buying them at the Coop and Schoenhof's or plain stolen books for resale to a dealer near to Central Square, which was something people did. He had acted on an impulse. Resentment had entered into it more than greed—that the best he could do was this little townie slut who wouldn't go all the way. But once he understood the mess he had made and its likely consequences, the more powerful sensation that made him go on took over, one of fatality, of being carried he didn't know where by a force he couldn't and didn't want to control. The cards were what they were; they had to be played out.

That in this incident, and certain others apparently unconnected with it, he might have been in fact pushing his luck, lunging headlong toward catastrophe like a test driver at a cement wall, occurred to him when, as a very young partner, he was flying back to New York from a recruiting session on the campus of a southern university where Wood & King had never tried to hire associates before. Unless what linked the incidents was nothing else but malice, the unique quality that turns a man against himself, his neighbors, and, of course, God. What a sense of relief! Legs stretched out, a second double bourbon before him on the pullout table, he was luxuriating in the comfort of his first-class seat. The hangover of the early morning, on account of which he had called American and put himself on a later plane to New York, was present only as a vague, not entirely unpleasant, feeling of increased sensitivity and alertness. He had been able to spread his papers on the seat next to him and was going over résumés of the students he had interviewed and his notes. Laverna Daly! Entitled "A Short Biography," her c.v. had been professionally printed and had clipped to its upper-right corner a color snapshot. It didn't do her justice. She had worked in summer stock and small repertory companies as a set designer until she was over thirty and then decided to study law. The rest was as you might have expected: A's and "Excellent" in soft courses taught by phonies—human rights, international legal order, legal problems of women, and a seminar on prison conditions—passing grades in the tough subjects that counted to Schmidt and at W & K: contracts, tax, civil procedure, corporations, securities law. On the other hand, she had to her credit an undergraduate degree granted with highest distinction in Renaissance studies at Berkeley, a year at the university in Grenoble, and what was said to be complete fluency in French and Italian. This was his last thirty-minute session of a two-day interviewing stint that ran from eight in the morning until six in the evening, in a windowless cubicle in the administration building. The demand to see the W & K recruiter had been so strong that he agreed to tuck in additional interviews over breakfast and lunch in the law school cafeteria.

He had read the Daly résumé along with the others the night before. She had no chance: the grades were wrong; that students who start law school late, after they've abandoned some earlier muddleheaded career, don't work out as lawyers was an axiom at W & K; he was put off by the "Personal Interests" listed in italics at the bottom of the second page—cooking, modern dance, and poetics. It was a waste of time for which the university's lottery system of assigning students to oversubscribed interviews was to blame. That girl might as well be applying for the space program. The thing was, though, that she surprised him. He had had trouble keeping his eyes open during the preceding interview and the one before. But as soon as she began to talk—stating, as he had asked her to, the facts and the holding of the most recent case she had read that caught her interest—he perked up, recognizing a remarkable sense for the structure of legal reasoning combined with unoffensive self-assurance. She continued to do so well that he didn't cut her off at the end of the allotted time and, in fact, was busy figuring out whether her cause would be better served by his inviting her right away, on his own responsibility, to a full set of interviews at the office in New York or getting the hiring committee to issue the invitation. In theory, only the strongest candidates were to be invited on the spot by the interviewer. She certainly didn't qualify on paper, and he might not be able to convince the committee, which would read her record with the same biases as he; whereas if he got her in the door, she might do exceedingly well.

Look, he said, I'm going to take a calculated risk. If I just looked at your grades and that sort of stuff, I should be telling you that this has been a very good meeting, that I'll report favorably to my partners, and that I hope we will be able to invite you to visit us, although the competition at your school is very stiff, and so forth. Instead, I am sticking my neck out and inviting you to New York right now because I want to give you a chance to overcome your record by talking to other partners the way you have talked to me. Don't get your hopes up too high, and don't disappoint me.

It wasn't a blush. She turned red and began to tell him about the fulfillment of her dreams, and how this was the first invitation from a top firm, when he stopped her.

Just call this lady. Here—he wrote out the name and telephone number and handed the paper to her—sooner rather than later. She schedules interviews. There is some advantage to being in the first wave to be considered.

She got up and shook his hand and then asked, Do you know this town? Have you been here before?

He told her it was his first time.

Then would you let me ask you to dinner with me? You're probably staying at the University Arms. I'll pick you up in an hour.

He looked at her in a new way now that she was standing up. It was all right; the clothes women students felt obliged to wear to interviews looked all right on her; she wore normal high-heel shoes. He had had his fill of footgear designed by mad podiatrists. In fact, he had no plans, and having dinner with a student you considered promising enough to interview in New York was quite within the rules. Since this was a woman, he supposed it would be better if he didn't have the meal with her alone, even though it was her idea. Therefore, he answered, I would love it, but I'm inviting you. By the way, if there are any other students you'd like to ask along—or anyone on the faculty—let's by all means have them too.

She made a little noise that sounded like ooh ooh, and said, No, there isn't anyone. I think we'll have a better time alone. Don't you?

The dinner, he discovered, was to be in her apartment. Just cheese, fruit, and wine. He didn't mind? She was tired of the dolled-up restaurants near the campus and the fake southern fare; if they were going out it would have had to be a roadhouse, way out of town, and she wasn't sure that was his style. Or maybe it was. The police were hell if they caught a student driving after a few drinks, and anyway she would rather have him at home. At home there were to be found, somewhat as he had expected, candles and Moroccan cushions and rugs and oversize heavy wineglasses. She excused herself to change into blue jeans and a top that tied in the back and left her midriff bare. The music was Vivaldi. After the cheese, she asked him whether he smoked. He replied he did, cigars, preferably, not cigarettes.

This made her laugh. I mean real stuff, she said. You know. Let me roll one for you.

That was just about as much marijuana as she had, enough for one joint. It was Schmidt's first. They smoked it half lying side by side on the rug, their backs against a pouf. She nestled her head on his shoulder. Quickly, his arm was around her, and he was playing with that bare midriff, teasing her navel. The smoke, if he could tell, wasn't affecting him, but the need to take her was unbearable. He worried about ejaculating.

Hey, I can't do it until I'm high, she told him suddenly, I just can't. It hurts. You got any in the hotel?

No, he answered, can't we get some? Can't you call someone? Is there somewhere we can go to buy it?

There was a whole list of numbers with occult marks beside them in her address book. She put on her glasses and started telephoning. Meanwhile, newly sober, member no longer tumid, he took stock. There he was, in a room that reeked of pot, with one hand in the shirt and the other on the crotch of a half-naked law student looking for a job in his firm, rubbing her up while she called every pusher in town for a delivery. The very portrait of a W & K partner on a recruiting trip. He had to be insane. Besides, the numbers rang busy or didn't answer. There was one thing they mustn't do, he decided: that was to start cruising bars, looking for a dealer.

Laverna, he murmured while she was dialing, this is a waste of time. Why don't we have a real drink instead?

That was all right with her, rum with Coke for her, neat for him, while they waited for a guy for whom she had left a message. She had taken off her jeans and gotten him to undress but kept on her underpants. No way he was going to screw her until she'd had her high. With each gulp of rum, that mattered less to him. The worrisome erection was somewhere far away, having its own good time. He heard himself, as though he were some ventriloquist's dummy, carry on about the taste and smell of her sweat. Hey, I want you to sweat more, he croaked, which was like carrying coals to Newcastle the way both of them were streaming. At last, when the bottle was empty, and they were each falling, at ever shorter intervals, into fits of snoring sleep, during a contortion that had her on top of him, sliding her torso up and down between his legs, he felt the wet, the release, and the gluey cold.

He timed a two-day business trip to Boston to coincide with her visit to Wood & King in New York, having asked Jack DeForrest, then his best friend at the firm, to shepherd her from partner to partner, which would have been his own normal responsibility. It was a safe choice: Jack was wonderfully obtuse about everything that wasn't a legal problem or a matter of firm politics. He left in his hands a note for Laverna that was carefully affectionate and impersonal, the sort of thing that couldn't compromise him and yet should serve to pacify her if that was needed. He didn't want to get her on the warpath. To his horror, a week later a job offer went out to her. A month or so passed, during which time he contemplated the monstrous inconvenience of her presence at the firm even if she acted as though nothing had happened. Then he received first a copy of a letter she had sent to the hiring coordinator in which she declined the offer and then a letter to him, about as bland as the one he had written to her, saying that in the end she thought she would be happier working for the government and was taking a job with the Justice Department. She'd be glad to get together if he ever came to D.C. The thought of her being available—not in New York but nearby, and out of the W & K context—powered for him erotic daydreams. In the end they were sufficient. He replied wishing her luck but made no move to see her.

And his much praised crushing rectitude? Schmidt thought that was a matter of emphasis if not definition. That he had beat his colleagues and clients over the head with demands his righteous zeal made of the practice of law was beyond doubt. Whether he had the right to cast the first stone seemed to him another matter. If there was a day to come when all sins would be revealed, there was one he knew would make him wish his tomb had remained sealed until the end of eternity. The financing of petrochemical facilities spread out along the coast of the Gulf of Texas turned on a series of contracts that bound to the supply of product a huge oil company with sufficient credit to back a borrowing of several billion dollars. How much product had to be bought and paid for in any given period, and the level of payments that were due even if the product became unavailable, were determined by contract provisions that alone came to a hundred pages. Within them, like the pit inside a plump fruit, was a series of algebraic formulae expressing what had been decided in words during the negotiations, and definitions of exquisite complexity. Of exquisite beauty, claimed Schmidt, who was their principal maker, in his role as counsel to the syndicate of long-term lenders. When the time came for putting the documents into final form, he took a benevolent attitude toward the oil company's last-minute requests for changes, most of them in his opinion unnecessary, on the theory that it was good policy to give its lawyers the opportunity to show that they were not always capitulating to the lenders and to Schmidt.

One such request, for a change in a formula, put forward solemnly by the senior partner of the law firm that was the lead counsel to the oil giant, threw Schmidt into a state of astonished amusement. He heard it prefaced with a personal appeal to himself, recalling the many hard cases that distinguished lawyer and Schmidt had worked on together as colleagues to such good effect. There was one small problem: the effect of the change, if a court let the contract stand as modified, would be unfairly adverse to the oil company. His friend, the oil company's lawyer, was making a grotesque mistake: he had turned himself one hundred eighty degrees around, pointing in the wrong direction. To be sure, it would not have been polite for Schmidt to point that out on the spot, in front of the very large group that included oil company businessmen gathered around the conference table, but he could have said something about taking the request under consideration and then explained first to his clients and then to his friend in private why the change should not be made. Instead, Schmidt passed his hand over his eyes, as though to chase away an incipient headache, and whispered to the associate who was keeping track of the changes to make it without a fuss. Thereupon, he excused himself and left the conference room for some minutes to take a turn in the corridor while his heart pounded. Fatally, the change was made, and the final agreements, signed the next day amid great pomp, incorporated it. Schmidt waited until he was quite sure that only he knew that they were flawed. It was then that he wrote, having told the lead lender that was what he would do, a letter to the oil company's lawyer, informing him that he had authorized the change in question as a matter of courtesy, although, immediately, he doubted its wisdom. Having taken the time to study it thoroughly, he was certain it was not something that his colleague or the oil company could have intended. He explained why, and how he had already recommended to his clients that an amendment to the agreements be signed correcting the error and restoring the originally intended text. Such an amendment was signed. The eminent opposing counsel spoke and wrote eloquently about Schmidt's remarkable, indeed exemplary, powers of analysis combined with rectitude rarely encountered these days in the profession. Several members of the lending consortium seized the occasion to write as well, with copies of their letter to old Dexter King, who was still the presiding partner, to go on record as being proud to have Schmidt as their lawyer.

It might well be that Dr. Renata hadn't the gift or training needed to break down a witness, force him to tell all until the last misdeed, the one that was to have remained buried forever, had been laid bare. But Schmidt had to hand it to her: she was no slouch when it came to getting him to examine his own conscience. All right, he was an abyss. Perhaps deeper and darker than Jon Riker. It seemed to him that it didn't matter. For one thing, he had never been caught. He strove to avoid doing evil. His own sins were no reason he shouldn't hold Riker to being honest with Charlotte. At most, they might temper his scorn.

XI

THEY WERE in bed, Carrie watching the Knicks game, Schmidt reading. He had abandoned *Phineas Redux*, for the first time unable to share Trollope's enthusiasm for Phineas or Lady Glen or Mr. Plantagenet Palliser, to feel that, across time and space, true English ladies and gentlemen were his spiritual comrades-at-arms. In the place of *Phineas*, he had taken up James's *The Awkward Age*, which he pored over sentence by sentence, if not word by word, struggling to make sure that he understood correctly the diabolical chatter over teacups: the virus of corruption spreading from Mrs. Brook's drawing room had really spared no one, not bewitching Nanda or even Mr. Longdon, with whom he would have liked to compare notes on more than one subject. He was also playing footsie under the covers with Carrie. For some time now, she had taken to wearing pajamas to bed and would resist taking them off when they made love. Love-making followed a different course too. She was always affectionate and attentive, but almost without exception she forced him to come before he made a move to take her. I want it this way, honey, she would murmur. Hey, I like it this way, don't spoil it. What's the matter? Your little guy sure likes it. Or she just kept her legs closed. No way to pry them apart.

Indeed, what was the matter? It wasn't a question he was eager to ask. Snuggling close, he put his free right hand inside her pants. That she didn't resist; in fact she moved her pelvis to help him and fell into the same rhythm with him. Very quickly, he felt her come. It was the break for commercials. She turned on her side; said Keep reading, stupid; covered his mouth with hers; and returned the favor. Did you like it? Come on, tell me, did you like it? When he groaned yes, she told him, You see how nice that is. Now go back to your reading. I want to watch.

Carrie, he said, maybe we should get away from here for Christmas and your school break. I thought we'd go to Paris, stay there until the end of the year, and then do something adventurous. Like Egypt. They seem to have stopped shooting tourists. We might as well take advantage of the pause. Mike Mansour could set things up for us.

He had been thinking about his spending habits and Mike Mansour's low opinion of his standard of living. Mike wasn't altogether wrong. With the money he had set aside for Charlotte's trust, of which he made himself the individual trustee having the power to decide on distributions, naming Gil Blackman as his successor—but really he must find a younger successor instead of leaving the choice to W & K if Gil died or went soft in the head—and the money he was leaving outright to Carrie, there was no reason he shouldn't spend more and give Carrie, and himself, a good time. He knew he would never do anything too wild. Even if the markets were bad, he had enough in treasuries to live out his life in great comfort. The unresolved question was whether the successor to Gil should be Mr. Mansour. There wasn't enough money in the trust to make him want to steal it—which the bank trustee, one could hope, wouldn't let him do in any case—and he might in fact be sensible about investment policy and when principal should be invaded. This was something to talk to Mike about. Yes, he was in a position to begin a life of irresponsible pleasures.

Jeez, replied Carrie, Christmas is just when they're going to be on this estate in the Dominican Republic that Mike's trying to buy. We'll be invited.

Oh, how do you know?

Jason told me. Don't you want to go? It'll be fun. They'll have a big boat to visit other islands and there'll be scuba diving. I'd really like to learn to scuba dive. Jason says it's really great.

I suppose Mike will have a whole lot of people.

That's OK. The house is big.

I see.

All of a sudden he wanted to pull his knees up to his chest, stick his head under the pillow, and pretend that he wasn't there and this thing wasn't happening to him. Nothing could be more natural. This passionate girl and the Viking bodyguard with brutally strong, huge hands of such astonishing gentleness when he wasn't out to hurt, why he was the dream partner for all the things she ached to do—dancing, scuba diving, the triathlon, and other pleasures she had not even thought of, hang gliding, perhaps, and motorcycle races. And in bed. Although they may not have done it yet in bed, only on a blanket stretched out on a dune or in the back of the Ranger he drove when off duty. There was no way he could keep her from Jason. She wasn't out for money, his or Mike Mansour's, or that of any of Mike Mansour's sleek associates who hadn't lacked opportunities to whisper to her at parties or to wander off to a corner of a vast deck, out of sight, out of hearing, and back up the proposition with a sudden and expert caress. If she was sleeping with Jason, the ignominy was in what they had just done, in the services she didn't refuse. But perhaps she wasn't sleeping with him; it might all be only in her head and his own. Not getting into bed naked, not letting him get inside her, these might be forms of purification and prayer and not her way of being straight with two men at once.

Carrie, he said, you're seeing a lot of Jason.

No, I'm not. He's traveling with Mike Mansour.

I know that, sweetie, I mean when he is here. And you're talking to him a lot. He certainly keeps you informed! What's going on between you? Don't be afraid to tell me, just this once I'm not going to blow up.

Jesus, Schmidtie, aren't you ever satisfied? I guess I didn't make you feel good just now, huh?

You did, honey, but you know that we aren't making love the way we did before.

Yeah, I'm keeping you out of my rear end!

This was said glumly. She moved as far away from him as the width of the bed allowed and, though the game wasn't over, switched channels until she found women's wrestling. There was a box of graham crackers on the night table beside her. She stuffed one after another into her mouth and chewed with her mouth open.

Oh, Carrie.

What's the matter? You're hurt because I told you what you really like? It's OK to do it, but I'm supposed to be ashamed to talk about it?

Honey, each time you told me you wanted to. You said that's what you did with Mr. Wilson. Am I wrong?

Yeah, and now I don't want to. You want to know why I let you? Because I know that's all you want. Out of my whole body!

He breathed carefully, not trusting the self-starting action of his lungs. A moment of inattention, and he would be dead. And with the man, with Mr. Wilson?

You lay off Mr. Wilson. He showed me the ropes. I did everything he said. Now leave me alone.

Then she added, and he heard in her voice that she was crying, It's OK. You can read. I'm going to sleep.

He heard her sob in the middle of the night, when he woke up because his bladder felt full, and tried to put his arms around her, but she pushed him back saying, You leave me alone or I'm getting out of this bed, so that he crept to the bathroom, making sure he was very quiet when he passed water as though there were a stranger on the other side of the door, got a sleeping pill, and returned to bed holding it between his fingers, not willing to take it before he knew that she was all right and there was nothing he could do for her.

She was in fact breathing quietly. Unless she was pretending, she had dozed off. He took his pill and didn't awaken until eight. It was past the time for her to get up, since she had a class that started in one hour, but he saw that her alarm clock wasn't in its usual place. That meant she had swept it under her pillow, so she wouldn't hear it. He wasn't going to interfere. Missing a class usually didn't matter to her all that much. For him, it was a question of life and death to speak to her without another outburst. He couldn't go on as he was, not after last night. Such a crust of resentment and bitterness when he had thought they were friends, with nothing but goodwill between them. He ran his morning errands. In the mail, among the bills and brokerage statements, there was a letter from Charlotte. It would have to wait until later, when he hoped he would feel calmer. Working toward that end, he squeezed the oranges and set the breakfast table. Then he waited, staring at the newspaper.

Finally she appeared, her face sullen and puffy as though she had not slept at all.

You let me oversleep.

I know. I thought you needed the rest.

Some rest. I needed to get to my class.

She ate and drank in silence. He kept quiet too, smoking a cigar until she had finished.

Sweetie, he said, we didn't go to sleep happy last night. You cried in the night. Couldn't we talk about it? Try to fix whatever is wrong?

She was hesitating. Then she said, It's like I don't know what to do. I don't know what to tell you. You're good to me, and Jesus, Schmidtie, I love you. But everything is such a mess.

You do love me?

He knew that was a stupid question, but his need to be comforted was so urgent he hadn't been able to stop himself from asking it.

Yeah, I love you. Come over here.

She took her elbows from the table, turned in the chair so she was sitting sideways in it, and wiggled out of the sleeves of her bathrobe so that she was naked to the waist.

It's nice and toasty in this kitchen. Come on, you can kiss me and touch me. Isn't that better?

It was awkward to lean down, so he pulled a chair up alongside hers. If only he could drown inside her, make the points of her breasts penetrate into his own flesh. He tasted in her mouth the savor of each thing she had eaten: the Rice Krispies with brown sugar, the croissant she liked to save for the last, the orange marmalade. You make me so happy, he whispered into her curls.

You make me feel good too. Shit, I didn't want to hurt your feelings. I didn't want any of this. I don't know what to do.

About what, honey?

About the way I feel. Like I said. I love you, you've been good to me, but I'm not like you and you're old. I mean you're OK, and in good health and everything, but Jesus, Schmidtie, you're older than my dad. Then I meet Jason, because you take me to see this rich guy he works for, and right away it's there. He's the kind of guy I could really be with, and he feels like that too, and what are we supposed to do? I don't know. Hey, you want to see why I've been wearing pj's to bed?

She put her arms back in the sleeves of the bathrobe and untied the belt. Look, she said, pointing to where the hair started.

There they were, right above the mons, a blue *C* interlaced with a blue *J*, with a red heart as background.

I didn't want you to see it. We had it done by this real cool guy in Riverhead, after the triathlon. Jason has one too, only bigger, over here.

She pointed to a spot high up on the thigh.

Sort of cute, isn't it?

Very, he said, feeling oddly distant from her and from himself. It'll show, I think, when you wear a bikini.

Yeah, that's the idea. You know, like rings.

She began to sob again and reached out for his handkerchief. It's so hard, Schmidtie, you wouldn't believe it.

What is hard? Love?

What to do, don't you get it? Like if Jason and I want to get together, he's got this job as Mike's head of security, so what's he going to do about me? I'm the girlfriend of the guy who's the best friend of the boss. How does that make me look? And like I told you, I still love you.

He was beginning to see. Downstairs love crossed by an upstairs-downstairs arrangement. It didn't really matter, but he asked anyway: Are you and Jason lovers? I mean do you sleep with him?

Judging by the look she gave him, he was every bit as obtuse as he had feared.

Honest, Schmidtie, I'm in your bed every night, aren't I? I lay him when I can. That isn't any too often. Anyway, I don't want to get you guys mixed up. You see what I mean?

I do see. Does he love you? Do you want to be really together, for instance get married?

He says he does, she said, looking down in what he took to be a display of modesty that could not be taught and was as entirely beautiful as all her grace.

And you?

She smiled.

All right, said Schmidt. This is very hard, but I think it can be sorted out if you both really want to. Meanwhile, do you think you want to go on living here, with me? Can you?

You mean I can? I thought you were going to tell me to get out. Like good-bye to this house and all that. You know. No more college or car. You really mean I can stay here?

I do.

Even if I'm with Jason, like I told you? Hey, Schmidtie, listen to me, if you let me stay, you and I can still be together. Like fool around. You know, like last night. That's OK with me. I won't be a bitch, I swear. Jason knows I love you. It's just different. The way I love him is different.

Extraordinary excitement and disbelief: he wondered whether he could think straight. Therefore, for Christ's sake, don't rush. Who are you anyway? The morals police? Grab the offer. She'll be in your house and in your bed. Nothing else matters. The shame of it isn't your business.

You can definitely stay, he told her. Let's just act natural and be nice to each other. All right?

After she left for her lab class, he hesitated over the red wine remaining in the bottle he had opened the previous evening, poured himself instead a bourbon, and reached for a knife with which to slit the envelope of Charlotte's letter. His hands were trembling. He put the knife down, looked around the kitchen where everything was in its place, quite in order, and tried again. There were two printed cards inside it. The one on top was some sort of variant on the change-of-address form. It announced, *urbi et orbi*, that as of a date that was more than a week past Charlotte again resided at the apartment that had been hers and Jon's. The telephone number was the one he knew. She could also be reached there by fax. It didn't say where she was moving from. The fax number was new, and, having underlined it to remind himself that he should enter it in his address book, Schmidt set that piece of cardboard aside. The other one was an announcement that Jon had become a member of a firm in New York with five name partners, four of them apparently Jewish and one Italian. This had to be good news. He threw the card into the wastebasket. Schmidt didn't think that he knew the firm—he would have to ask the W & K librarian to send him information about it—but surely Grausam, the first of the names, was the fellow who was always listed as appearing on Bar Association bankruptcy programs, and the Italian, Mazzola, was the divorce lawyer. Well, they had gotten themselves a first-rate bankruptcy litigator—indeed, an excellent all-around litigator, if Jack DeForrest was to be believed. Wood & King had also started out small. One lawyer, the venerable Mr. Wood! Perhaps, before long, Jon and his new partners would be giving Wood & King a run for their money. It was not exactly the kind of outfit Jon Riker had aspired to when Schmidt recruited him at Yale, but what the hell, he was damaged goods and lucky to have someone willing to take a chance on him. Schmidt took it to be one of those firms where the partners eat what they kill. Riker would have to find clients. The best sources, when you leave a top firm, are your former colleagues, who will send you cases that are too small or have a tight budget, and an occasional good project from an established client they can't take on because of a conflict—unless they want to make points with a big firm, by referring the client to it instead, which means they take the risk that the big firm may snatch the client and keep him. One had to hope that Riker still had friends left at W & K in spite of the unanimous vote to throw him out. Possibly some partners who felt guilty about what they had done. Schmidt examined the envelope again, went so far as to shake it. No, there wasn't a personal note sticking inside it, nothing, absolutely nothing, not a word.

Fine. This was like a discharge in bankruptcy, artfully arranged by his bankruptcy-specialist son-in-law. There wasn't a thing he had to do—except to write down that fax number, which was of doubtful usefulness to him since he did not own a fax machine—and there wasn't a thing anyone was asking of him. He had entered a state of expanding personal freedom. Another libation was definitely in order. The brown liquid had not yet touched his lips when the telephone rang. Who could it be—Mr. Mansour's assistant? Mr. Blackman's assistant? Some surly voiced retired cop soliciting contributions for the conference of retired police chiefs? Oh no, surprise, surprise! He recognized the voice of Renata Riker at once but waited until she had identified herself before pronouncing a greeting.

Aren't you thrilled, she asked.

He lied, About what?

Charlotte. Jon. Both of them! You were so right, Jon has got a job, a partnership with a New York firm he likes. I am so happy! I don't think I was any happier when he made partner at Wood & King. And he and Charlotte have gotten back together. Oh, Schmidtie, this is so good, so right. Are you going to come into the city to celebrate?

My dear Renata, I have received the news from you only this very minute, and I haven't heard anything about a celebration. In fact, I was just sitting here, having a quiet drink.

You mean they haven't called you?

They haven't.

It was pleasant to get back on the solid ground of unchallengeable facts.

That's bad, very bad, but you've got to forgive them, it's been such a whirlwind. Of course, they were hesitating—I mean Charlotte was hesitating because Jon had no doubts—until the partnership came through, and then, the last couple of weeks, you can imagine! So many plans to make, organizing the reentry into their old life. They were very nervous about how their friends would react.

Of course.

All I can say is that I told them to call you, and it's my fault that I didn't make sure it was done. Please, please, don't sit there thinking bad thoughts. Bad thoughts have such power! Schmidtie, we're one family again.

It was good to have taken that second drink. It gave him the determination to do a thing he had never done before, honest to God, not even to one of those police chiefs who got him to the telephone off the toilet seat. He hung up.

That same day, late in the evening, already in his pajamas and bathrobe, he brought the stepladder to his bedroom and took down the box stored on the top shelf of the closet. There they were, wrapped in tissue paper. He was surprised by the care he had taken. He unwrapped them one by one, the photographs that were the story of his family, from portraits of Mary and him at their wedding to the snapshots she had taken in the last months, when they had already moved to Bridgehampton, but she was trying to carry on as she always had; the illness had not yet tightened its vise. He had put them away when Carrie came, so they wouldn't stare down on the bed in judgment. Now they could return. Except for the pictures of Charlotte after she had met Jon, and the pictures of Charlotte and Jon together. For a moment he considered putting them in the living room, where he almost never sat, preferring the library, but really there were enough mementos there already, and of all sorts. He didn't want them in his closet either. He put them back in the box, not bothering with the tissue paper, and, because he was too tired to rummage around the attic for a suitable place, set the box down for the night in one of the spare bedrooms. The room he liked best in the whole house, better than his own bedroom, was the room that had been Charlotte's, and then

Charlotte and Jon's, directly across the landing from him. Carrie was in it. He paused outside the door. Not a ray of light, not a sound. Sleeping like a baby.

She had called from the college, after a class, and told him she had reached Jason. Mr. Mansour was in the city and was going to dinner at a restaurant, so the other guys could cover. If Jason drove out to Bridgehampton, could he come over, like to say hello. Schmidt said yes, that was just what he would have recommended. Hey, she giggled, I'll pick up a couple of pizzas. It'll be like the old times, remember? Indeed. It made him ache to see her burst into the house all flustered and eager, worrying about where to set the table—in the kitchen because it was just pizza or in the dining room because this was like a big event—and what table service to use. The dining room, was his judgment, with the best tablecloth and silver and crystal glasses. She liked that. Ah, yes, like old times, like the first meal she had eaten in his kitchen, at the time of his great happiness. How beautifully they assumed their roles: Schmidt, the fallen ogre; his child mistress, more expert than Hecate and yet as pure as a vestal, her body newly branded with the mark of the invader, her hair heavy with musk and the secrets he had whispered in spasms of unendurable pleasure; the blond hero destined to conjure the spell. The boy would kill him, just as he, Schmidt, had killed Mr. Wilson. The method chosen for the execution remained to be revealed, but everything in its own good time. If he explained it all to the boy, made clear the circumstances, it could perhaps be a single blow to the neck, the trick of mercy Mr. Mansour bragged about, delivered in the library. The lifeless body would sink onto the Chesterfield sofa, and there, in the smell of corruption, await the chorus of mourners, his Polish cleaning ladies. Except that, righteously, unexpectedly enraged by the tale Schmidt unfolded, he might choose to hack off his hands, feet, and penis, crush the skull, and throw the offal into the pond at the garden's edge for the delight of crabs gathered at its slimy bottom. How much did the boy know? Had she told him also about Mr. Wilson's initiatory practices, his transformation into "the man," the fetid hobo to whom she lovingly ministered until the end? How strong was Jason's stomach?

Gee, Mr. Schmidt, said Jason, this is real good. I don't think Mr. Mansour serves better wine. Anyway, none I've managed to taste!

For the third time, Schmidt asked to be called Schmidtie. Capture the lad's benevolence and reduce the ridicule. He wasn't, after all, the father of the bride.

Look, Jason, he continued, it's very nice that we are here, all three of us. That was a very good decision, to come to see me. You know how I feel about Carrie. She has been good to me, she has made me very happy, but she's very young. I've always known things would change. I am glad it's you. I've watched you at Mike Mansour's—while you were watching me—and I believe you're OK. Best of luck to you both.

Thanks, thanks a lot, Mr. Schmidt.

Schmidtie. And what happens now? Have you thought about that?

Carrie broke in. We've got no plans, Schmidtie. We just kind of got together.

Please, let Jason answer my question.

It's hard, Mr. Schmidt. I make a good living with Mr. Mansour, but you've seen how it is. I'm with him, like most of the time, and when he travels I go with him. That's one thing. The other is that if he finds out about Carrie and me I'm out. That's his rule.

I think he's got his own idea about what goes on.

Yeah, I know, he gets a kick sometimes out of needling you. But that's because right now all he thinks is that maybe we kind of did something behind your back. Once it's in the open, let me tell you that will be something else.

Perhaps I could talk to him.

Nah, that won't do any good. He's very strict. Like with all the staff. I'm not an exception.

I suppose you could quit and get another job.

Yeah, in security. That's the same problem all over again. You get no time off; you have no life. I've been thinking of starting a security business of my own. I know a lot of reliable guys, well trained, and I could help people who don't have an organization like Mr. Mansour or that friend of his, Mr. Perle. Even those guys might like that. Sort of get the problem off their hands. I've been saving to do that, but I'm not there yet. Not by a long shot. He laughed.

Do you think it's a good business?

Oh, yeah. The demand is there.

Well, is that something I might want to invest in? I mean if it was helpful.

Gee, Mr. Schmidt, I don't know, I never thought about anyone helping me out.

It wasn't clear to Schmidt whether there was more Jason might say, because Carrie broke in.

You guys are nuts. Lay off, Schmidtie.

All right, does Jason have any other ideas?

Yeah, I'm good with bikes. I've thought of running a bike shop, but I don't know. The competition is real hard. I know this guy who used to be on Route 27. He was on the force, he knows what he's doing, but after a couple of years he gave up and moved to the North Fork. He's doing OK, but just OK.

And Carrie, what do you think?

I don't know, Schmidtie. I don't think it's up to me.

Do I take it then that you don't mind if Carrie goes on living here? For the time being? With me?

Man, no. I mean that's great if that's all right with you, Mr. Schmidt.

Schmidt looked at Carrie full in the face, but she seemed to be studying the weave of the tablecloth, and her eyes didn't meet his. He decided to concentrate on the pizza and the ice cream that followed. The permutations subsumed in the proposition that she would stay at his house were numerous. He didn't think they could be discussed with Jason in her presence or with her while Jason was there. Perhaps they couldn't be discussed at all. She added to Schmidt's puzzlement by asking them to stay with her in the kitchen while she did dishes. He had thought she might chase them out to the library, to let her clean up, or find another way to give him a moment with Jason. But perhaps she knew better. When the dishes were finished, she told Jason it was time for him to go and told Schmidt she'd be right back; she wanted to say good-bye to Jason. It turned out to be a long good-bye. He imagined its being performed in Jason's car or in the servants' quarters of Mike Mansour's house, if such things were allowed on the premises or could be done on the sly.

He turned out the lights in the kitchen and waited in the library. During his last visit to the mall he had bought a CD of *The Marriage of Figaro* to replace the fading tape. The vinyl LPs had not traveled from the New York apartment to Bridgehampton. In fact, he wasn't sure he knew whether they had been thrown away, sold, or given to a thrift shop. It didn't matter; he no longer owned a turntable on which he could have played them. The scanning feature of the CD player was a lovely convenience. He found in the fourth act the aria "Aprite un po' quegli occhi" and played it over and over, although he knew that, even if Carrie was a witch and had enchanted him, that was not really the point; he hadn't been fooled, and no one need open his eyes. It was just a way to let off steam, since, like Figaro—and Almaviva!—he felt sorry for himself. *Basta!* He poured a brandy and was considering having another when he heard the front door slam. Carrie rummaging in the front hall, going upstairs, coming down. She had changed into the pair of black silk pajamas he had given her to mark the beginning of the new college term. Her feet were bare. She sat down on the Chesterfield sofa, catty-corner from his armchair.

Hey, I took a bath.

That, thought Schmidt, could be simply because it's cold out.

I'm all clean.

The first hypothesis was put in question, but not necessarily defeated.

Schmidtie, you're going to talk to me?

Yes, I'm just shaking myself awake. Or something like it. I guess I don't know what to make of the conversation with Jason. I don't understand where you and he stand. I would have imagined he had some idea—how you might live together, married or unmarried. Anyway, an idea of living as a couple. I didn't hear that.

It's heavy for him. You know, when he quit the PD he was like in the detective section—her tone rose, questioning, because she didn't know what she was talking about and whether she was saying the right thing. He did it because Mike Mansour pays a lot. A lot, maybe twice what he was making. But, like he said, Mike could fire him. So what's he going to do?

And you, what do you think?

I told you, Schmidtie. I don't know. It's like this. I want to be with him, but I don't want any pressure. It's crazy.

Could it be that you want to find out whether it really works for you to be with him?

Oh, it worked just fine, she told him, but there was no way to be with him except when he was off duty, and then they had to look for a place to be alone. Thereupon, she squirmed around on the sofa as though she had a big itch. Schmidt began to see that if he thought all he had to do was to say yes to a suitor asking for the hand of his child mistress he was wrong. In that case, the question had to be put to Mr. Schmidt: Where did he stand? Schmidtie thought he knew the answer.

Carrie, I've told you that you can stay with me, he told her. As a member of my family. Nothing will change in that regard. But you and I can't sleep together if you are sleeping with Jason. I know I told you once, long ago, that I wasn't asking you to be faithful, but that was before I loved you so much, before we had lived together. So if you want to be with Jason, you and I can be best of friends; as I said, you'll be a member of my family. Or if what you've had with Jason is off, we can be just the way we were before. It's up to you, baby.

She came to sit on the arm of his chair and put her arms around his neck. It's not off with Jason. But I love you, Schmidtie. Like I said I want to stay here. As long as you let me. Hey, can I still get in your bed? If we keep our pants on? Honest?

XII

NO SOONER had Gil Blackman disembarked at Kennedy from his Los Angeles flight and gotten into his car than he telephoned Schmidt.

I'm back, he said, just landed. How about lunch tomorrow at what's that place in Bridgehampton? I'm spending the night in the city, but I'll be out first thing tomorrow. We have to talk.

Such eagerness on the part of the great filmmaker to see his fuddy-duddy old college roommate was without precedent in recent memory. You would have to go back to the time when Gil positively needed him, such as when he had decided to leave his first wife and, being as yet unacquainted with the divorce lawyers celebrated in the tabloids, had asked Schmidt for help.

O'Henry's, said Schmidt, very gladly. I'll see you there at one.

There was no longer any reason, it seemed to him, to avoid that hamburger joint, which of late had also taken to serving lobster and chicken-salad sandwiches on pita bread with diced avocado on the side. Certainly not if he went there without Carrie, to meet the glamorous Mr. Blackman. And even if she consented to come with him, surely a de facto statute of limitations had begun to apply. There was the owner left to remember Carrie—and the fun he had humping her, if he was to believe Bryan—and Pete, the bartender, so far presumed innocent. The waiters, a bunch of aspiring actors and actresses with no imaginable talent and overly familiar manners, were practically all new, hired after her time. Half-breeds most of them, like Carrie. Ah, cauterize the wound with scorn, obliterate the past: how she would lean, when she brought his food, on the empty chair at his table and speak in a voice so hoarse his entire body strained to hear, how she let her hand sometimes brush against his shoulder when she hurried by, how this willowy, sallow-faced, gallant kid from the slums let him love her.

The kid, as he set out to meet Gil, was already behind the steering wheel of her car on the way to her art class, speeding dangerously, he was willing to bet, on the back roads. Drawing from the model! He could draw her with his eyes closed—each lineament, shade, and hollow. These were the last weeks of college courses; the semester would be over soon. What to do about the Christmas vacation worried her; that was clear. Schmidt had accepted Mike Mansour's invitation for the holidays at his Dominican Shangri-la as soon as it was extended. It was what she said she wanted, but now going there as Schmidt's girl, as though nothing had changed, while Jason lugged bags from the tarmac to the car, drove to the beach house, lugged the bags again to the bedroom, and watched over the master and his guests frolicking in the water or feasting at table, all that was hard, even humiliating. Scenes of the goings-on in the bedroom shared by Carrie and Schmidt—in reality strictly nothing, a sword lies between them—would pass before Jason's eyes, behind those reflecting sunglasses. And Mike Mansour's amused glances! How much does he really know, and how much will he confide to a chosen guest or two, and how the word will spread! That is a problem for Schmidt too, although a small one, really a pinprick. But all things weighed, early on he said to her, Let's tell Mike we won't come. It won't upset him or his plans; this sort of house party is like a picnic, you don't count the guests, not with a house like that. We'll go to Paris instead, and to Egypt if that is still possible, and, if it isn't, to Morocco. The Mamounia or Fez or both; you decide. But the kid does want to go to Mike Mansour's, because she's never been to such a house or traveled in a private jet or plunged into a sea of liquid blue and gold off a great, big yacht. Also, above all perhaps, because Jason will be there. She can't get enough of that perfectly formed head and face, with its brush of blond hair, the blue eyes, pert nose, white teeth, and believe it or not a cleft chin, and this is before you take in the rolling shoulders, pectorals of a discobolus, and, Jesus, the biceps. There is, of course, much more to descant upon that Carrie knows in detail and Schmidt prefers not to think about. All right, he told her, if you don't want to give up the trip, we're going. The most interesting question may be what does Jason think, what does he want? Being the strong and silent type isn't the same as having no point of view. The boy is an enigma to Schmidt.

There must be some sort of test for armed bodyguards; certainly there are intelligence tests you must take before you become a New York City detective—assuming Carrie got that right—and it's unlikely that Mike Mansour would have hired him if Jason tested dumb. Perhaps it's a special sort of smarts, an aptitude for the chokehold grip and the quick frisk: to Schmidt, he doesn't seem nearly as smart as Carrie. But then he has an unnatural, perhaps excessive, respect for Carrie's brains. Intelligence raised to a greater height by sensitivity and intuition: an unbeatable combination.

Finally, with Jason, Schmidt gives up. There may be nothing at the core of the enigma other than class difference. He'd say that the boy has the attitude and the outlook of a servant, if you were still permitted to use that noun. One would like to understand, though, his point of view on having sex. Carrie is at home every evening, except when she goes out with Schmidt, and the few times, really very few, when she tells him she's going to the movies with Jason. Schmidt thinks she really sees the movies, because she tells him about them, with an eerie knack for imitating the noise of explosions, whistling bullets, and car chases. Also, she doesn't get home that late. A quick one in the backseat, or perhaps in the back of one of those panel trucks the security detail uses, borrowed for the evening? Something or other between the end of classes and Carrie's reappearance for dinner? That was easy before the weather turned cold. All the empty dunes thick with the smell of sea grass. There remain as solutions the perennial back of the car, a motel room rented by the hour if such a thing is possible in Suffolk County, or the pad of some pal. He hasn't heard of any such person. No, sharing the equatorial bedroom with Carrie—sure to be air-conditioned—isn't going to be a problem for Schmidt. She's gotten into the habit of coming to his bed anyway, although he has bought a television for her room, so she can watch hockey. He might just as well have given her his set, since he almost never turns it on, but he didn't want her to think he was depriving himself. She slips into his room, therefore, late, and very silently, when he has put his book down and is almost asleep. Often he is not aware of her presence until her arms are around him, her body pressed to his. He protested at first, saying this wasn't the deal, but she told him, Darling, it is, we're keeping our pants on, let me, I like it. In every respect but this he treats her like a daughter, a daughter he loves and who loves him back, but, after all, she isn't his daughter. Not in the least. She is his Hecate.

One o'clock sharp. Mr. Blackman has been delayed. A matter of minutes. He has telephoned from his car. Mr. Schmidt will not complain, provided he can have at once his dry martini with an olive. After all this time, he has come to savor the pleasures of a retirement unencumbered by obligations. If you want a martini before lunch, have it. Two martinis? That's all right too. Similarly, there's no need to be worked up because you are made to wait. It's time you have to yourself, when you can think your own thoughts undisturbed, and observe your more active fellow human beings. In this season, they aren't very numerous during lunch at O'Henry's. Of the monstrous Weird Sisters, widows of writers once resident in the East End, who used to be there almost every day, sometimes with an equally aged and seedy male intellectual, two are dead. The survivors have taken their business to a greasy spoon as yet undiscovered by summer people and tourists, or are bedridden or too impoverished to afford the newly inflated prices, or, quite simply, aren't there because this is not the day when they meet. Schmidt's connection with local gossip has become too tenuous; he couldn't venture a guess. In fact, there is no one in the restaurant he knows except the barman and the florid real-estate man with a bad case of shakes, eating at the bar. The rest of his fellow lunchers seem to be retired bodies, no more active than he, former lawyers and doctors probably, for whom, just as for himself, a summer house has become a year-round residence. Had he remained a member of the stubbornly anachronistic tennis club, so unwelcoming to Jews and the likes of Carrie, where these good people probably play golf, they might be his friends. The privilege wouldn't seem worth the cost of the yearly dues. But *en garde!* Pushed with more than usual vigor, the front door flies open, and into the restaurant strides Gil Blackman.

Schmidt gets out of his chair. Quite untypically they embrace. Seated again, they begin to order lunch—no mean affair, since habit has put them, already at first sight of each other, into a high, expansive mood.

Schmidtie, you old scoundrel, said Mr. Blackman, I've done it. *Chocolate Kisses* is ready to go. The reaction, each time we've shown it, has been fantastic. And I'm not just talking about studio drones. Real people! It's just possible we've got a winner. You should hear Elaine. And for that matter, your best friend, Mike Mansour. That guy's over the moon. He hasn't even noticed we haven't taken a single one of his suggestions. I tell you, it's a dream. You still own a dinner jacket? Yes? Stupid of me to ask. Well, get it ready. You're coming to the opening of openings. With Carrie, of course. We shall feast!

God bless you. That's really fantastic. What the hell, you're great.

I am. By the way, Elaine is arriving tonight. She wants you at dinner tomorrow. Can you come?

With bells on. There's nothing I would rather do.

Good. By the way, you've got Mike bent out of shape—I mean nothing serious, it's just that the guy is going ape. No kidding.

Oh?

Absolutely. He's flummoxed. First, he offers you the presidency or whatever it is—the top job—at his foundation. You know he's bananas about it. The foundation's going to get most of his money because he's cut out his kids and so forth. He thought you were going to fall into his arms and weep from happiness, gratitude, whatever. Instead, you turned him down. Apparently he's got Holbein working on how they can coax you into changing your mind. I must say, I think you're nuts. This is a great opportunity. The greatest. Then, and this he told me in strictest confidence—I've got to hand it to him, I never knew he had any sensitivity or tact—he's worried that Carrie and his head gorilla, that blond fellow, you know, his Nordic Ajax, may have a little thing going. He thinks you're on to it, but isn't sure. Anyway, he doesn't know what to do. Fire the guy, because that's against house rules; keep it quiet, because why rock the boat, maybe it's nothing; speak to you and ask you what you want him to do; and on and on. It's a funny thing. I think Mike Mansour has a crush on you—I don't mean anything sexual, that boychick is queer all right but not that way. You know what? He likes being with you. So what do you say?

You know? I'm at a loss—completely. The stuff about the foundation is a crock. No, it's weird. Of course, I'll take the job if he really means to offer it. I thought he was pulling my leg, so I kept my distance so as not to come out looking like a presumptuous ass. And as for Holbein! He wrote to me what I thought was a buzz-off letter. If that's his idea of coaxing someone into doing something, he's got to have his head examined.

You'll see Mike tomorrow night. You can straighten it out then.

I'll try. Honest.

You do that. If you don't, I'll think you should have your head examined.

Schmidt nodded. He would have to tell Gil about Carrie. With some omissions.

The stuff about Carrie is very complicated, he said. She is having—frankly, I'm not quite sure whether it's still going on—an affair with your Ajax. Jason's his name, actually. I talked to her about it kindly and calmly, because I can't blame her. She's not even twenty-five! So I offered to have her stay on with me if she wants—as a friend, no sex, no problems. She liked that. Still likes it, I guess. Thereupon I had a visit from Jason. Nice. Polite, didn't beat me up or anything, just tucked away a half of a big pizza. I explained the situation to him and in a sense tried to get him to take her away. I don't mean that I necessarily expected him to ask for her hand—why ask it of me anyway?—but at least to get her out of my house into his, or however they can arrange it. But nothing came out of him. Nothing. Didn't even rise to the bait when I asked whether he wanted perhaps to start some business I might invest in. Or maybe I would have gotten a nibble out of Jason with that if Carrie hadn't come down on it like a ton of rocks. She really snarled at him!

Amazing.

She's a remarkable girl. I realized immediately that she didn't want me to buy him for her. Can you believe it? How do you bring up kids to be like that? For example, where did Mary and I go wrong with Charlotte? One way or another, that one wants me to buy her everything and everybody.

Where does that stand?

It depends on your point of view. Objectively, I have to say it could be worse. It seems that she and Jon have patched things up and gotten back together. He's become a partner in one of those pushy small firms that's trying to be a boutique, but you don't know what they've got to sell.

Pushy, you said. Schmidtie, I know your code. You mean it's Jewish.

You guessed it. On the other hand, do you know how I got the news? Charlotte sent me two printed announcements, one that she was moving back into their apartment and the other of Jon's partnership in that firm. Not the tiniest personal note. Zero. I got the background briefing from the ineffable Dr. Renata.

Holy mackerel!

Precisely. Now you're up-to-date. Do you understand it? You've always been a man of imagination. All these personages in your films you manage to think—feel—your way into. What is one to think of a child like that? You observed her being brought up, from a distance to be sure, but still. You know that she was loved, by me as well as Mary. Of course, Mary did a better job. Charlotte has brains; she's been given all the opportunities; we've denied her nothing. Why is she treating me this way? In the process, she is making her own life less agreeable, surely she realizes it. Why is she so bitchy?

You know, it won't surprise you that I've turned that problem over and over in my head—not apropos of Charlotte but of my own cutie pies and also darling step-Lilly. Actually, the closest I've come to dealing with it in a film was when I made *Rigoletto.* Funny, isn't it? I was too young then to get even near the bottom of the question, and anyway I wasn't exactly writing on a blank page! Little Gilda is quite a number, including as a daughter, when you think of it. The girl who fucks and sings too much! The truth is that I haven't got an answer, just some observations. One: I don't think it's mostly in upbringing. There is some genetic fatality at work—don't ask me what it is, I don't know beans about genetics. More and more, though, I don't see upbringing, the way you and I have understood it, and the circumstances of childhood as the dominant influences on a kid's strength and serenity. Hell, being able to be happy and having a good character. Two: I wonder whether the upper class—if I may have the chutzpah to include myself and my two wives—hasn't lost the knack of bringing up kids. I realize that this goes in the opposite direction from point one, but all you've got to do to test my thesis is to go sometime to the candy store, next door from here, order a nice rum-raisin ice cream, and watch the little waitresses. They're fourteen? Sixteen? A couple may be no more than thirteen. I've gotten out of training when it comes to kids' ages. You'll see those terrific genuine smiles, a sparkle in the eyes, politeness to take right to Buckingham Palace, and they're working their tails off without feeling sorry for themselves. Who are their parents? I've never asked, but I would bet it's the local, more established blue-collar types or people just a tad above. The small-time painting contractor, the hardware-store owner, maybe the exterminator. They've managed somehow to keep a balance for themselves, and anyway for the kids, between expectations and personal effort. And a space for a sense of personal achievement and gratitude. Quite frankly, I love them. There is some of that in Carrie, I think. Three: This is the most bizarre, heartbreaking part. I've noticed that being good to your kids isn't rewarded. You can see this in divorced couples. It isn't the mother or the father who have broken their backs for the little buggers—always responsible, always there when they are needed—on the contrary, it's the awful parent, the one who never stops making scenes, gives them a birdhouse out of the L. L. Bean catalogue or wool socks for a wedding present, who is the mummy or daddy they treat with tenderness and respect. Anyway, they're scared of those bad mothers and fathers. They pussyfoot around them for fear of provoking an attack of rage. That's already something—better than what you and I get. So what are you going to do about Carrie?

I don't know. More and more I think it's her call.

That evening he told Carrie about *Chocolate Kisses* and the invitation to dinner at the Blackmans'. Gil and she got along. Right away, she telephoned to congratulate him, spoke instead to the answering machine, and afterward fell to thinking. One could always tell. She would curl up on the big sofa in the library with her legs under her and her arms crossed over her head as if she were doing a baby version of the backstroke. After a while, she said she was going to the kitchen to telephone. When she returned she thought some more and said, Hey Schmidtie, it's OK with you if I don't go to the dinner? I talked to Jason. He's not driving for Mike tomorrow evening. I'd kind of like to see him. Go to a movie or something.

That was all right, he told her.

You're going to call them?

Yes, but not right now. I'd rather not have to leave a message.

You're not going to forget?

Promise. Anyway you can stick a note on the kitchen telephone. It's not a big deal, you know. He said they were inviting only Mike Mansour. They'll have Blue Felt Slippers put out four settings instead of five.

It's a big deal to me. I don't want to screw it up for you with your friends.

Don't worry.

He went over to her, knelt down, and kissed her hands, because it had become clear how she felt trapped, and how in fact she might be wondering whether she hadn't screwed it up for herself. Poor little tramp! There were so many ways he thought he could help her, but he feared that if he made one false move most of them, perhaps all, might be refused. For instance, if she would only change her mind and agree to marry him. He knew that the chances were close to but not quite zero. She too would be better off if she had a few more decent years with him, no different really from the way they were living, and then she could leave him with a good settlement, if that's what she wanted. Alimony or capital, it didn't really matter. A few years wouldn't make a dent in her looks or figure and she was capable of learning a lot fast—not only at courses. He had worried about her being a fish out of water if she became his wife. Quite right, just as she had been as his mistress. But a corner of the curtain had been lifted, he had had a peek at what her life might be as Mrs. Jason. Putting aside Jason's qualities as a stud—he was willing to assume they were at least average and, therefore, given Jason's age, superior to his own—and the joy of worshiping at the temple of his body, there wasn't anything he saw to recommend such a life. Perhaps he should renew his own suit officially. Cool it, Schmidtie, he admonished himself. Haven't you learned, beginning with Charlotte, that kids want to be with other kids and do what other kids do, even if old Mom and Dad are up to something much more interesting, and above all more refined?

Perhaps because Carrie had begged off from the dinner, and the light of the candelabra would not be transforming into a theater of Chinese shadows the nervous play of her long magician's fingers, the Blackmans decided to add to their table an ornament of another sort. They invited Caroline and Joe Canning, a writing couple with a house on the way to Sag Harbor and an insouciant habit of displaying in public their fondness for each other and stony if polite indifference toward everyone else. In fact, in Joe's case, the politeness was only intermittent. The layer of his good manners was considerably thinner than Caroline's, and his own person clearly the principal subject of his attention. Lord Harry, said Schmidt to himself. What's Gil trying to do? Snow Mike? It won't work; he doesn't know who these two are. Broker a deal for Joe's novel? He doesn't need to ask him to dinner for that; a call to the agent will do it. Or is it a deal for Caroline's book? The last one was a biography of Louis XIV's mother. They'd have to turn it into the untold story of the Three Musketeers! He shook Caroline's hand and noticed that her fingers were no shorter than Carrie's and pleasantly warm. Unlike the other women he used to see around the baked ham and runny Brie of his and Mary's Fourth of July parties, she had become more handsome with the passing years. Her bearing did it, and her laughter, which carried you along irresistibly even if you couldn't make out the joke. The intriguing question was how Canning, whom Schmidt remembered from college as a turkey with literary pretensions, had gotten this splendid woman to marry him in the first place, after their divorces, when they must have both already been in their forties, and how he had kept her. It couldn't be his looks or reputation—she shone brightly enough herself—and he had no money. Besides, at the time of their marriage, he hadn't written the novel of his grandmother's invented life that got short-listed for every prize and even won a few. He was a busy something or other in the upper management of New York's stodgy biggest insurance company. Depending on one's point of view, the marriage was a colossal piece of luck or a colossal injustice.

A small drink that looked like vodka in hand, Canning lurked between a large Chinese vase and Gil and Mansour without seeming to be included in their conversation. Their physical proximity may, nonetheless, have given him countenance, like a sideboard to lean against or an artifact on a wall that can be made the subject of a prolonged examination. Schmidt felt Canning's eye pass over him and flee. That was par for the course. Undeterred, he headed in their direction and shook Gil's and Mansour's hands.

Congratulations!

Accepted. Has Gil told you how we worked together? You didn't believe it, that I had it in me. Huh?

No, I mean yes, I did think so.

Pas de problème, the question to ask yourself is this, Do I have talent or is it just force of will or a freak accident? What do you think, Mr. Canning?

Joe, please call me Joe. I've no idea. I've not seen your work.

You're going to see it. Gil will get you an invitation to the opening. I want you there. Your wife too. You'll tell me what you think later. Schmidtie's going to be there, I hope with his girlfriend. By the way, Gil's been telling me about your books. You should pay him a commission. I began one on the plane back from the Coast and it's on my desk now, in my office. What's its title?

That depends on which one you're reading.

It's about this older guy who's screwing a young girl. Ha! Ha! Ha! What we all want to do.

Gil laughed too.

All his books, except the first one, are about that.

Then I don't want to read the first one. Schmidtie, you know Joe? Mr. Canning?

Schmidt and Canning nodded.

No kidding.

We were all in college together, explained Gil, except that Joe is younger. Two classes behind us.

I see. A Harvard reunion. Myself, I went to NYU, which taught me all I needed just then. Now what I don't know I don't need. Joe, you should talk to Schmidtie about your favorite subject. He's quite an expert. Screwing little girls! You're killing me. We'll join the ladies.

Evidently, Canning had come to the same conclusion as Schmidt, that there was no acceptable way to part company at once. He was the first to collect his wits and break the silence. I am truly sorry about Mary. I might have told you sooner.

We haven't seen each other.

No big loss. We're making up for it this evening.

Elaine had Mr. Mansour on her right and Canning on her left and gave Caroline to Mr. Mansour, which put Schmidt between Caroline and Gil. Canning's parting shot preoccupied him. Unless he had misunderstood, it was a piece of insolent nastiness. Gratuitous, or was there a reason? He would have liked to ask Caroline, but the table was too small and Canning's hearing, he was sure, acute. His own silence weighed on him. It was too bad, he wished he had refused the invitation to this dinner. Carrie might have made her date with Jason anyway, but if he had to eat and drink in such isolation, he would just as soon do it at home. Just then taking part in the general conversation became unnecessary and even impractical. Mr. Mansour was questioning Canning about the art of fiction.

Caroline, Schmidt muttered under the cover of the huge voice, did you hear what Joe said to me just before we sat down?

She nodded.

I don't know what to make of it. Why should he attack me? What have I done to him?

Nothing at all. It's best not to pay attention. Half the time, he doesn't even know what he is saying. He might have meant he'd rather be at home working. Or something like it.

She laughed.

Excuse me, as you know I haven't read your masterpieces, thundered Mr. Mansour. Just the beginning of the novel I had on the plane, before I had to work the phone. Elaine says your first book is the best. Is that what you think?

Does it matter what I think if you haven't read it?

Although Canning had spoken, only Caroline, who had to live with him, and Schmidt seemed to have heard what he said. His voice was low, and he took no trouble to force it.

So what's your answer?

I just gave it to you.

Joe, intervened Caroline, Mike Mansour didn't hear you. Nobody can hear him, Mike. He said that it doesn't matter what he thinks because you haven't read his novel.

He's got a point there, said Mr. Mansour and laughed.

Caroline laughed too. Ha! Ha! Ha! replied Elaine and Gil, Elaine throwing in an extra Ha! Ha! as soon as Gil subsided. She had always been a very attentive hostess.

Is that where you describe sex with little girls?

Oh, young girls. Very artistically! If you do read me—I don't especially recommend it—you'll see. You might find it amusing, replied Canning, apparently convinced that he was shouting.

Amusing! said Elaine. Don't listen to him. He's a great writer. You know, he reveals so much! Gil's always thinking he should film one of his novels.

He's never mentioned it to me and I'm his partner. I will want to be consulted. These revelations Elaine just talked about. I mean I'm sorry to ask you while your wife's right here. Are your books autobiographical?

I write novels.

But if you're revealing so much it must be because it's you, what you've done.

Not necessarily. I could have just dreamed it, don't you think? Why do you care?

Gil, let's you and I talk another time about what we do with your friend Joe. Maybe our people could put together a package. Lay it out, so I can focus. And Mr. Canning, thank you for your courtesy.

Afterward, on the back porch, Mansour put his arm around Schmidt and said, I just hate this guy. Canning. He was trying to put me down. That doesn't go down well with me.

He's prickly.

You mean he's a prick. I think he's an anti-Semite too.

There you may be wrong. He's one hundred percent Jewish.

Jesus, with that name! All right, so he's an anti-Semitic Jew. The wife, she's something else. Superb! That's the kind of woman you should be with, Schmidtie, do you get what I mean? A real class act. You can go anywhere with her.

Yes.

I have an idea she's OK in bed too. I'm psychic about that. Ha! Ha! Just like you. But she's got it all. She'd be OK even for me. How did a schmuck like that find her?

That's what I've been asking myself too. Dumb luck.

I hear you. I want to change the subject. With all due respect, the question is, Why did you turn me down on my foundation? One, I need you; two, you've hurt my feelings.

But I haven't, Mike, really, I didn't mean to. I guess I felt overwhelmed.

All right. Then you're on. I'll have Holbein send you the paperwork. When can you start? Early in the new year? Whatever suits you.

Mr. Mansour's arm reclaimed its place on Schmidt's shoulder. He continued: You're coming to my place for the holidays. Let's say right after we get back. And listen, I've got to talk to you about you know who. I'll call you.

He returned Mr. Mansour's squeeze and said, Thank you, Mike, thank you very much. You can't imagine how happy this makes me.

Carrie's little BMW wasn't in the driveway or the garage when he got home, but the house was lit up, haphazardly. He went from room to room turning some lights off, turning others on. There was still hope; any moment he might hear her car wheels on the gravel. Another half hour passed. He went to bed.

XIII

How was the movie? he asked the next morning. She had no class, but she was up anyway, and the breakfast table was set.

OK. No, it wasn't OK. It was lousy. How was your dinner?

He laughed. Mediocre. No, midway between mediocre and OK. Food was OK. The usual Chinese dishes. Gil and Elaine were OK minus. There was another couple I think Gil invited to take your place. Two for one, I guess. She's a nice woman, but I've never been able to stand the husband. He went to work for an insurance company after college and stayed there until he retired, but when he turned fifty-something he began to write novels. Many people find them unpleasant. Politically incorrect and so forth with great sex scenes. If you like that sort of thing. And of course Mr. Michael Mansour. He was OK plus. First, he got into a literary discussion with the novelist, and then he offered me a job. I think the offer is real. He wants me to run his foundation! I'm supposed to start right after the Dominican holiday. We have to talk about this, honey. I've kind of told him I'll take it, but it will mean making some changes in the way we live.

Yeah. I guess.

Her face shut down. It had been a mistake not to speak about the foundation before, but he hadn't wanted her to know he'd made a fool of himself when the job first seemed to have been offered and then feared making a fool of himself if he revealed that he still hoped it could be salvaged. Besides, with everything between him and Carrie so up in the air, he hardly knew how to put any plan forward, especially one with so many contingent outcomes.

What I mean is that I will probably have to get some sort of apartment in New York and be there during the week—anyway, some weeks, perhaps most weeks—and will have to travel to visit offices overseas. That sort of thing. Mike said he wants me to take a look at their offices in Europe right after I begin. I said I would, because it makes sense. But these won't be really long trips. I can break them up and come home for rest and recreation.

He waited for her to say something, but she didn't. It could be that she was going to sulk.

I don't think you would really mind being here alone during the semester, he continued. The rest of the time, you could come to New York or travel with me. Think of all the places we might get to visit!

A quick glance to see how she was taking this. No change. She might just as well have been in a lotus position, meditating. Schmidt poured another cup of tea for himself and a cup of coffee for Carrie and returned to the newspaper. Suddenly, she spoke.

You won't need to get an apartment. There is one for you to use, on Park Avenue. It goes with the job. It's furnished, but you can bring your own furniture or they'll redecorate.

The information about furniture was proffered in a voice so flat that it could signify either considerable respect for the munificence with which he was about to be treated or scorn.

How do you know that?

Jason told me. He's been to see it with Mike. Mike wanted to make sure it was good enough for you.

Oh. When was that?

First time they went over? I don't know, before Thanksgiving. And as soon as he got back from L.A. They're redoing the bathrooms. He wants you to have a bidet.

For heaven's sake! What else do you know?

Plenty. Like Jason talks to Bernice. Shit, they all talk to each other.

Bernice was Michael Mansour's head secretary, known to Schmidt principally on the telephone and from the Thanksgiving lunch, on which occasion she had seemed to be in charge of the household, rearranging the place cards on the table and giving orders to Manuel.

She said Mike is real worried about you and this job. He thinks you can do it all right, and it would be good for you.

What's he worried about then?

Who knows? He says maybe Schmidtie's got used to not working. He might quit or something.

I guess I'll have to watch my step and prove I'm still an eager beaver. Carrie, why haven't you told me these things before?

She played with her Krispies and poured herself another cup of coffee. Jeez, Schmidtie, I don't know. You didn't talk to me. Isn't it sort of the same?

That was surely right. He nodded.

All right, at least we're talking about it now. It's OK with you? I mean being here alone during the week?

At once she was at his side and put her arms around his neck. Hey, move, dopey. The table's in the way. I want to sit in your lap. OK like this? Schmidtie? You're not going to get mad or anything, are you?

Why should I? What's happened or what have you done?

Like the way you go crazy about Bryan.

It was so good to have her against him, her breath on his cheek when she talked, that he only managed a shrug.

He hasn't fucked up, I swear.

All right. Tell me anything you want. I'm ready.

You know, it's kind of hard to know where to start. Bryan's been living in Springs, doing odd jobs. Like all summer he was washing windows and refinishing decks. He'd rent this power machine that sprays water and gets all the mold off and then he sands down the wood and paints it with a finish.

No, I hadn't realized.

Yeah, he made good money this summer and got some good customers. Like people who have bought houses and don't have anybody steady working for them. He's watching houses when they're away, the way he used to, doing the trim or taking care of their cars. Shit, he can do anything with his hands.

Yes, yes, he and his hands.

Schmidtie, you're not fair to Bryan. He's changed. Honest. She wiggled in his lap.

I knew you were going to be like this.

All right. I won't. Please go ahead.

OK. If you promise. OK. Bryan's been working for this guy who's got a marina in Three Mile Harbor. Helping him with the dock and the workshop and also with the boats. You know, things that need to be fixed. He can do that too, like if you don't need to take the boat to a real boatyard. This old guy wants to sell his business, or maybe take in a partner or a couple of partners and let them buy in, over time. He'd even help the new guy get established. It's a good business.

I can imagine that it might be. Have you seen the place?

Yeah, with Bryan and Jason. It's cool.

And how old is this guy?

Oh, he's real old, maybe sixty-five. But is he strong! His wife's got arthritis so they want to like go somewhere warm, maybe Arizona? Her voice turned up at the end of the sentence, signaling they were in the realm of invention. The thing is if you keep boats for customers, you've got to be here in the winter. That's when her arthritis is real bad. This guy's got no kids.

Lucky bastard, thought Schmidt.

So Jason thought if he had that marina he'd build the business, maybe get some boats he could rent out, on charters, and maybe give lessons, you know, driving motorboats and sailing. All the summer people want to do it.

Ah, he's a sailor as well as a trained killer.

Cut it out, Schmidtie, Jason's from Nova Scotia. He was brought up to be a fisherman. That's what his folks do. It's real cool. So what do you think?

Perhaps this was it. Steady, he said to himself, it's not the time to get out ahead of them or to scare them off. Easy does it. This has to be their show, and if they are going into business they should use their brains.

What do I think? As I said, I can imagine that it's a good business. It obviously helps that Jason knows boats and boat repair and can do these other things, like running a motorboat or sailing on the side. But he's got to think this through. Giving lessons, you know, is not a one-man job, particularly if you're also taking care of boats. You've got to have a staff, insurance, maybe even a license. I don't know about the license part, I've never looked into it.

His speech had turned out to be pompous, not friendly, but it didn't seem to matter.

Jason has thought about it. He's been real careful.

That's terrific. Then there is the business part of the deal. What does this ancient guy really own, is there a mortgage and what kind, how much is the marina really worth, and so on. Probably Jason has thought about this too. There is one thing that does bother me. Bryan. How come Jason wants Bryan in this business with him? A kid who has pushed dope and gotten himself into some sort of trouble in Florida? How does that fit with Mr. Clean? That's part one. Now part two. How much does Jason know about you and Bryan? Nothing? Everything? Somewhere in the middle? If he knows, does he mind? If he doesn't, what kind of surprise will he get and what will he do about it? Please answer the question, Miss Gorchuck.

Gross, Schmidtie, I knew you'd get pissed about Bryan. OK. All right. Yeah, I've told him. I've told him everything, like I've told him about you. So there. And I've told him about Mr. Wilson. Jeez, sometimes I can't figure you. What do you think I am?

A magnificent young woman. It's just that these things are tough to talk about so almost anyone might be tempted to play them down. It wouldn't have been good policy in this case. Now explain to me why Jason wants this guy.

All right. Bryan's clean now. He's OK. Jason says so and he should know. He was in the narcotics unit. This stuff in Florida was chickenshit. Like nothing. He's looked into that too. Jason wants him because the guy really knows how to work and knows what he's doing. How is that?

Chickenshit. That was the expression Bryan used. Schmidt resisted pointing out the coincidence and said: Pretty good. I've got to hand it to you. Thank you.

You're welcome.

She wiggled off his lap and moved back to her chair across the table. Hey, you want to hear something? Mike Mansour said if Jason sets this up he's going to buy a big speedboat, you know, and let him take care of it. Wouldn't that be something? You know, like being able to say to a customer, You got nothing to worry about, Mr. Mansour himself keeps his boat here!

Not bad at all. So Mike knows about this plan.

Yeah, Jason talked to him. Mike said he'd get some of his people, like an accountant or something like that, to check on the books. Just like you said.

He should rejoice but couldn't. Final judgment had been entered in the remaining great case of his life. As though that did not suffice, Mr. Mansour's powerful, long arm had shoved him aside. These young people already had all the advice he could have given.

Good for Mike. Is he going to invest in this business?

He says that if Jason needs it he'll make him a loan. I don't know. Jason thinks he can get money from the bank.

That's simply terrific. I guess I have to ask you one other question. What will this plan mean for you personally?

Schmidtie, I want to live with Jason. Mr. Mansour said if he gives notice now he can let him go before Christmas. We'd go to see his folks. It sure will be cold!

In Nova Scotia? I don't think so. Not so bad as all that. Anyway, you know what they say: "I've got my love to keep me warm!"

Yeah. Then I'm going to help them, like do things around the office. I want to finish college too.

Well, that seemed to be it. It was he who got up this time, waddled ponderously over to her chair, and planted a kiss on the top of her head and then another. She hugged him, as if in response. All this is so strangely chaste, thought Schmidt. In this kitchen, in this house. When he looked at her he saw she was crying. Don't, sweetie.

It's OK. I'm going to get a Kleenex.

Her face, when she returned, was a beautiful blank.

Hey, can I say something?

He nodded.

Schmidtie, I didn't sleep with Mike Mansour. Never. Isn't that something? What a weird guy! He really turned me off. I guess I was real lucky.

He held out his cup, pointing to the coffeepot, which was almost full. To hell with tea!

She busied herself with the coffee, filling their cups, getting milk for hers.

Hey, I guess you and I aren't going to make it anymore either. That's too bad for the little guy. Huh, Schmidtie?

He nodded again.

So what do you say? Now you can do it. That's if you want to.

Of course, there it was, the change in circumstances. He should have understood right away. Whatever he did, he was on his own and so was she.

Sweetie, he said, I think I owe you one million American dollars.

You really meant it! You're going to do it!

Of course. I'm putting my money where my mouth was.

Oh! Oh! Oh!

It was she who began to laugh first, but then he laughed too, uncontrollably, the marvel of it being that he had begun to feel pretty good. In fact, he had misread the holding of the judgment; he too had been delivered.

Look, he said, I can get that money to you very quickly. I'd like to. Is this money going into the business? Should I talk to

Jason? I want to see him anyway—offer my congratulations. Why not, over a bottle of champagne. We could break one, like when they launch a ship.

I haven't told Jason. Schmidtie, if you really do this, don't you think it should be kind of between you and me? Like it's something I can tell him later. You know, the marina's OK. He and Bryan don't think they need any money for it. Could you like set it up so it's for me? She giggled. Invest my money for a rainy day?

For a retired financing lawyer, he was spending an unusual amount of time setting up trusts. With his own money, too. At last, though, he had a contented beneficiary. This was the holiday season, when for as long as Schmidt could remember, whether by reason of the ever longer lunches, carol singing, and other such useful activities, combined with the demands of inconsiderate clients intent on squeezing in tax-saving gifts before the end of the year, having postponed until the last minute the pain of parting with their funds, Dick Murphy and his other Wood & King trusts and estates colleagues were unwilling to do any work at all. The very thought of it provoked a fit of foul humor. Especially if it was work for retired partners. Schmidt resorted to the ultimate threat—he would take his will and Charlotte's trust, and therefore his estate, away from Wood & King. What other firm might want a client like him, who wasn't going to make any lawyer rich, he had no idea. But he had pressed the right button. Murphy didn't relish the prospect of Jack DeForrest's mentioning the matter at firm lunch. Partners might ask questions, for the pure pleasure of needling Murphy, even if they didn't give a hoot about Schmidt, alive or dead. A week later he drove into the city with Carrie—not that it was necessary to take her to see Murphy, there being nothing for her to sign except investment authorizations and bank cards that could be handled by mail, but to make her feel that what he had done was quite real and irreversible, meriting a special expedition. He wanted to have fun too. Let the receptionist and Murphy take a good look—why not DeForrest too, he thought at first and then relented. Really, Carrie didn't deserve that, although the notion of showing her off to that horse's ass about to taste for himself the joys of retirement was almost irresistible. She looked as good as the million dollars he had just handed over to her, far better in fact than an equal amount in any currency. No stack of cash had ever smelled so sweet or had a body that exuded such nice even warmth. When you slid your hand under her arm, just above the elbow, for instance to guide her along the corridor, you wanted to stop, take her by the shoulders, turn her toward you, pry her lips open with yours, and drink from them until the world ended. He was thrice and four times blessed. Still, even dying swans must eat, before they head for the East End of Long Island. He decided he would take her to lunch at his club, where she had never been, and, he supposed, would not have occasion to visit in the future. Rituals and greetings to soothe the bruised soul: shake the hand of the jovial hall porters, introduce to them Miss Gorchuck, and enter Miss Gorchuck's name in the great guest register; wave to acquaintances with whom he used to lunch at the members' table; mount the green-carpeted stairs to the dining room, pausing on the way to point out to Carrie the club's memorabilia and portraits of its past presidents and other notables glistening in their good black broadcloth.

This place is cool, she told him once they were at table. You're going to come here a lot when you move to the city?

I don't feel it will be a real move. More like camping out between weekends. But yes, I'll come here. You get a meal and, while you're at it, you remind a bunch of other old geezers you're still alive. Two birds with one stone. Whether the second bird is worth a stone is open to question.

You'll want to see people again.

Probably. I'll miss you.

Hey, you'll see me on weekends. If you want to.

She picked at her eggs Benedict, took a sip of the wine, and put her glass down.

You think I can have some mineral water? Any kind is OK.

Sure. In that case I'll drink your wine and let you drive.

He knew, of course, that wine or no wine she would want to drive, listening to one AM station after another while he dozed. But he felt grateful and happy.

That's the life! he continued. But first we're going to do some serious shopping. I'd like to buy something nice for you, your Christmas present—I've been thinking of a fur jacket for Nova Scotia. That way you can leave your red parka in the house. It will be like a silver cup I've won.

Her foot found his under the table.

Is that OK to do here? She giggled. Hey, no one's looking. I wonder what else you can do. Schmidtie, you remember everything. I wore that parka when I came to see you the first time—in the middle of the night. I was one fresh kid! You almost brained me.

That's because I thought you were a burglar. I was right. You were. You broke into my heart.

I did? Then keep me there.

If only he could keep the use of some of his old freedoms. He pressed her foot.

Schmidtie, can you be serious one minute.

The smile that had been spreading from ear to ear turned shy.

I want to tell you something. I wanted to tell you yesterday, when I got back from school, but I kind of thought I should wait until we'd seen the lawyers. I know it sounds crazy, but I didn't want it to like make any difference if you like wanted to change your mind or something. You want me to tell you now? OK. After my first class, I went to the hospital.

She waited for the effect on him.

Come on, Schmidtie, guess!

I can't. I had no idea that there was something the matter. You didn't tell me.

Yeah, I know. I was worried. That's why. I'd gone there twice before.

Carrie dear, should I be worried? No, it's too late now, I am worried. Tell me what's going on.

But as he spoke those words, he already understood. There was no need to tell. This was a conversation with a pattern as fixed as that of the minuet. How odd that he should be the wrong partner to bow to her now, having completed his own leisurely turn. Had she already had the same conversation, on the telephone of necessity, with Mr. and Mrs. Gorchuck? Had Jason spoken to his seagoing parents and siblings? Mike Mansour and Bryan could contend for avuncular standing, but surely he, Schmidt, had every chance of becoming the supernumerary grandfather.

No, it's OK. Except that, can you believe it, Schmidtie, I'm pregnant! Hey, he heard the heartbeat!

Love, that is simply wonderful! He took her hand and kissed it. Congratulations to you and to Jason! What an absolutely fabulous event. Can I ask you a stupid question? How did it happen? I thought you were on the pill.

She turned red. I kind of lied to you. I took it like most of the time. This summer I thought I was getting a fat tummy! Hey, imagine the tummy I'm going to have. So I stopped. I figured nothing would happen. I didn't take it with Bryan. Or with Mr. Wilson. Shit, was I scared then.

And what about the owner of O'Henry's, the waiters, busboys, and everybody else, wondered Schmidt. Bodies are just bodies. No more questions for the moment, no more true confessions.

Well, you've been a very lucky young lady—from beginning to end! I guess the thing to do is to get right to work on your wedding. I want the bride to look like a bride when I dance with her.

She giggled and hid behind the napkin. Schmidtie, I want to put the wedding on hold. I didn't want to talk about the baby until I was sure everything was OK. I guess it's OK now, that's what the doctor says. I'm past the third month.

You get it? It's like this. Jason hit on me right after that time you got pissed off about Mike.

The dining room had been emptying. It was all right, although her voice carried. There was no one at the tables near them.

I went out dancing with him. Remember, you didn't want to take me. I liked him all right, but I wasn't sure. So I was laying the both of you. Then I missed my period and had the test. Boy, let me tell you, I was confused. It was getting real heavy with Jason, like I knew that this was really it for me, but I was still fooling around with you. God, Schmidtie, right now I wouldn't know if I was getting married to the right guy. That's why I didn't talk to you yesterday.

Of course. Now he understood that too, her bewildering delicacy. She thought he should have every chance. Because certainly she was right about him; it was more than possible. Was Jason's candidacy as strong? In novels he had read about such matters the girl always seemed to know, but they were just novels. One thing was clear to him. If he said one word, out of the boundless savoir faire he had acquired as a lifelong contributor to birth control causes, one word about how this was the time to act, she would go for his eyes with the dessert fork.

Love, he said, how absolutely extraordinary. I may need another glass of wine. To drink to you—and the baby. Have you told Jason?

Yeah, last night. When I saw him.

But I mean also about not knowing?

She shook her head. He's not like you, he doesn't carry

on about getting married. It's not like his number-one priority. That's OK with me. So I think I'll kind of cool it until the kid is born. If you ask me, it'll be beautiful and look like Jay. But if it has red hair and a big nose—jeez, I'll have to say the stork brought it. Maybe Jason won't care. Who knows?

He didn't think he should tell her right then that more certain methods exist of discovering the answer to this particular riddle. There would be plenty of time for that. Besides, even on that subject he would probably be telling her nothing she didn't already know. He had once fervently wished for grandchildren. If Charlotte and Jon really did get back together, and managed to keep their marriage going long enough, that wish might yet be fulfilled. He preferred not to ask himself whether the issue of their union would in fact give him the joys he used to imagine beyond the abstract satisfaction that Charlotte wasn't at a dead end. It was easier to foresee the heartache and desolation of remaining on the outside of their lives. But a child of his own now, at his age—he would need more than the six months and then however long it took for the appearance of a definite family resemblance to get used to that idea.

You don't think it would be more prudent to tell him you have this doubt? So he won't feel later that he has been somehow misled? That he's done things he might not have done if he had known? Like quitting his job with Mike and going into the marina business, to take one example, or the two of you living together? By the way, is that what you plan to do?

There was also the minor or perhaps not minor at all matter of the visit to the seafarers in Nova Scotia. He decided he wouldn't mention it.

Shit, Schmidtie, get off this. A baby is a baby. Jason knows about you. He loves me. So, big deal. If the kid isn't his it's mine, and he's the stepfather.

Presented that way, the thought was intolerable to Schmidt, but he kept quiet. After all, he wasn't likely to ask for custody.

Jason's had it with running Mike's security anyway, she continued. We want this marina. Come on, Schmidtie, relax. And listen, do you think we could live in your pool house when we get back from seeing Jason's folks? Like while we're looking for a place near Three Mile Harbor?

He smiled yes.

Oh, Schmidtie, I can't wait to tell him. Can I call him on the car phone when we hit the road?

There was a message on the answering machine at home. Mr. Mansour's Bernice wondered whether Mr. Schmidt could drop by the beach house at eleven the next morning, for coffee. Mr. Mansour was sorry not to invite Mr. Schmidt to stay to lunch. He would be flying back to the city. It was all right to call to confirm even if it was late. She or Vicky would be at the office. Seeing Mr. Mansour just then, coffee or no coffee, was not on Schmidt's wish list. He was about to advise Bernice or Vicky, whichever one happened to answer, that he was busy for the rest of the day (he was wary of Mr. Mansour's tendency to insist, and of his nocturnal habits) and would be busy all of the following morning, when consciousness of a new reality intruded. Mike Mansour was no longer merely the eccentric billionaire with whom he hung out when he felt like it; he had become his prospective employer and could be summoning him as such. He called to say Mr. Mansour could count on his presence.

It was a cold and completely clear day. He drove to the main beach, left his car in the parking lot, and walked west on the sand which, close to the ocean's edge, was as smooth and hard as the sidewalk on Fifth Avenue where Mary and he had had their apartment. There had been an elevator man in the building, a squat man with a Slavic-sounding accent, a bald head, bulging friendly eyes, and a lack of front teeth so complete that it made him drool when he talked—the sort of man, in brief, who could have emigrated to the United States under an assumed name after a career as a guard in Treblinka or Auschwitz or as an inmate there—with a particularly engaging habit of replying, when thanked for depositing you safely on the tenth floor, It is my pleasure and duty, and thank you gentleman—or thank you, lady, depending on the passenger. Oh, they had all made fun of John, the elevator man, and loved him, Mary, Charlotte, and Schmidt himself, and always remembered to have a small present for him at Christmas, a necktie or wool gloves, in addition to the cash distributed to him and the rest of the staff. One day there was a pimply replacement in the elevator cage, to whose smell they would have to become accustomed. Where is John? Today is his day on. Ah, John, he is dead. There was no one to whom they could offer condolences or a little sum of money.

An Orthodox church somewhere in Queens saw to the burial. That had been a model employee and an example for Schmidt to emulate and ponder.

Mr. Mansour, installed in an Eames chair in his study, telephones on a side table within the reach of his right hand, was all business once Manuel had served coffee and the pound cake cut into little cubes that accompanied the magnate from roost to roost between meals. Here it is, he said, your employment agreement. Holbein walked me through it. I'd like to sign you up before Christmas. The question is whether you want some lawyer to review it before you commit. We'll pay the lawyer's fee.

Give me a few minutes to read it and I'll tell you.

Study, study. Take your time.

Unlike Mr. Mansour's telephone conversations, the document wasn't long. During a break that ensued between a call Mr. Mansour placed and a call he took, Schmidt said, Mike, this is very generous. I don't need a lawyer to tell me that. I'll sign now if you like.

Let's go. You're doing the right thing. Like they say, *merde!* I'll be at your side all the way. You'll have a great learning experience. We'll have a drink to your success. Then I've got to leave. We're closing a deal on a property down in Miami. A fabulous deal. I stole it from those guys.

Schmidtie, said Mr. Mansour after a pause, having looked around first, apparently to make sure Manuel had left the room, Jason's told me you're going to let him and Carrie stay in your pool house after Christmas while they're looking for somewhere to live. I'm not going to say it's none of my business, because you need me to help you. Don't let them stay there too long. Give them a deadline. Before Easter. Then if they're still there, you can extend it for a month. They can find something they can pay for, but it won't be as nice as your place. And—ha! ha!—it won't be rent free. You've got to get them out of there before that baby is born or they'll never leave.

Schmidt nodded.

It is no problem, but that's not all. You should give that girl some money, so she's independent. I don't know for sure if you can afford that, but I think you can. The question is, Should Jason know about it? In my opinion, he shouldn't. Among other things, he'll start running the business like that money was his. It's a good business, but he's got to watch the margins, and that means he's got to watch the overhead. The other aspect is right now he knows you two have been living together and he accepts that. You give her money, and it's more than a couple of thousand dollars, right away he'll start thinking maybe there's something more to it. Once a cop always a cop. You can't take the blue out of him!

Again, Schmidt nodded. It was nice to see that Carrie in her own way could keep up with the great tycoon. He said, Thank you. I've already taken care of this exactly as you recommend.

You see! You're getting smart. That's because you're spending time with a smart Jew. By the way, do you think you can invite the Cannings to the Dominican Republic? Do it on my behalf? That Mrs. Canning—what's her name, Caroline?—is one attractive woman. Brilliant too! That's the kind of woman I could go for.

XIV

IN MID-FEBRUARY of the following year he began the tour Mike Mansour had asked him to make of the foundation's offices in Central and Eastern Europe and the new republics that had detached themselves from the Soviet Union. As he got acquainted with the local staff and the Life Centers' work in the field, no doubt remained in Schmidt's mind: Mr. Mansour had hit the nail right on the head when he decided at the outset that the populations of these countries, given the nature of the catastrophes they had gone through since the Great War, needed better research and better teaching in the humanities even more urgently than new hospitals and orphanages, additions to housing stock, modern steel mills, personal computers, and improved telephone service. He couldn't help though regretting a bias that came along with this call to life, one that he hoped might be attributable to Eric Holbein and the school of economics to whose drumbeat he marched. The failure of the Communist version was beyond dispute, the solutions of Holbein's teachers might be sound, but Schmidt found himself irritated by the slogans of market capitalism the centers were under instructions to repeat as part of otherwise commendable activities, and quite unable to share the conviction, put forth with such cheerful enthusiasm, that expelling everywhere the state as manager and owner and handing the keys over to newly minted local captains of finance were the necessary premises of a resurrection, let alone the good life. Sleeping badly, raiding the minibar of hotel after hotel, he wondered: Instead of worrying whether his new hire would quit, having become unused to work, should not Mr. Mansour have asked himself whether his protégé was still willing to espouse, with the requisite lawyer's zeal, the positions of his employer? Had he become too independent? The question, Schmidt felt, didn't require an immediate answer, and he couldn't in any event give it, before figuring out where precisely Mr. Mansour himself stood—if indeed such a thing could be known.

His last port of call was Prague, the seat of the first of the European centers, established soon after the events that carried Václav Havel to the presidency. It had moved recently into new quarters on a steep historic street leading to the royal castle. Amid the smell of wet cement and the noise of sawing and hammering, the former dwellings of minor court functionaries that lined it were being converted into chic offices and residences for foreign businessmen and newly rich Czechs. In the countries he had already visited, he found that interviews he conducted during office hours with directors of the centers and their program officers quickly took on the character of a catechism—the questions and responses equally predictable and monotonous. It was no different in Prague. If he was going to break through, he had better wait for the moment of relaxation—in his case, it may have been torpor—induced in equal measure by the meal of national delicacies and variants of vodka or plum brandy to which he treated them, and rapid exchanges on the subject of the American society and its failings. Only then was there a chance of penetrating the callus of evasiveness and suspicion built up over years of dodging informers and cajoling despotic superiors. There was a new barrier as well, a mixture of resentment of his undeserved good fortune, bestowed upon him simply by virtue of his being an American, and determination not to let him forget whose territory he was on and according to whose rules he would have to play. All the same, he took these people to be good, on the whole. They had hung on to as much decency as was consistent with not getting into really bad trouble and obtaining a modicum of comfort and pleasure: in fact, their readiness, once they had been loosened up, to argue into the night about any subject that did not put in question their performance and prerogatives made him think they bore a skewed resemblance to the hapless *intelligents* he used to encounter in Dostoyevsky and Gogol. Schmidt and the director of the Prague center were setting out on their way to just such a meal when Schmidt stumbled in the historic cobbled street and turned his ankle. The pain was so acute he thought it was broken. Many hours and X rays later, he found himself with a bandage wound around an ankle that had been officially pronounced only sprained. By the next morning, he was also in possession of a carved walking stick that the director told him had been his father's. He begged Schmidt, in the name of their newly formed friendship, to keep it.

Favoring as best he could his bad leg, wondering whether he should substitute a crutch for the cane, he went from Prague to Paris to attend meetings sponsored by an international organization and to catch his breath. Mike Mansour had told—ordered—Schmidt to stay in the hotel he used himself, so that, instead of the establishment on the Left Bank he and Mary had frequented, he found himself at a palace sparkling with marble and polished brass, in an accommodation, moreover, that was permanently rented to Mr. Mansour and overlooked an immensity composed of the sky and, underneath it, the great public square, the unbelievably narrow and tame river just beyond it, and gardens that stretched on both sides. It was still early in the afternoon. He went out on the terrace to warm himself in the sun. It had rained all morning and there was a nice smell of spring in the air in spite of the traffic swirling below. His memories of Paris, since the first time he went there as a student, were principally of long walks. He had always wandered about tirelessly, disregarding the heat, the rain, and the fatigue, and also the blisters that formed so easily above his heel, where the shoe cut into the tendon, sometimes to discover or revisit a monument or site, sometimes for the simple pleasure of spending time in a particular *quartier*, often without any plan, quite content to lose his way until the lateness of the hour or his legs' refusing to carry him farther forced him to stop and study one of the marvelously detailed maps displayed at every metro station. The big red dot marked where he was. The rest was simple.

On a day such as this in April, it seemed inconceivable that he should not be out striding toward the stalls of the *bouquinistes* on the other side of the river, perhaps continuing afterward along the rue St. Jacques past the Panthéon to the Val de Grâce, one of his favorite buildings in Paris, before doubling back to the Luxembourg. The possibilities were limitless. He had to admit that, in truth, there was a certain sweetness in his circumstances: from this front-row seat he could look on the city he loved and call up images that moved him without suffering from inconveniences of his own injured and weary body, the bustle of the streets, or alterations in the urban aspect that, contradicting those images, would baffle him and interfere with his happiness, a city being apt to change even more quickly than a man's heart. Besides, lame or not, he was going out soon. He could follow his trajectory from the terrace. Hobbling along the place de la Concorde to the rue St. Florentin, he would pause to look at the mansion where Talleyrand, triumphant in Napoleon's defeat, had received Czar Alexander I. Then as soon as a red light stopped the murderous traffic—just long enough for someone in his condition to cross the rue de Rivoli—he would press on to the Tuileries. Charlotte was to meet him at the *bassin*, already crowded, he hoped, with toy sailboats.

Before leaving New York in February for Sofia, he had sent her his itinerary with the addresses and telephone and fax numbers at which he could be reached. At the top of the sheet he wrote: Just in case you should need to reach me. This was done as a matter of principle and good order. He did not expect to hear from her. There had been no contact between them at Christmas, nothing at all since he received those printed announcements, except the telephone calls he continued to make to her. The unvarying question—How are you?—answered: Just the same. That's good. Good-bye. He would not have claimed, if Gil Blackman had asked, that his awareness of the grief was constant; far from it, he went about his business for days at a time without necessarily remembering Charlotte. It was only when something—hearing the word "daughter," or in the street or in a restaurant he entered the sight of a young woman of her age and bearing—made him think of her, or when his mind was not fully engaged with some other subject, or when he consciously directed his thoughts toward her, that he realized he was in mourning.

By contrast, Carrie proved a profligate correspondent. Jason had installed a fax machine in the pool house. Rare was the day that passed without a message from her, in the fine schoolgirl's script he had admired so when she took down his orders at O'Henry's, and beautifully free of mistakes in spelling. Education was not wasted on Carrie. Had he been able to make the acquaintance of Mr. and Mrs. Gorchuck, if he only knew their street address, it would have pleased him to write them a postcard about their child, perhaps enclosing a sample letter. It was thus that she kept him informed of the tranquil development of the fetus, including its heartbeat and stupendous kicks, Jason's undiluted joy at the prospect of becoming a dad, the purchase of the marina, the myriad repairs Bryan, at times assisted by Jason, made in the house, which she was sure were going to blow his mind when he returned, the way she looked after the health of his Volvo, taking it out for a run each week, and—the subject of his most frequent inquiries and her detailed replies—the progress, physical and moral, of Sy, short for Siam, the Siamese kitten quickly approaching the age when he must be neutered that she and Jason had presented to him upon his return from the Dominican vacation.

They had moved into the pool house during his two weeks at Mr. Mansour's estate. He supposed that if they were at home they must be awake since it was lit up, in which case it was odd that they had not come to greet him, but it was possible that they had gone out leaving lights on, which was his own custom. The notion of knocking on their door or calling them did not appeal to him. It was a very cold evening, unusually cold for Bridgehampton; he was still suffering from a sunburn that had turned his skin the color of verdigris, and he missed Carrie all the more, he thought, for having found himself totally alone for the first time after a holiday in a house full of guests. At least, she had sorted his mail. It lay in neat piles on the kitchen table: bills, magazines, junk, and everything about which she was in doubt. He took a bath, changed into clean warm clothes, and poured himself a bourbon. Each of these remedies had the desired effect. Encouraged, he poured a second drink and got to work on the unclassifiable mail. It wasn't going to be a long project. His stomach was rumbling from hunger, but he decided he wasn't going to dine off tuna fish or any other Schmidt staple he might find in the pantry. It was better to drag himself to O'Henry's than to endure the humiliation of those two seeing him—if they had in fact gone out and happened to return just when he was eating—attack in solitude hard-boiled eggs and whatever he had forked out from a can. He was almost ready to leave when he heard the doorbell and then the front door being opened and Carrie's voice: Schmidtie, it's us, we've come to say hi! Hey Jason, shut the door. You're letting in the cold. Of course, she had opened the door with the latchkey. Carrie in a maternity dress! He was unable to take his eyes off it.

Don't act surprised, dummy. I'm pregnant, remember? We've got a present for you. Wow, you haven't even noticed.

Jason was carrying something like a little red duffel bag. She took it from him, set it down on the kitchen table, and unzipped a side panel. In a moment, he saw what it was: a kitten the color of sand, with mottled blue eyes, brown ears, feet, and tail, and a cheerful face that made you think that the little cat, getting ready for the carnival, had decided to wear a brown Venetian mask.

Aren't you going to pick him up?

Of course.

Schmidtie, he's Siamese! He's got a pedigree and everything. Jason, show Schmidtie. A Siamese prince! He's going to keep you company.

Indeed, his very own pussycat. There was nothing he could do about it, he realized, not a chance of his giving up this warm soft thing with a huge heartbeat that had at once licked his hand and purred as though the crook of Schmidt's arm had always been where he belonged. He made the evident objection: who was going to take care of the cat when he was away—as he would be, very soon, for a number of weeks. That had been worked out; they would, and later, when they moved out, Bryan was taking over. It was a joint purchase and a joint gift, but Bryan had found the breeder, looked over the litter, and picked out this little guy. It shouldn't have been a surprise to learn also that Bryan's mind had been racing ahead. When he came to take care of the cat, he wouldn't stay in the pool house, because Schmidt might need it for guests. But there was the space above the garage that could be fixed up so it would do fine, and he wouldn't be in Schmidt's way. Would that be all right? Schmidt did what was expected of him. He nodded agreement.

This was his first cat. By the time Schmidt left for Europe, he thought he discerned in this talkative little animal not only intelligence—that the kitten came when Schmidt whistled and had mastered both the topography of his new dwelling and Schmidt's habits so well that he could be counted on to gallop to any place in the huge house where, according to his mysterious calculations, Schmidt should normally be at that moment and get there ahead of Schmidt, was solid proof of the resourcefulness of the brain inside that little head—but also moral qualities of distinction. Sy would see to it that he was fed when he felt hungry. That was very clear. He jumped first on a chair and from it onto the kitchen table and followed every move of Schmidt's that should result in food appearing in his dish, sometimes rising delicately on his hind legs for a closer look, waving his long thin right paw. But his interest in Schmidt's company did not seem principally connected to hunger: out of what Schmidt took to be quite simply the satisfaction the kitten found in his company, Sy would curl up in Schmidt's lap or in the armchair next to Schmidt's when Schmidt read, or, when Schmidt was busy in the kitchen, in a basket on top of the refrigerator, the bottom of which Schmidt lined, once he had noticed the kitten's interest in that lookout point, with one of his old sweaters, and, for that same reason, would rush to meet him at the front door whatever time of day he came home. This last demonstration of friendship was the one Schmidt found the most touching of all. Among those moral qualities in response to which Schmidt felt growing inside himself a blend of loyalty and tenderness, Schmidt included also Sy's love of pleasure and insistence on respecting pacts. Thus, in the morning, if Schmidt was shaving, the kitten would appear in the bathroom, jump on the toilet seat, sit down, and expect to be brushed. If by chance Schmidt, having for instance just finished soaping his beard, were to say, Please wait, Sy's wail of outrage left no doubt about the wound to his pride—something unknown, the importance of which he could not admit, had taken priority over an appointment he made and, for his part, had kept. Schmidt didn't doubt that when alone in the house, Sy relented and actually drank the fresh water that was always set out for him. But never if Schmidt could be found. Roused by meowing of a timbre Sy had taught him signified thirst and recalled their covenant, the kitten and Schmidt proceeded to the nearest faucet, preferably in a bathtub, where, after Schmidt had reduced the flow of water to the thinnest of rivulets, the kitten would sit down, cock his head skeptically, purr approval, and begin to lap. Mysteriously self-reliant Sy, coveting no reward, and refined in every gesture: whatever the facts were, Schmidt considered him Carrie's gift. He looked forward to his life with Sy. Each of them was still, so far as the other was concerned, without sin. Tabula rasa. Once before, it had been given to him to write on a clean slate: his daughter's. He hoped to do better with the cat.

The message he received from her in Prague was so unexpected that, when the hotel concierge handed it to him, his mouth momentarily went dry. Brought back to his senses when he realized that a fax bearing her name as sender could not be the one that would alert him to an accident or something else truly awful that had happened to her, he opened the envelope and read. The letter was not an attack; it was a surprise of a different kind telling him that she and Jon would be in Paris more or less at the same time as he, celebrating an anniversary. She wondered whether he would like to see her, perhaps take her to lunch. He wondered in turn what anniversary that could be. Certainly not of their marriage or of the disastrous day of the accusation that Jon had mishandled the sealed brief. Were they perverse enough to mark the beginning of their infidelities or their coming to light? Never mind, he would soon find out. The great thing was that she had asked to see him. He answered at once. One week later he rose to greet her in the restaurant where he had proposed to

Mary and she had accepted, at a table next to a window from which they could look out on the garden of the Palais Royal.

You're lovely, he told her.

Thanks. Renata picked out this suit. I thought you'd go for it.

Renata's name was not one he had hoped to hear immediately. A moment passed before he said, How very nice.

There was an edge in her voice when she next spoke, which frightened him. Yes, it really is. I don't think you realize how much Renata is doing for me. It's like Mom, if she were still alive.

You're a lucky girl, he answered; let's order lunch.

She told him in rapid succession that Jon had business in Paris, which was in part the reason for their being there, that he was happy at the new firm, and that she might change jobs, as soon as something attractive came her way. Now that she was back with Jon it made her even more uncomfortable to be surrounded by people who knew all about Harry Polk. And she could hardly bear running into him every time she ventured out of her office. There was a possibility that one of the museums might want someone with her experience to organize special events—parties for openings, exhibitions, and dinners for big donors. She thought she'd like that.

Schmidt murmured assent. Perhaps it was a false alarm: this lunch might yet run its course to the accompaniment of harmless chatter. Set a sort of precedent that might help them get along. He told her about almost breaking his ankle in Prague.

How old are you Dad? Going on sixty-four? Sixty-five? I guess you're getting up there. It's kind of early to be having trouble with your balance, but if you do you should start using a cane.

He pointed to the walking stick, which was leaning against the empty chair.

I mean like all the time, she replied. That's what the doctor told Jon's father. Well, I see I missed your birthday. Thanks, by the way, for the check you sent for my thirtieth. I guess I never thanked you. Sorry about that.

I'm sorry too.

Hey, you haven't asked me what kind of anniversary this is. I'll bet anything you don't know. Do you?

He shook his head.

That shows how much attention you've paid to me. Think hard.

Really, I have no idea. Please tell me.

She giggled unpleasantly. No kidding. It's the anniversary of the party you threw for your insurance company geeks and office nerds. That's when I met Jon! It figures you forgot. You probably wish it had never happened.

His ankle, which had been satisfactorily quiet since he sat down, began to throb. He leaned down and rubbed it for a moment between his thumb and index finger. Really, there was no point in letting her goad him.

Look, Charlotte, he told her, the food here is particularly delicious. Let's not spoil it by squabbling. Why don't we eat it in peace and discuss what's the matter between you and me when we get to coffee. Since this is my day off, I might even have a brandy. In the meantime, tell me how Jon is doing in his new job or, if you prefer, let's talk about the weather or the stock market or the movies.

He had used the same tone of voice, the same deliberate diction, that had proved so effective during the summer when she was about to turn ten and threw regular tantrums after pony camp—weeping and wheezing so uncontrollably that Mary and he wondered whether she might be developing asthma—if a particular girl a year younger and about half her size was given a livelier pony ride or was praised more warmly than she for going over the series of little jumps they worked on. Pavlovian response to a stimulus? Involuntary memory? He didn't care which it was. She started to extol the virtues of Jon's new firm, telling him how funny it was, considering the years he had spent at W & K, and especially his never having had another job, except as a counselor at the soccer camp, that he had taken to it immediately, didn't mind the dreadfully long work hours, worse than anything he had known at the old firm, or the partners yelling and screaming at one another, because it all felt like one big family—partners, associates, secretaries, everybody. Not like those gentlemen, she pronounced that last word scornfully, at W & K who couldn't wait to condemn him, never thought to give him a chance.

Perhaps, thought Schmidt. At lunch in the city, in January, a word or two Lew Brenner, that subtle and cautious man, had let drop may have been susceptible of some such interpretation. Schmidt smiled at Charlotte and said, This is excellent. All is well that ends well. I wish him luck and great happiness. Now let's talk about the reserved subject. You and me. Why do you treat me so badly? I have nobody in the whole wide world except you.

You're forgetting Carrie. She snickered.

Never mind Carrie. Please tell me.

You really want to know? Because I feel I never had a father. You were married to Mom, you didn't always treat her right, and when briefly you weren't at the office you hung around the house. Sure, you paid for my education, or maybe Mom paid for some of it. I don't care. Is that all I was entitled to expect? When did you act like a father? I didn't know what families were like, so I thought that was kind of normal—maybe only Mom was supposed to be a human being. Now I know better. I've seen the Rikers when they're together. Do you realize that they actually talk to each other? Myron understands what's going on in Jon's head, what Jon does, what he wants. The same goes for Jon's brother. It's not just Renata. It's a father they can go to. I can go to him too. Can you imagine it? With you it's zero. All right, now I've told you. That's what makes me sore. It makes me choke. It makes me want to puke.

He looked around, caught the eye of the headwaiter, ordered another coffee and a brandy—since she wanted neither—and thought about what he might tell her.

Charlotte, he ventured finally, is that really true? I remember so many talks, so many outings to this or that museum or opera or concert, so many times I've helped you when you thought you were stuck—even with your Latin homework.

Or the days I spent with you on the beach. That was me, not Mom. I taught you about the surf. Or playing tennis. Who drove you most often to the stable? All of that can't have been worthless or without meaning. I don't understand.

I can see that. I'm not saying that you didn't go through all the motions. The trouble is they were only that. Your mind was elsewhere. On your big-shot law practice. On Mom. Or on some woman you were screwing on the side. Do you know that in all your life you've never, I mean never, had anything to say to me? No insight, no wisdom. Sure, you were great at all the mechanics. Which train or plane I should take. Get me to the train or plane. Get me picked up on arrival. How to make sure Miss Schmidt has the right traveler's checks. Anyway, that wasn't even you. It was your goddamn secretary! And you think I can forget what you did to Mom.

There was nothing he could do. Say good-bye. But to put an end to this conversation condemned him, he thought, to a nightmare worse than going through with it.

Honey, he said, I've never stopped regretting the incident with your baby-sitter. Now that I know that you realized what was going on I regret it even more. But Mom forgave me. We stuck together—there wasn't a moment's question about that, she wanted it as much as I—and we went on to have a good marriage. Until the very end. I would think that you know enough by now about men and women and sex to understand such things. They can be forgiven. Sometimes they are. After all, it seems that you and Jon have forgiven each other.

She interrupted, We don't have any kids, remember?

I do know you have no children, and that has certainly made the last year easier. But please, let me finish. The rest, I don't even know what to call it—my failure to teach you more, or listen to you better, really I'm at a loss—that's something I've worried about more than you can imagine. Look, I am me, not someone else. All during those years you talk about, I was, in fact, working very hard. I did try to be a successful lawyer, as I suppose Jon does and will, even after you have children. And I'm not an easy, communicative person. I'm not like Mom. I'm not like the Rikers. But I've tried and tried to do well by you, and maybe you've even noticed that I love you. Sure, it's my love, not some other person's, not the love of some ideal father. Can't you accept me such as I am?

If I do, I don't know where that puts us. Nowhere you would like. That's what I think.

He called for the check and paid it.

But you must have had some purpose in asking to see me. Tell me what it was. Right now it's quite beyond me.

She nodded. I'm wretched too, she said. I just wanted to tell you what I think.

She was staying in Paris another few days, she told him, whereupon she and Jon would drive down to Nice, slowly, making many stops, and take the plane from there to New York. He listened carefully and asked her to meet him the next day on a park bench. He did not think he could risk asking her to another meal.

He got there early, picked a folding chair next to the *bassin* that was in full sunlight, and waited. He'd read the paper in the morning. It would have seemed grotesque to him in any case to have brought one, or even a book. Far better to draw lines and circles in the sand with his stick. He saw her from far away, walking fast, swinging a little pocketbook like a miniature doctor's satchel. So wonderfully American: he admired her blue jeans and brown suede jacket, the dark glasses she wore like old-fashioned motorcyclist's goggles pushed up so they rested on her hair. Probably she had not seen him, thinking he had meant literally a park bench. Before he stood up and waved to her, he saw also that her brown laced-up shoes were shined, as they used to be when she went off to her riding lessons.

Let's sit here, he said. The sun is just right. It's warming every one of my old bones, and they are each and every one grateful.

I'm glad.

He went on drawing his lines and circles.

Dad, she said suddenly. I'm not sure you think I'm so great either. Let's make a deal. I will take you as you are, you take me as I am. For now. We'll see where that puts us.

You've got it, he said, and held out his hand.

Almost at once she left him to meet Jon at the pyramid of the Louvre. He stayed in his chair for a good long while, because there was no hurry, and then limping carefully left the Tuileries, retracing his steps to the rue St. Florentin. There were no taxis at the stand. He continued, wincing until the ankle warmed up and the pain turned into a dull, stupid ache, to the rue St. Honoré and turned right. A couple of blocks farther was the apartment of the widow of a younger partner of his who had run W & K's Paris office, retired early, and died. The widow had invited him to tea. He reached the gate of the building and stood before it studying the polished brass plates, uncertain whether after all he would press the buzzer next to her name.

Schmidt Delivered

Louis Begley

A Reader's Guide

A Conversation with Louis Begley

George Andreou *is an editor at Alfred A. Knopf.*

GA: When did it first occur to you to write a sequel to *About Schmidt*?

LB: I first thought that continuing Albert Schmidt's story was possible, and would be fun, when I was finishing *Mistler's Exit*, the novel that followed *About Schmidt* and preceded *Schmidt Delivered*. I knew the ending of *Mistler's Exit*; it was just a matter of getting it down on paper. So I did not feel guilty about flirting with another project.

GA: How has your hero, Albert Schmidt, evolved since the days of the first book? It was particularly amusing to observe someone so temperamentally at odds with the culture at large—has that gulf widened?

LB: By "culture at large" you must mean popular culture. I have never thought that Schmidt was at odds with American culture, as the word used to be understood, before people began to talk about such things as the culture of a particular big accounting firm or investment bank specializing in junk bond financings.

If you are referring to *popular* culture, the gap has narrowed. Carrie, his half–Puerto Rican waitress friend, who is approximately forty years younger than Schmidt, has taught him quite a lot about how the rest of the world lives. Loving and admiring her has made Schmidt far more tolerant.

Yes, I do think my friend Schmidtie has matured—a word I prefer to "evolved"—like plums that you buy at a fruit stand when they are hard and leave to ripen in the sun on the ledge of your kitchen window. That, too, is the effect of love, as well as time.

GA: Do you think this book clarifies, or further complicates, the much commented-upon question of Schmidt's anti-Semitism? Were you surprised or influenced by the reception he received with the appearance of the first installment?

LB: In *About Schmidt*, I presented a portrait of a man of Schmidt's age and milieu at the time the action of that novel takes place, which is the beginning of the 1990s, with a great many flashbacks to the preceding decades. It would not have been unusual for such a man, the product of a New York Anglo-German middle-class family with some plumage—the parents lived in a house on Grove Street, the father was the senior partner in an admiralty law firm with a Greek ship owner clientele and some money—and of an education in a Jesuit high-school and Harvard College and Law

School, to have the sort of mild anti-Semitic feelings I have ascribed to Schmidtie. Bear in mind that his is not an active sort of anti-Semitism. He does not practice it in his law firm; on the contrary, I have him be particularly decent to Jewish associates. He does not trumpet his feelings, and he is not proud of them. He knows that they get him in trouble with his wife, Mary. But, they are part of the prism through which he looks at the world. Please bear in mind also that my portrait is not of the sort you hang on the wall of the bar association library: it does not flatter. Instead, here and there it caricatures the subject's traits. I thought that this particular trait was worth mentioning, for the sake of realism, for the sake of seeing Schmidt's anti-Semitism dissolve as he becomes deeply involved with Carrie (who is the object of similar prejudice), and quite simply for the sake of poking fun at people I have known.

I duly noted, when *About Schmidt* first appeared, that many reviewers seemed to concentrate their attention on my protagonist's anti-Semitism—although anti-Semitism is not, in my opinion, the most interesting aspect of his personality—but I am not sure whether I was surprised.

In order to be surprised, I think I would have had to think in advance to what the reviews of my book might be. But I didn't and I never have. When reviews do come out, with exceptions, for instance when I know the reviewer or have special admiration for the reviewer's work, I only scan them.

I should add that, in my opinion, an author who thinks how his book will be treated by reviewers while he is writing, and, worse yet, tries to "correct" his work to anticipate criticism, is in bad trouble. I think I am responsible to only one critic, and that is myself.

GA: Did you ever consider letting Schmidtie live out the rest of his days with Carrie? (He wouldn't be the first man his age to accomplish such a feat!) Or did you regard it as inevitable or meaningful that he "set her free," and if so, why?

LB: Of course, I could have done just that. But I didn't really consider such a solution because both Schmidt and Carrie are too lucid to have accepted it. Carrie recognizes the powerful sexual content of her relationship with Schmidtie and refuses to have a future in which caresses are not followed by intercourse. Of course, couples can have a happy and fulfilled relationship after the man's ability to perform has waned, but these are couples in which the age difference is not so great. Couples united by interests more profound and more nourishing than those that Carrie and Schmidtie seem to share. Schmidtie certainly knows that.

Yes, I think that Schmidt's generosity and elegance when he lets her go with Jason are very important. They let the reader see his intrinsic decency.

GA: Schmidt seems to be your only protagonist whose story does not involve some fundamental deception. Your other heroes seem either to be living a lie, passing for someone they are not (I think of Maciek in *Wartime Lies*, Ben in *The Man Who Was Late*, even, to a degree, Max in *As Max Saw It*), or otherwise concealing a more discrete but terrible truth (as with Mistler in *Mistler's Exit*). Does Schmidt's authenticity, so to speak, set him apart in your mind? In what ways, if any, does this make it a different type of story to tell?

LB: You are right, and you have asked a very difficult question. Schmidt is different from my other protagonists. I would say that he is more ordinary. I know a number of men like him. His story is not tragic—except in the way all lives are tragic. Most of us lose to illness people whom we have loved; we all age and must face the decline of our powers and our own illness and death; we make bad decisions the consequences of which cannot be undone; and we have heartbreak relations with our parents and our children even if, on most levels, they go well.

I would say that is where the difference lies between telling the story of Schmidt and that of my other protagonists. Schmidt requires a lighter tone, suitable for comedy. In the end, the tone dictates the choice of incidents to be related.

GA: You have come to be identified by some as a chronicler of the rich and powerful. Even among this elite, billionaires, a fixture of the nineties and of the so-called new economy, seem a breed apart. How typical is the Egyptian tycoon Michael Mansour? Are the rich different by degrees, or are the super-rich truly an "exclusive spiritual brotherhood," as you say? Do they have a code of their own?

LB: Ah, the anointed of Mammon! I do think the super-rich are a class apart, and I think I have done a pretty good job lampooning them. What is their essential defining characteristic? Perhaps there are two: certainly, their prodigious sense of personal entitlement—the right not only to the pursuit of happiness but also to guaranteed instant gratification; and a belief in their own well-deserved omnipotence. Since, on a whim, they can summon jets and helicopters and buy houses and works of art, why can't they also buy people? They do—with money. If that is so, why shouldn't they be able to direct those people's lives, for their own good as the billionaire patron perceives it?

As I say in one of my books, Vespasian was wrong: money does smell. Its aroma acts as an aphrodisiac. In sufficient concentration, sniffed by your fellow billionaires, it confers on you admission to the "exclusive spiritual brotherhood" and its many domains on private islands and mountain tops, in deserts and historic palaces.

GA: One inevitably hears your writing described as "elegant." Does that always describe your goal in crafting prose, or do you sometimes find yourself writing against the grain of such expectations?

LB: I never write against the expectations of others or in order to meet them. I simply try to do my best. It is true that I correct and rewrite compulsively, sometimes until I am quite discouraged. I try to get to the point at which I can read the text to myself word for word without wincing.

GA: You call this book *Schmidt Delivered*, but though it begins with Schmidt living in bliss, he is aware almost from the start that his heaven with Carrie can't last, and indeed it ends before the book does. In what sense should we see Schmidt as being "delivered" in these pages?

LB: I think that "delivered" as applied to Schmidt in this book has at least three meanings. Wouldn't I be wrong if I imposed any one of them on the reader? Shouldn't the reader make his or her own choice? And isn't it possible that more than one of them or perhaps all three are valid?

GA: At the end, Schmidtie seems literally on the threshold of a further adventure. Do you have a plan for another installment of his story?

LB: Yes, to be written after my friend Schmidt and I have lived a few more years.

GA: As a late-blooming writer you have developed with astonishing speed into a literary veteran, now with this sixth acclaimed book to your name. What has been your most interesting discovery about the writing process since your first novel? Has your way of going about it changed at all?

LB: I hadn't realized how hard it is to write. I can't imagine that breaking stones to build pyramids in Egypt together with my ancestors was harder.

No, my way of going about writing a novel hasn't changed. I put together in my mind the essentials of the story and try to find the voice in which it can be told. Once I have found it, I get going.

Reading Group Questions and Topics for Discussion

1. Why won't Carrie marry Schmidt? Do you believe she loves him?

2. In the first chapter, Schmidt considers the scene at Sesame, the local grocery store. What does his vision reveal about his neighbors, and about him?

3. What do you make of Schmidt's anxieties preceding Charlotte's arrival? What worries him the most? Why isn't he more pleased that she is turning to him in her difficulties?

4. How do Charlotte and Carrie compare in Schmidt's mind? What is revealed about these two women as individuals in the way they treat each other?

5. What do you make of the way Schmidt is treated by his former law partner?

6. What does Schmidt remember about life with his parents? How does it color his relations with Charlotte?

7. What do you think of the arrangement Schmidt proposes for investing in Charlotte's business venture? Is Charlotte justified to be upset? Is one or the other to blame for letting money come between them? Compare Schmidt's reaction later to Carrie and Jason's

business proposal. Is there a double standard at work? If so, why?

8. What kind of man is the billionaire Michael Mansour? Why is he so eager to be Schmidt's friend? What do they have in common? What does each value about the other? Why do you suppose Schmidt takes Mansour into his confidence?

9. Is Carrie guilty of bad behavior when she visits Mansour in New York City? How do you judge her relations with men other than Schmidt?

10. Why does Schmidt draft his letter of bequest? Do you think he is treating Charlotte fairly?

11. Schmidt resists following Mansour's advice about how to handle the conflict with Charlotte. Do you think Mansour's tactics make sense when applied to family relations?

12. How do you understand Renata's motivations in her lunch with Schmidt? What tactics does she employ and how effective are they? Is there a winner in this duel?

13. "Generosity begins and ends with gratifying the giver," the novel tells us. Do you agree? Why does Mansour offer Schmidt the job as head of the Man-

sour Life Institute? Why does Schmidt hesitate? What does his initial reaction reveal about his view of human nature?

14. For what reasons did Schmidt as an undergraduate try to cheat the shop girl in Cambridge? Why does he now remember that story, and the one about Laverna Daly, whom he recruited and bedded as a young partner? How do these recollections inform his view of his son-in-law's behavior?

15. Do you think Mansour has encouraged Carrie and Jason's relationship? If so, how do you explain his motivations?

16. How does Schmidt react to Charlotte's reconciliation with Jon? How does he react to Jason and Carrie's coming together? What can we learn by comparing his reactions to these two developments? Where do they leave Schmidt?

17. In the last few chapters, what change occurs in the way Schmidt views Carrie? And what corresponding change do you detect in his view of himself? How would you describe the transformation his life undergoes?

18. What was your reaction to Schmidt's final meeting with Charlotte in the novel? How much has been

resolved between them? In what ways have this father and daughter each found substitutes for the other?

19. In the conversation with Louis Begley preceding these questions, the author suggests the title may be understood in at least three ways and leaves it to the reader to decide. In what sense do you understand Schmidt to be delivered?

20. How do you imagine the life ahead of Schmidt?